ISBN-13: 978-1-335-62951-7

Awakening the Shifter

HARLEQUIN®
™ www.Harlequin.com

Printed in U.S.A.

W9-DBO-940

Arms folded across her chest, Sarange stood in the doorway, blocking his entrance to the room. "You can start talking now."

"I was hoping to shower first. Maybe find some clothes."

"You turned into a tiger." Khan wasn't sure whether the wobble in her voice was caused by anger or shock. It didn't matter. She kept going, coming toward him until he was pressed up against the balcony rail and she had to tilt her chin to look up at him. "I need to know what's going on."

He caught hold of her upper arms, and as soon as he touched her, she collapsed into his arms. The feel of her body against his drove every other thought out of Khan's mind, and a harsh groan of surrender was dragged from him. His whole body was entranced by her. His eyelids half closed as if weighted and he lowered his head, compelled by a force beyond his control to graze Sarange's lips with his.

I don't want to control this.

Jane Godman writes in a variety of romance genres, including paranormal, gothic and romantic suspense. Jane lives in England and loves to travel to European cities that are steeped in history and romance—Venice, Dubrovnik and Vienna are among her favorites. Jane is married to a lovely man and is mom to two grown-up children.

Books by Jane Godman

Harlequin Nocturne

Otherworld Protector
Otherworld Renegade
Otherworld Challenger
Immortal Billionaire
The Unforgettable Wolf
One Night with the Valkyrie
Awakening the Shifter

Harlequin Romantic Suspense

Sons of Stillwater

Covert Kisses
The Soldier's Seduction
Secret Baby, Second Chance

Harlequin E Shivers

Legacy of Darkness
Echoes in the Darkness
Valley of Nightmares
Darkness Unchained

Visit the Author Profile page at Harlequin.com for more titles.

AWAKENING THE SHIFTER

JANE GODMAN

HARLEQUIN® NOCTURNE™

Dear Reader,

I'm so excited to share the first of my rock-star shifter books with you!

Beast, the rock band with a difference, first made an appearance in another of my Harlequin Nocturnes, *The Unforgettable Wolf*. Don't worry if you haven't read that book; it won't affect your enjoyment of this one (although it *is* a great love story!).

Awakening the Shifter is the story of Beast's lead singer. Arrogant, unpredictable and temperamental, Khan is the charismatic bad boy of rock. When he meets well-behaved singer-songwriter Sarange, the attraction between them is off the scale, but there's a problem...

Khan is a tiger shifter and Sarange is a werewolf. Cats versus dogs? Claws versus fangs? How can they be mates? The fates have got it all wrong this time. Particularly as Sarange doesn't even know she is a werewolf.

When his mate is threatened, Khan is forced to put his antagonism aside and go to her rescue. It's an act that leads him halfway across the world on a journey of discovery, during which he finds out about his own tortured past as well as the bonds that tie him to Sarange.

If they are to have a future together, the tiger and the wolf must work together, as they did in the past, and rediscover the love that once founded a great shifter dynasty.

Look out for more rock-star shifter stories after this one!

I'd love to hear from you. You can contact me at www.janegodmanauthor.com, on Twitter, @JaneGodman, and on Facebook: Jane Godman Author.

Happy reading,

Jane

This book is dedicated to my friends Gill, Karen and Andrea. I won't embarrass them by saying how long we've known each other...but it's been a long time!

Chapter 1

This was where Khan felt alive. The only place he knew for sure he existed. The heavy, thumping beat of the drums pounded in time with his heartbeat. The screams of the crowd pulsed along his nerve endings. Exhilaration fizzed through his bloodstream, sending his energy levels into overdrive.

In front of an audience of thousands, or in this case, tens of thousands, with millions more watching on TV or live streaming…this was the only place his life had any purpose.

He didn't move. Head bowed, arms outstretched. Fire and fury exploded around him, but Khan waited. Pumped up the expectation beyond fever pitch and kept it hanging. Teased and tormented until the yelling and pleading from his fans became a fervor in his blood.

When he finally raised his head, he felt his own vigor pulse through the audience. The devil horn sign was

repeated over and over as far as the eye could see. Two
fingers at the side of the head. The sign of the beast.
Our sign. Nothing matched this…except maybe sex.
The two experiences were similar, with the need for release becoming overwhelming. The climax came when
he delivered his performance, poured himself into his
spectators, gave them everything he had.

Dense smoke rolled like fog from the stage and,
within it, colored strobe lights danced in time with the
drumbeat. Giant LED screens at the rear of the stage
projected alternating images of fire, close-ups of snarling animals and the band's logo, a stylized symbol re-
sembling three entwined number sixes. At the side
of the stage, explosions went off at random intervals,
shooting orange flames high into the night sky.

The other members of Beast were unleashing a storm
around him. Behind his vast, gleaming circle of drums,
Diablo exuded raw, brooding vitality. His chest was
bare and his tattooed biceps bulged as he hammered
out a manic beat, his blue-black hair flopping forward
to hide his face.

At the front of the stage, red-haired Torque, on lead
guitar, was all burning drama and flickering movement.
The air around him glowed with life, and he matched
the sweeping arc of his hand on his guitar to the explosions at the side of the stage. In contrast, Dev, on
rhythm guitar, held his body statue still, the movement
of his flying fingers the only sign of life. His white-
blond hair and pale skin added to the illusion that he
was carved from ice. Slightly to the left of center, just
behind Dev, Finglas was lost in his bass guitar, a faraway expression on his face.

"Unforgettable." Khan felt the stadium still as he
elongated the word, starting on a whisper and ending on

a screech. He knew the power of his own voice, knew what people said. *Is Khan the best rock singer ever? Does he have the greatest vocal range of all time? Or is he just a showman?*

Khan didn't give a damn about speculation and comparisons. Tonight, in Los Angeles—and at the simultaneous concerts in Manchester, England, and in Sydney, Australia—as long as they were talking about him, that was all that mattered.

"Unforgettable" was their bestselling track from the album of the same name. As he launched into the number and the crowd sang along, Khan gave them what they expected. Throwing back his red-gold mane of hair, he swaggered, swayed and jumped around the stage in skintight leopard print pants and a flowing white shirt slashed to the waist. His voice ranged from husky purring to wild yelping, with acrobatics to match.

He ended the song in one of his favorite ways. Approaching Diablo, Khan howled out the final chorus while dry humping the drum kit. It was always a crowd pleaser. It was less popular with Diablo, whose expression became even more tempestuous. Ged Taverner, Beast's manager, frequently warned Khan that he would one day push Diablo too far.

"When I'm asked to identify your body, Tiger Boy, there'll be a drumstick through the center of your eye."

Acknowledging the adulation of the crowd, Khan returned to the front of the stage. Before he could speak, he was conscious of a change in the atmosphere. A curious hush fell over the packed stadium, something Khan had never known. He wasn't sure he liked it. Silence? Where was the validation in that?

A slender figure swept onto the stage. Sarangerel Tsedev, known as Sarange, was unmistakable. One of the few people in the world who, like Khan, needed only one name. Even if that hadn't been so, her place on the stage was assured, her ability to silence thousands well established.

Although she was one of the most famous singer-songwriters in the world, Sarange was also the organizer of this concert. The Animals Alive Foundation was her nonprofit organization. Tonight was about raising awareness of endangered species. She had driven forward this vision, persuading the biggest names in the entertainment industry to come along with her. All across the globe people were watching this spectacle unfold and donating millions. The final tally was likely to be billions. Against all the odds, she had succeeded in uniting the world in a common cause.

It had always been the plan that Sarange would join Khan for the official Animals Alive anthem. This was the finale, the culmination of all her hard work. What was striking about this encounter was that it was the first time two of the biggest names in the music scene had met in person.

Khan had seen Sarange on screen many times, of course. He had heard her described as one of the most beautiful women in the world, and that accolade had piqued his interest. Yes, she was stunning. He had acknowledged it and promptly forgotten about her. Now, as Beast played the first few bars and she walked toward him, he realized she was a whole lot more than stunning.

She wore a simple full-length white shift dress. High-necked at the front, swooping almost to the cleft of her buttocks at the back, slit to the thigh on both sides. The evening breeze molded the lightweight material to her body as she walked, highlighting the perfection of her figure. Her waist-length hair was iron straight, its blue-black sheen emphasized by the strobe lighting. As Sarange drew closer and raised her microphone, singing the first few lines of the song she had written—a love song to the creatures of the planet—he caught his first glimpse of eyes that were like chips of blue ice.

Forcing himself to focus, he circled her, growling out his response. The audience went ballistic. Could they feel it? Sense what he had experienced the moment she walked into view?

Khan knew what was happening, knew what the legends said. It was like a mantra imprinted into every shifter's psyche.

When you find your one true love, you will mate for life.

He had heard the stories about how a shifter instantly knew its mate. How the sudden hit of attraction and lust was like nothing he, or she, had ever encountered before. It was said to be irresistible, an injection of pure, molten heat straight into the bloodstream.

Yes, he'd heard other shifters talk about that feeling. He'd just never believed it. Until now. Until he'd seen Sarange. Breathed her in. Felt her touch his soul.

And now he was in deep trouble. For so many reasons. The thoughts tumbled over themselves as he continued to perform on autopilot. As far as the world was concerned, he was Khan, charismatic lead singer of the hugely successful rock band Beast. And that's exactly who he was. Who his *human* was.

But, like all shifters, Khan had two equal sides to his psyche. They existed in harmony, the traits of one complementing the other. He was a weretiger. Half human, half tiger, he had the ability to shift seamlessly from one form to the other. Because of the life he had chosen

when he met Ged—if "met" was the best word to use
to describe the encounter—he spent most of his time
in human form, but that didn't mean his inner tiger had
been subdued. Those instincts were as powerful as ever.
For Khan, as for all shifters who chose to live among
mortals, day-to-day living was a constant balancing
act, a striving to maintain anonymity.

Rock star by day, tiger by night. He was the mightiest of the big cats, with teeth, claws and a personality
to match, but that was his deepest, darkest secret. He
wasn't about to reveal it to anyone, particularly not Sarange, darling of the paparazzi. It didn't matter how
much she made the blood in his veins sizzle, or how
much she triggered a zipper-straining reaction farther south. It didn't even matter that she had her own,
equally compelling secret.

Because, as soon as he saw her, he knew. Sarange's
secret was the same as Khan's. She was a shifter, too.
Khan had scented her before he saw her. That gorgeous
face and stunning body hid the soul of a werewolf. That
knowledge made everything Khan was feeling right
now so far beyond screwed up he thought he might just
be going crazy.

He was a tiger. She was a wolf. Cats and dogs? They
were natural enemies. Put them together and the claws
came out and the fur flew. Even if Khan had been able
to do what the legends said—settle down, take a mate—
it would never be her.

The tales about the unbreakable bond between true
mates hadn't foreseen this particular problem. They
dealt only in success stories. Happily-ever-afters. It was
always possible Khan's dilemma had never arisen until
now. He needed answers. Having found a mate he didn't

want, a shifter couldn't walk away—could he? Once the bonds were forged, could they be broken?

He was about to find out.

There had never been any question about who the headline act would be. Never any doubt about who would sing the Animals Alive anthem as the concert closed. Beast was the hottest rock band in the world. Although Sarange hadn't been to any of their concerts, or met them in person, she intended to tap into that raw power.

Even if the lead singer was a total jerk.

She had watched enough footage of the band over recent weeks to reach a simple conclusion. Khan was a strutting, narcissistic show-off. She knew better than anyone that that was the perfect qualification for a rock star. Unfortunately, there was enough evidence to prove he was exactly the same offstage. She'd been hoping to enlist Beast's continued help after the concert. It made sense. *Beast.* It had the potential to be the perfect partnership. Their name combined with hers, their pulling power, the two contrasting audiences…between them, they could have taken awareness of the plight of endangered species to a whole new level. Having watched interviews with Khan and done her research into his lifestyle, she'd changed her mind. Promiscuous, arrogant, conceited, he just about summed up everything she disliked in a man…in a *person*. Khan described himself as "the guy who dived head-on into hedonism." Yeah. He was a jerk.

As she walked out onstage, she gave herself a firm reminder. This was for the Animals Alive Foundation, the non-profit organization she had founded. Its mission was to maintain the environments of endangered

species through fundraising and education. All she had
to do was get through one song. Five minutes out of her
life to get the attention of Beast's followers. She didn't
have to like this guy to sing with him. Performing was
what she did best. She achieved a melting expression
as she sang the first lines of the anthem that meant so
much to her.

Sarange was used to crowds, but this was an emotional high like nothing she had ever experienced. This
was the culmination of over two years of hard work. Of
being told it would never happen. Big fund-raising gigs
were last century. Austerity measures meant there was
no spare cash. People, not animals—that was the way
nonprofit worked these days.

Kicking open slammed doors. Pulling down barriers
with her bare hands. It was one of her strengths, but it
had been hard. Fighting the establishment one interview
and rally at a time. *If we don't care for animals, how can
we care for each other? When they are extinct, your re-
grets will be worthless.* Sound bites. Slogans. Pins. Ban-
ners. Every album she made, every photo shoot, every
gig…like a general rallying her troops, she used each
as another opportunity to get more people on her side.

But the feeling that tore through her as she reached
Khan had nothing to do with the triumph or relief of
this night. It had nothing to do with viewing figures or
pledges. It was about *him.* Something crackled in the
air between them and around them. It was electrifying,
thrilling and scaring her at the same time.

The film footage she had watched hadn't done Khan
justice. He was startlingly handsome. Tall, with a lithe,
muscular grace, his features almost perfect. He had
high, carved cheekbones, a straight nose and breathtaking amber eyes. Almost perfect because his mouth was

too full and sensual for perfection. But those eyes…they were mesmerizing. Set under slanting brows, they reminded her of a cat's in the way they drew her in and refused to let her go. As he closed the gap between them, he was staring at her with an expression she couldn't fathom. He could have been playing a part for the audience, but, if he was, he was good. Frighteningly good. Because she was instantly swept away by the hunger in his gaze.

This song wasn't supposed to be sexy, for God's sake. But the way Khan was standing behind her, not touching her, but almost touching her, his body moving in sinful time to the music…nothing had ever affected her this way. It was as if he was an illegal high and she was dragged into addiction after her first hit.

As they sang the last verse, Sarange was barely aware of the other acts who had performed throughout the course of the evening joining them on the stage. This night would go down in history. It would be remembered as the night she had alerted the world to her cause. And in her own life it was the night everything would change because she had met Khan.

When the song ended and the sound of Khan's voice died away, she felt bereft. He still hadn't touched her. Not once had he placed a hand upon her. She closed her eyes, willing him to do it now. To wrap his arms around her waist as he stood behind her on the stage. To let her feel the warmth of his body as they swayed in time to the music.

She opened her eyes to see a close-up of her face projected onto the giant screen at the rear of the stage. To the watching millions, the look of enchantment in her eyes had to do with the concert. Only Sarange knew the truth. She wondered if Khan had guessed. He was the reason for her rapture. Turning her head, she sought his gaze for confirmation.

She didn't get it. Khan had already left the stage.

Because of the number of acts performing in the stadium, there hadn't been enough dressing rooms for everyone, and Beast had been forced to share. They had arrived in Los Angeles that morning at the end of a three-month tour. Now that the concert was over, their tour bus would be taking them to New York, where the band was based. Predictably, the roads around the stadium were blocked. Their security team had advised them to remain in the dressing room, and they faced a lengthy wait before they could depart.

It was always the same when they were together for any length of time. At least on the bus there were sleeping compartments where they could escape each other's company. Now there were five massive egos competing for space in a small room.

"This sounds like the start of a bad shifter joke," Dev said.

Diablo scowled at him from under lowered brows. "What does?"

"Us, all crammed into this room. You know. A tiger, a dragon, a black panther, a snow leopard and a wolf…" Apparently sensing he had lost his audience, Dev shrugged and lapsed into silence.

The atmosphere had reached the point where sizzling tension was about to become boiling animosity, when Sarange burst through the door and jabbed a finger into Khan's chest. "You arrogant jerk!"

Khan, who was stretched full-length on the only sofa in the room, opened his eyes as she leaned over him.

Although her presence made his pulse soar, he managed to hide the effect she had on his emotions.

"I'm an arrogant jerk who is trying to get some rest." He closed his eyes again.

"How dare you walk off that stage like it didn't matter? Like you had someplace more important to be?"

Khan sighed and uncurled his limbs. Stretching, he got to his feet and looked down at her. Her hands were on her hips, and her lips were drawn back. Werewolves generally steered clear of confronting him. The hierarchy that existed in the animal world also applied to shifters. Tigers outranked wolves. It was a simple matter of superior size, strength, razor-sharp claws and lethal teeth. Even so, Sarange was displaying clear signs of wolf rage. Snapping and snarling. Normally he found it so unattractive. On her it was hot as hell.

"I thought I was a volunteer out there on that stage." Khan kept his voice light, knowing how much it would annoy her. He needed to infuriate her further if he was going to push her away. "Pardon me for not realizing I signed up to the slavery option."

Her indrawn breath was so harsh it sounded like a growl. He had to grip his hands hard at his sides to stop himself from shoving her up against the wall right there and then before hauling up the hem of that too-sexy dress.

"I think this is our cue to leave." Torque jerked a thumb in the direction of the door.

"Really?" Dev looked from Sarange's furious expression to Khan's watchful one. "Looks like this could get interesting."

"No need to go, guys." Khan tossed the words over his shoulder without breaking eye contact with Sarange. "Our visitor isn't staying."

He saw Torque wince at his dismissive tone. That distaste was the effect Khan wanted to have on Sarange. He needed to drive her away. Right away. Make her view him with hatred and contempt. If he couldn't make this aching, burning longing go away, he could at least make sure nothing ever came of it.

Although she was looking at him with scorn, Sarange wasn't going anywhere. She had come here with a purpose, and with classic wolf tenacity, she was going to see it through. His bandmates had clearly recognized her intention and, following Torque's lead, were heading for the door. Khan couldn't even call them on it. Couldn't question their loyalty. Over the years, his relationship with them had become the closest thing he had to friendship. But he was a tiger. A big cat loner. Powerful, sensual, selfish and controlling. His need to dominate the group was far greater than his human need to be liked.

As soon as the door closed behind them, Sarange was back on the attack. Like a beautiful wolf gnawing on a bone. "I was warned about you. Narcissist. Playboy. Jerk. That's what I was told. I don't know why I thought you'd be different."

"Nor do I."

A strangled sound of fury issued from her throat. "You are the most infuriating man I've ever met."

He laughed. "This is nothing. I can get a lot worse."

She drew a breath. "You made a commitment to this concert. You were the headline act. When you walked out on the finale, you gave a message to the audience that it didn't matter—"

He flapped a hand at her. "I get it. Let it go, wolf girl."

Her brow furrowed. "Wolf girl? What the hell is that supposed to mean?"

Khan stared down at her, incredulity jolting him out of his attempted nonchalance. She appeared genuinely confused. What the hell reason could she have to pretend *not* to be a werewolf? Was it possible Sarange didn't know she was a shifter? He'd never heard of that happening before, couldn't believe it was conceivable. Yet she was looking at him as though he was crazy.

Maybe that was the explanation. He might just be crazy after all. Had he gotten this all wrong? Could it be that she *wasn't* a werewolf? He dismissed that thought instantly. Khan's shifter instincts were pure and true. Beneath the expensive perfume she wore, the scent of Sarange's skin made his nostrils flare. She smelled of female wolf. Of lichens and berries, frost and pine. Of dark, sharp evergreens and ice-hard ground. It was an aroma that should have been alien to his inner cat. Instead, it was making his mouth water.

He wanted to taste her so much it hurt. And Sarange felt it, too. It was there in the depths of those unusual light eyes, in the flare of her nostrils, the way her nipples tightened and pressed against the thin cloth of her dress and in the warm, honeyed scent of her arousal. In the way her breathing came hard and fast as she faced him with a mixture of confusion and passion clouding her features.

Sarange moved first, wrapping her arms tight around Khan's neck and pulling his lips down to hers. She kissed him hard and hungry, claiming his lips as anger and lust powered through them both. Khan was helpless. No matter how hard he tried to resist, his need for her was too strong. His large hands seized her toned buttocks through the cloth of her dress, squeezing hard as he pulled her tight against him.

It was more conflict than kiss as Sarange squirmed desperately in his hold, her hands clawing at his shoulders. Their mouths clashed, tongues fighting, caressing, battling for supremacy. Khan was instantly rock hard, harder than he'd ever been. As he pressed his erection into the soft curve of her belly, Sarange moaned and broke free.

A dozen conflicting thoughts chased around in Khan's head as, breathing hard, they glared at each other.

Tigers and wolves...cats and dogs. How can she not know?

Make her leave.

Beg her to stay.

Kiss her again. This time make it last forever.

Just as he lifted a hand to slide it behind her head and draw her back to him, Sarange stalked out of the room.

Chapter 2

Sarange didn't know what she was feeling. So many emotions were competing for dominance inside her she couldn't begin to single out or categorize any individual one. Generally, her temperament was even. She didn't have mood swings. Yet after one brief encounter with Khan, her senses were swaying like a barometer needle in changing weather.

It was a relief to reach her dressing room without encountering anyone who wanted to talk to her. As the concert had approached, the demands on her time had increased. In the past few weeks, she had barely had a minute to call her own. Tonight had been a whirlwind of questions, requests and suggestions, all of which appeared to require her personal intervention.

Sarange had endless patience. It was part of her makeup. Her birth parents, whoever they were, must have bequeathed it to her with their genes. But right now she didn't want to cope with someone else's problems. Even for the sake of Animals Alive, the organization that had been her life's work for so long. The thought caused her a pang of guilt, and she managed to quell it. Just for once, she was going to put duty aside. She was going to spend a little time alone analyzing what had just happened to her.

How had she managed to let the most arrogant, infuriating man she had ever met get to her? *And by "get to me" I mean turn me on so much I almost burst into flames.* Just the thought of how Khan made her feel had her breath catching in her throat and a renewed thrill of desire pulsing through her body.

What is wrong with me? She closed the door behind her and leaned against it, releasing a long sigh. Despite his devastating looks, Khan was not her type. She didn't like overtly dominant men. Sarange had no desire to settle down. Now and then, she speculated about the reason. Did she have abandonment issues linked to her strange past? By ensuring she was the stronger partner in any relationship, was she making sure she couldn't be hurt? Although it made a strange kind of sense, she didn't feel it was a valid explanation for her choices. Perhaps she was just cold-hearted? It wasn't something that affected her strongly enough to probe deeply.

Now she thought about it, her brief relationships had all been with men who conformed to a certain category. *Undemanding* was the first word that came to mind. Did she deliberately choose partners who wouldn't challenge her? It wasn't a question she had considered until now, and she didn't like it. Didn't want to start psycho-analyzing herself just because Khan had strutted onto her horizon. *So what if, up to now, I've chosen sweet, considerate guys? The sort any woman would have no problem taking home to meet Mom and Dad?*

Not that Sarange had a mom and dad. She had an uncle and aunt who did the same job. She tried to picture taking Khan home to meet Bek and Gerel Tsedev. The thought made her choke back a laugh. It was never going to happen, but the image was amusing.

It wasn't just his arrogance that triggered a warning about Khan. It was the way he stripped away her control, and did it with such relish. *Wolf girl.* That was what he had called her. What had he meant by it? One thing was for sure, it wasn't a compliment. The tone of his voice had been scathing, while the look in his eyes had scalded her. She assumed he meant she liked to be in charge. He had judged her on first impressions, likening her to the leader of a pack. It was a curious analogy, but their encounter had hardly been conventional. If she hadn't walked out when she did, heaven alone knew what would have happened next. She had a feeling it would have led to passion beyond her wildest imagination followed by a world of regret.

Hadn't she been equally guilty of basing her opinion of Khan on sensational reporting and the antagonistic, thrilling clash from which she had just walked away? She pushed herself off from the door and made her way to the refrigerator. Snagging a bottle of water, she drained half its contents in a few quick gulps.

This violent attraction she felt toward Khan, this uncertainty and angst about her feelings, the burning restlessness that made her want to turn right back around and finish what they'd started…it was all new to her. New and frightening. She didn't like feeling this way. Sarange's life was neat and tidy. She liked it best when everyone knew what they were supposed to be doing and no one deviated from the script. This felt wild and unrehearsed. Khan had thrown her so far out of her routine she couldn't see a way back. And the scary thing was, she wasn't sure she wanted to.

Her whole body was still trembling with a combination of excitement and outrage. Curiously, she felt as though the electricity coursing through her veins was there to stay. How could that be so? The answer was simple. It couldn't. Put a little distance between her and Khan and she could forget him, get back to normal. It wasn't as if he could have any sort of lasting effect on her life. Was it?

A knock on the door startled her into spilling water down the front of her dress. Instantly, she wondered if it was Khan, and her feelings went to war over the possibility. Excitement trilled through her at the thought of opening the door and seeing him again. At the same time, anger flooded through her. There could be only one reason why he would follow her. He must be confident she would fall into his arms again.

And won't you? She hated this. Hated the way her body was pulling her in two different directions. Because she had no idea what she would do if she opened that door and Khan was standing on the other side of it. There was a strong possibility she would launch herself at him, but whether the outcome was a kiss or a punch remained to be seen.

With a hand that shook slightly, she turned the handle and opened the door. Her initial reaction told her everything she needed to know about her feelings. The man who stood there was most definitely not Khan. Shorter, slighter, with dark hair and sharp features, his smile oozing charm. It wasn't his fault Sarange wanted to slam the door in his face because he wasn't the person she longed to see. Her heart gave an uncomfortable downward lurch. She had a wretched feeling it was a signal. A warning that no one else would ever be good enough. From now on, the only person she would open a door to with a willing smile would be Khan.

This was straying into the realms of the absurd. This man, whoever he was, had begun to regard her with a slightly bemused expression. "Your manager said this would be okay. I'm Gurban Radin, owner of Real Planet Productions. We spoke on the phone last week."

Forcing herself to concentrate, she dredged up a memory of the conversation. "Of course." She held out her hand and he shook it enthusiastically. "Come in, Mr. Radin."

"Just Radin, please." He stepped into the dressing room. "I wanted to stop by and congratulate you on the success of tonight's concert. After what I've just seen, I'm even more keen for us to work together on the project we discussed."

Sarange nodded. "I'm looking forward to making the documentary with your company. Obviously, returning to my home country of Mongolia will be exciting for me. Even more important than that will be the focus on the plight of the blue wolves. They are one of the most endangered species on the planet."

Radin paced the small room excitely. "I don't know if you're aware of it…if you've had time to check yet?" He held up his cell phone. "But the response to your duet with Khan has been phenomenal. Social media is going wild. The electricity between the two of you was incredible."

"We are performers. That's what we do." Sarange hoped her voice didn't sound too cold, but at the same time, she wanted to dampen some of his enthusiasm.

And maybe some of her own. She also had no idea what her performance with Khan had to do with the wildlife documentary she was supposed to be making.

"Exactly." Radin's eyes shone with zealous light. "We need to use that, and also capitalize on the public enthusiasm."

"How do you propose to do that?" Sarange had a feeling she wasn't going to like the answer.

"By getting Khan to make the blue wolf documentary with you."

Being a rock star meant living on his nerves. The life was high-energy, high-profile and high-stress. Khan was permanently in the public eye and on someone else's agenda. He had known how it would be when Ged helped him escape from captivity. This was the life Ged had offered him, and he had embraced it with gratitude. Khan was good at it—the best—but it didn't always suit his big-cat temperament. His inner tiger craved solitude and supremacy. Juggling the two sides of his persona wasn't easy, and he had been looking forward to this time after Beast's tour as a chance to unwind before they started work on their new album. It hadn't happened.

It had been weeks since the Animals Alive concert, and the intervening time had taken the madness of his fame to a whole new level. The entire concert had fired the public imagination, but his duet with Sarange had been the highlight. The chemistry between them had been tangible to those watching. Rumors of a romance between the bad boy of rock and the world's most glamorous singer had persisted ever since. They couldn't look at each other that way and *not* be in love; that was the argument that pervaded every website, magazine and TV program.

Always the subject of paparazzi attention—the press was desperate to catch him out in bad behavior…and they often succeeded—Khan had been unable to move out of his New York apartment. Ged had advised him to lie low.

"Something else will come up in a day or two to attract their attention, and this will all be forgotten."

It hadn't happened. *Kha-range*—Khan wanted to put his foot through the TV screen the first time he heard *that* celebrity fusion name—had become a media obsession. Hotels and restaurants, keen to boost business, fanned the flames by hinting at sightings and bookings. Engagements, weddings, a secret baby, breakups…the whole range of stories had hit the headlines in the last few weeks.

And the job offers had rolled in. The moneymen, seeing the opportunities in a collaboration between Khan and Sarange, had come up with an eye-watering range of ideas. Films, TV specials, a record deal, interviews, photo shoots, advertising, even a book.

Khan had lost count of the number of times he had said no. Today was different. Today he would get to say the word to Sarange herself.

"No." He tilted his chair back so he could rest his shoulders against the wall. At the same time, he placed his feet on the glossy glass surface of the meeting table. The gesture was calculated to annoy Sarange. From the way her light blue gaze grew even icier as it dropped to his scuffed biker boots, he guessed he'd succeeded.

"I don't think you've quite grasped the concept." Gurban Radin, the guy who was in charge of the production company, leaned forward earnestly, resting his clasped hands on the table. "What we're proposing is unlike anything that's ever been done before. Two major stars being filmed as they travel together to a remote region of Mongolia to see the blue wolves in their natural habitat—"

"What part of 'no' didn't you understand?" Khan had no problem being rude to this guy. He hadn't asked for this meeting. He'd started out polite, but now they were taking up his valuable rehearsal time, and they still weren't listening to him.

"The Animals Alive Foundation would benefit from your contribution." Ged's eyes held a play-nice warning. Khan saw that look on his manager's face on a regular basis. Sometimes he felt a pang of pity for Ged. He worked so hard to keep Khan, his most famous client, out of trouble. He didn't always succeed.

"I'll write a check. Name your price." Khan yawned. "The answer is still no."

He could see Sarange fighting to keep her temper under control. He could read her emotions, even though he didn't want to feel that connection to her. Part of the reason he had agreed to this meeting had been to test his resolve. The last few weeks had been torture. Every minute of every day, his body craved her. It wasn't like going cold turkey on an addiction. It wasn't getting easier as time went by. He didn't have any periods when he didn't hunger for his fix. If this was the rest of his life, he was screwed.

He really shouldn't be here. Keeping away from her would have been the wisest move, but the rest of the world was conspiring against him. Even Ged was giving him some powerful reasons why he should consider this latest offer. In the end, Khan had taken a break from precious rehearsal time so he could look at Sarange and see how she was coping with the whole fated-mates, enforced separation situation. He hoped she was doing better than he was. And he wondered if she'd gotten a handle on her inner wolf yet. Because that whole denial thing was seriously weird.

Now that he was up close to her, he could see she was suffering. His gaze lingered on her face, drinking her in. Today her hair was drawn back in a thick braid that hung to her waist and she wore a crisp white shirt. Her jeans were tucked into soft leather boots. Even in casual clothing she managed to look like a Mongolian princess. Her face was heart-shaped, with flat high cheekbones tapering to a pointed chin. A broad, arrogant nose and full mouth added to the regal look. The only giveaway to her werewolf heritage was her eyes. Set under thick, soaring dark brows, they were twin chips of blue ice. Khan could see pain and confusion in their depths. Unlike him, he could tell Sarange still had no idea why she was hurting.

Life could be hard, and Khan knew from experience that went double for shifters. He experienced a brief, dangerous pang of sympathy for Sarange. Someone should sit her down and explain how these things worked. Not him. No way was Khan going there. But he wanted to take away that lost, hurt look in her eyes and replace it with the cynicism she would need to develop if she was going to survive as a werewolf in the human world. Maybe Ged could talk to her. The guy who had dedicated his life to rescuing damaged shifters had the experience and the skill.

"Are we done here?" Khan placed his hands on the table, indicating he intended to leave. Because he couldn't put his body under this strain for much longer. There was only so much torment he could endure. And fighting the need to drag Sarange into his arms was just about the worst torture he had known. Coming from Khan, a weretiger who had endured capture, imprisonment and near death, that was quite an admission.

"Wait." Sarange's voice was quiet, almost pleading. When she raised her eyes to his, it was as though there was no one else in the room. "Just hear me out. Please?"

In spite of the voice in his head urging him to get right away from her and do it fast, Khan sank back into his seat. There was a tiny flare of gratitude in her eyes. And, in that instant, he was lost. He understood how medieval knights of old felt when they performed heroic deeds to prove their worth. Climbing beanstalks, defeating dragons—although the only dragon he knew was Torque, and he was generally harmless—and breaking magic spells. She wasn't going to ask him to do any of those things. But he knew she was going to test his resolve.

"After to the red wolves, the blue wolves of Mongolia are the most endangered in the world. This pack has been gradually decreasing over the years so that now there are fewer than a hundred left." Her voice was low, passionate. It was obvious how much this cause meant to her. "I agreed to travel to the region to make a documentary to raise awareness of their plight. Now the production company—" her eyes flickered to Radin "—have said they will withdraw the funding…unless you and I make the film together."

"Why would they do that?" Even as Khan asked the question, he knew the answer.

"Isn't it obvious?" Sarange gave a bitter little laugh. "They'll draw a huge audience because of the recent public interest in us." She said the word "us" the way

Khan thought it. Within bitter quotation marks. "It all comes down to money."

Radin spoke up quickly. "We will, of course, be making a substantial contribution to the Animals Alive Foundation."

Sarange ignored him. "Even if this film gets made, it may be too late for the blue wolves. The prediction is that they will be extinct within five years. But if we can raise awareness, begin a breeding program…who knows? There may just be a chance we can save them."

"Why not make the film yourself using Animals Alive Foundation funds?"

"We couldn't allow that." Radin's voice was smooth. "My company owns the rights to the documentary. How it is made is our decision."

The sensation of being trapped was beginning to prickle along Khan's spine. They thought they had him. Conscience, publicity, environmentalism, guilt…they thought they'd pressed all the right buttons and gotten him where they wanted him. Even Ged, his *friend* Ged, was expecting him to agree.

Well, to hell with this. Swinging up from his seat, Khan stalked out of the room without saying another word.

Chapter 3

"Can I show you something?"

Sarange was so angry she wanted to barge past the man who spoke. She wanted to do a lot more than that. She wanted to eradicate anything to do with Khan from her life. If only it was that easy. Ever since she'd met him, it was as if he'd taken control of her thoughts as well as her body. For weeks now, she had been functioning only in relation to him. He was the first thing she thought of on waking, and the last image in her head at night. He occupied her whole attention in between, and then she dreamed of him while she slept. Her entire being burned with longing for this man. A man she had met once. A man she intensely disliked. It was the wildest, scariest, most wonderful feeling she had ever known.

Coming here today, knowing she would be seeing him again, had made her feel like a school kid with a crush. For days, she had been battling the butterflies in her stomach and the clamminess of her palms.

Will he remember the kiss? Does he wish it had ended differently? She had repeatedly tried to force her thoughts onto the most important thing. *Can I persuade him to change his mind about collaborating?*

When Khan had first walked into this meeting room, the roller coaster of her emotions was almost too much to bear. She had nearly convinced herself that her imagination was playing powerful tricks on her. She couldn't possibly have fallen as fast and as hard for Khan as her body was telling her she had. The guy was an overbearing, conceited jackass. No woman in her right mind could find him attractive. Okay, his face and body were incredible...*oh, heaven help me, I've been taken in by his pretty face and mouthwatering biceps.*

Sarange had been at the pinnacle of fame for over a decade. If good looks and muscles were what she wanted, she could have taken her pick. And, now and then, that was what she had done. Brief, pleasant relationships that had ended without regret or recrimination. But what she felt for Khan? This wildness? She had no idea what it was. All she knew for sure was she had to fight it. If she didn't, it would take over her life.

This issue with Radin and the documentary was a complication she could do without. Over the years, the Animals Alive Foundation had grown beyond her own desire to protect the endangered species about which she cared. Sarange's driving passion had become a global nonprofit organization, her primary function. Recently, her singing and songwriting had taken second place to her role as a wildlife ambassador.

Even so, she couldn't explain why she was so drawn to the plight of the blue wolf pack. *What the hell is wrong with me?* First there was this restless longing for Khan. Now she wanted to storm in and help a subspecies of wolf that was probably doomed anyway. There were bigger challenges facing the animal world. Ones that would attract far greater attention. Elephants, pandas, tigers…*fight the sexy fights.* It was no good. She didn't understand why, but the blue wolves called to her. Sarange would do what she could to save them.

It was her desire to protect the blue wolves that had brought her face-to-face with Khan again. She tried to tell herself that was why she had flown from Los Angeles to New York for this meeting. It wasn't out of any overwhelming desire to see him. And he had just rejected her. Again. She had created a situation in which he could storm out on her like a moody teenager…

She drew a deep breath and forced her focus back into the room and onto Ged Taverner. As he rose from his chair, Ged kept unfolding until his big, muscular body towered over her. As she looked up at him, it occurred to Sarange that she could have felt intimidated. Although her bodyguard was standing by the door, this guy looked like he could wrestle a bear with one arm tied behind his back. Instead, Ged radiated a curiously protective aura.

What was he saying? He wanted to show her something?

"I'm sorry. I don't have time…"

"This won't take long." He placed a hand under her elbow, his touch gentle but firm. The sensation of being swept along by forces beyond her control took over again. What was it about these people? Ever since she had encountered Khan, her life hadn't been her own. Did that extend to his whole entourage?

They left the meeting room and Ged led her to the

elevator. As he gestured for her bodyguard to wait, Sarange tried another protest. "I've wasted enough time
traveling to New York for a meeting that has proved
pointless. I can't see any reason to hang around."

"Five minutes." She capitulated, nodding to the
guard to meet her at the car. Ged smiled as he pressed
the button for the basement. "Thank you."

After exiting the elevator, they followed a short corridor. "Although the members of the band come from
all over the world, once Beast became famous, they all
moved here to New York. We tried a number of different recording studios before we settled on this one."

"If they come from all over the world, how did they
get together?" Sarange didn't want to be intrigued by
Beast. Didn't want anything to do with the world's
greatest rock band and its purring, strutting, infuriating frontman, but Ged's words interested her in spite
of herself.

"I brought them together." Why did she sense a huge
story lay behind that simple statement? In spite of their
dynamic personalities, Beast didn't give much away
about their private lives. Biographical details about the
band members were scarce. In the past, Sarange had
curled her lip at what she believed was a publicity ploy.
The enigmatic tough guys of rock. She wondered for
the first time what they were hiding.

Ged held open a door, motioning for her to precede
him. When Sarange stepped inside, she was in a recording booth. From behind a clear glass panel, she could
see a small, circular stage. Khan was seated on a stool
in its center. He had drawn his wild mane of red-gold
hair back with a simple elastic band, and his head was
bowed as he clutched a microphone to his chest. His
whole attitude was despairing.

Sarange turned to regard Ged. This didn't feel comfortable. It felt a lot like she was intruding on Khan's privacy.

"I've known him to spend hours perfecting a single note." Ged's voice was quiet as he looked over her head at the lone figure on the other side of the soundproof glass. "This side of Khan doesn't fit with his public image. The stage persona, the guy who'd laugh in the devil's face? That takes a hell of a lot of hard work."

He flicked a switch as he spoke and Khan's voice filled the booth. The song wasn't one of Beast's. It was an old love song, with a sweet melody, haunting in its intensity. Khan didn't apply any of his usual vocal fireworks to this performance. Alone, unaware of his audience, and with no backing music, he closed his eyes, pouring his heart into the song.

As she listened, tears burned the back of Sarange's eyelids. What *was* it about this man? Where had this invisible thread that pulled her to him come from? And how the hell was she going to sever it? She didn't know whether to be glad or sorry that Ged had shown her Khan had another side to him. Would it have been easier to walk away believing he was shallow and self-absorbed? Khan had given her no choice. She had to walk away. It was never going to be easy.

Ged waited until Khan had finished singing before he spoke. "His vocal range is unique. Khan can sing opera just as easily as rock."

As if to demonstrate, Khan started to sing again. The same ballad with a slightly different emphasis. There was something rawer in the emotion this time. God, he could tell a story with that voice! The last version had made her think of unrequited love. This one was a whole lot hotter. It conjured up visions of steamy sex and crumpled sheets…and it made her whole body burn.

"Who is he?" She tilted her head back to look at Ged. The question, coming out of nowhere, surprised her.

Ged didn't falter. "He is Khan." Ged said it as though it clarified everything. And maybe it did. Khan was one of a kind, defying explanation. "This campaign you have with the blue wolves, is that because of your own heritage?"

"I certainly have an interest in their plight because I was born in Mongolia, but that's not the only reason I want to help." She still wasn't sure why she felt so fiercely about this pack of wolves. Her homeland, heritage, Mongolian folklore…none of those things could quite account for the intensity of emotion this cause aroused in her.

"You must know that's not what I meant."

Sarange frowned. "What else could you possibly mean?"

Ged's expression was unfathomable. It reminded her of the look in Khan's eyes when he had called her "wolf girl" just before she initiated that devastating kiss. *What is it with these people and wolves?* Was it to do with the name Beast? Were they looking to use wolves for some sort of gimmick? Ged was staring at her as if she was an alien being. As if he couldn't make up his mind what to do about her.

Enough was enough. Whatever his problem was, she really didn't have time to spend analyzing it. On balance, she decided she was glad Ged had shown her this other side of Khan. Although her pride was still stinging, it helped to know he wasn't the one-dimensional jerk of first appearances.

She turned toward the door. "You're Khan's friend. Why does he hate me?"

Ged took a last look at the lone figure. "Khan doesn't really do friendship. And it's not you he hates—" he flicked the switch, and the booth went silent "—it's himself."

Beast had won Best Band at the Rock the World Awards for the last two years. This year, when they burst onto the stage to receive the award for the third time, Khan looked out at the sea of faces in the vast audience with a feeling close to apathy. The great and good of the music industry were gathered under one roof to honor their own, but there was only one person he wanted to see. He already knew Sarange wasn't there. If she'd been there, he'd have felt her.

They were in her town, yet she'd stayed away. It was her message to Khan. He knew she felt this invisible, unbreakable thread as powerfully as he did. By not attending this prestigious ceremony, she was showing him she was stronger than he was. She didn't need to see him. Didn't need the buzz that came from his nearness. This was what he'd wanted, yet the despair he felt was like a giant rock sitting on his chest. How could he miss what had never been his? All he knew was there was an aching hole in his life that could only be filled by Sarange. How was he ever going to learn to deal with this constant gnawing pain?

Beast was closing the award ceremony with a number from its new album. It was time to don his rock star persona and do what he did best...drive this crowd wild. Doing it when his heart had just been ripped out and his limbs felt like lead? That would be a new experience.

The way the band played together had always been

creative and intuitive. Each member was individually talented, but when they came together they became so much more. Maybe it came down to what they'd all been through before they got together. Their music did the talking because their emotions had been shredded. From Khan's raw yipping, screeching tones, through Diablo's wild drumming to Finglas's haunting bass lines, their unique sound pulsed with primal energy.

Physically they complemented each other perfectly as well. Each member of the band had his unique, onstage personality. Khan was all strutting, purring egomania. Diablo was solitary, stealthy and quick tempered. There was Torque with his quick-fire restlessness and Dev, in contrast, who remained cool and aloof. Finglas was the newest addition to the band. The young Irish werewolf had replaced Nate Zilar, the long-standing bass guitarist, and was just finding his place among the big personalities. Finglas often appeared detached, but he could raise as much hell as Khan when the mood took him. As a cast of characters, the band came together with a power that couldn't be manufactured. Beasts in the true sense of the word, they were one of a kind.

Behind them, giant LED screens played recordings of their signature three-sixes logo, roaring flames and the snarling jaws of wild animals. The cheering audience enthusiastically demonstrated the horned sign of the beast by pointing their fingers at the sides of their heads. The number ended on a wild note when Khan climbed to the top of the lighting installation at the rear of the stage, hanging perilously by one hand as he howled out the final verse.

He sprang back onto the stage, landing in a crouch at Torque's feet.

"And that, my friend, is how to bring the house

down," Torque said, as they walked off the stage. "I thought it might be literally. That set didn't look very stable."

Khan shrugged. "Remember Moscow?"

Dev caught up to them. "How could we forget? Although I blame Ged for booking us into a theater with balconies. He must have known you'd climb into them."

"How was I to know that building was unsafe?" Khan scowled.

Torque draped an arm around each of their shoulders. "Those were the days. Collapsing balconies. Irate Russians. Hot women. Cold vodka."

"Talking of which—" Dev steered them toward the bar at the back of the vast auditorium "—Ged is waiting for us. Best behavior, guys. The press is out in force tonight, always looking for the money shot of Khan in a compromising position."

Khan cursed under his breath. He wasn't in the mood for socializing, and he was never in the mood to have his behavior regulated. Over time, he had learned to strike a balance between his human and tiger personalities. On occasions like this, he drew on his human need for company, suppressing his cat desire for solitude. And there were usually compensations. On a night like tonight, he could generally find an outlet for his wild sexual appetite. The problem was, his body had decided it had found his mate, meaning his desire for sex with anyone other than Sarange had deserted him. It was a highly inconvenient side effect to an already out of control situation.

Until now, Khan's sexual instincts had mirrored those of a tiger in the wild. He supposed humans would call it promiscuity. Tigers would call it common sense. Find a female, have sex with her as often as possible within a short time frame until she was carrying his cubs, then move on to the next female. It was a simple rule for big cats in nature to ensure fertilization. As a human, of course, Khan was meticulous about using protection to ensure that didn't happen. Thankfully, his inner tiger didn't take over completely.

Monogamy wasn't part of the tiger social structure, but despite his inner cat, Khan wasn't all wild animal. He didn't get to be that lucky. Being a shifter, he got to live within a set of expectations that applied to all shifters. Ones that said he needed a mate. It seemed there was no right of appeal. Even though there were so many things wrong in this case. The mate the Fates had selected for him was the wrong species. She didn't know she was a shifter. *And don't get me started on who I am...*

Khan bit back a smile. Monogamy without a partner? Wasn't that called celibacy? That should keep Ged happy. At least there would be no sensational kiss-and-tell stories tomorrow morning.

"Come and join me, Tiger Boy." As if in answer to his thoughts, Ged appeared at Khan's side. He was carrying a bottle of brandy and two glasses. It was always serious when Ged got the brandy bottle out.

By some miracle, they found a quiet corner table and Ged sloshed brandy into the glasses. Around them, celebrities were getting drunker and noisier. Finglas was locked in an embrace with one member of a girl band, while her bandmate wrapped her arms around his waist from behind.

"That guy is after your reputation as the bad boy of Beast." Ged tilted his glass toward Finglas.

"The way I feel right now he's welcome to it." Khan leaned back in his seat, draining his glass in one gulp.

"Does this newfound apathy have anything to do with Sarange?"

Khan stared at his manager, the man who had rescued him from a cage and given him his life back. For long, unblinking seconds he said nothing. Then he sighed. If Ged wanted information from him, he would get it. He might as well cut out the part where he tried to resist.

"You've heard some crazy shifter stories in your lifetime, Ged. Shall I tell you a new one? One that takes screwed up to a whole new level?" He dropped his voice, glancing around to make sure they were the only ones who could hear. "How about I tell you the story of a tiger who fell for a wolf? If that wasn't bad enough, it gets even crazier. It turns out she didn't know she was a wolf."

Khan reached for the brandy, planning to pour himself another glass. To hell with it. He drank long and hard straight from the bottle, wiping the neck on the tail of his designer shirt when he finished. "I know."

Khan's eyes narrowed. "You know what?"

"I've met Sarange. I know she's a werewolf." Ged took the brandy from Khan and tilted the bottle to his own lips. "And I agree with your assessment. She has no idea what she is."

Khan slumped down in his seat. "Has that ever happened before?" If anyone was going to know the answer to that question, it would be Ged.

"Not that I'm aware. Violet, Nate's wife, lost her memory for a while." Violet was a werewolf who had joined them on tour recently. When she and Nate got married, he had left the band. "Part of that memory loss meant she forgot how to shift. That was temporary, but this is different. Sarange seems unaware that she has *ever* been a werewolf."

"What I don't understand is how she can be a shifter yet not want to shift. It's the most powerful urge we have. Right up there with breathing and sex."

Ged had been about to take another drink, but he lowered the bottle. "Judging by some of the situations I've had to bail you out of over the years, I'd say sex is the strongest urge *you* have."

Khan stretched his long legs in front of him. "I'm a cat. We enjoy the hunt."

"Yet you're not hunting tonight?" Ged raised a brow.

Before Khan could tell him to butt out, the music was lowered and the sound turned up on the big screens that were located on each wall. "You might want to listen to this, guys." Torque came to lean against the wall next to them.

The screens were all showing the same news story. The announcer's voice filled the room. "We're returning to our main story. Earlier this evening a group of four men broke into the Los Angeles home of singer, songwriter and animal rights activist Sarange—"

Khan was on his feet in an instant, his heart rate kicking up to explosive new levels. "What the...?"

"—although the men fled when the singer's bodyguards came to her aid, Sarange sustained minor injuries in the attack. It is believed the intention was kidnapping—"

Khan didn't hear any more. He couldn't think straight. Someone had tried to abduct Sarange. She had been hurt. His mate had been in danger and he hadn't been there to protect her.

Ged's hand was firm on his shoulder. "Go to her."

Chapter 4

How many different ways was she supposed to answer the same question? Tiredness and frustration were getting to Sarange now. It was beginning to feel like she was the suspect as the detective waited with his notebook open and his pen poised.

"I've already told you, Detective Kidd." Sarange thought she did a pretty good job of keeping the annoyance out of her voice. "They came into my bedroom through the balcony."

He tapped his pen against his teeth. It was a mannerism he'd already used a few times. If it continued, he might find himself eating that pen before too much longer. "See, that's where I'm struggling." He shook his head, and Sarange decided he'd modeled his mannerisms on various TV cops he'd seen. "You're saying that four men climbed up the front of the house and in through the balcony to this suite in broad daylight without being seen and without triggering the alarm system?"

"That's exactly what I'm saying."

Sarange had decided not to go to the Rock the World Awards. She hadn't declined, she had just decided she wouldn't turn up. Even though it was one of the biggest nights in the music world's calendar, she wasn't going to put herself through the humiliation of seeing Khan again. She might spend every private minute fighting the cravings, but she didn't have to do it publicly. She couldn't trust her emotions around him, and no way was he going to get another chance to humiliate her.

Even if he didn't reject her this time, what did she anticipate would happen between them? A one-night stand? She shivered at the thought. Spontaneity, stepping outside the boundaries, seizing the moment...they were all alien to Sarange's nature. She played by the rules. That, and the fact that she lived her life in the full glare of the public eye, were probably the reasons she'd never hooked up with a stranger. *I don't do wild.* An image of Khan came into her mind, bringing with it a surge of longing to break free of her self-imposed constraints. Although she thought she knew her own mind, her treacherous body kept giving the idea of a one-night stand an enthusiastic thumbs-up.

Her resolve had held firm. Vowing to avoid social media, she had spent the day in her office, doing her best to focus on Animals Alive paperwork. The attempt had been futile. The white-hot desire and almost insane longing for Khan weren't going away, no matter how hard she tried to push them aside. Knowing he was in the same town made it so much worse. It was as if an endless recording that could not be turned off was playing inside her head. Khan had entered her soul like a mind-altering drug, meaning she was no longer responsible for her actions.

Eventually, she had succumbed and checked her cell phone. Almost with a will of their own, her fingers found images and recordings of Beast arriving at their hotel. And there was Khan. Her heart melted at the sight of him. Glittering, feral, predatory. With his usual grace, he bounded from the limousine ahead of his bandmates. The sunlight turned his hair to burnished copper as he acknowledged the shouts of the crowd with a wave.

Who was she fooling? Of course she was going to the awards ceremony. There was no way she could stay away from him. That invisible thread that drew them together was pulling her to him harder and stronger than ever. It had been as she was in her dressing room, trying to decide what to wear, that the men had burst in from the balcony.

Sarange could understand Detective Kidd's confusion. It matched her own. Her luxurious home was secure. She lived in a gated community. She had three live-in bodyguards. Her security system was the best, and most up-to-date, that money could buy. There was no way four men should have been able to get close to her house, let alone inside her personal suite. She should not have a sprained ankle and a bruised cheek because she had fought them as they tried to drag her back out onto the balcony. It was only because she had her cell phone in her hand, with its personal attack alarm enabled, that she had been able to summon Marco, her head of security.

Her bodyguards had rushed into the room while calling the police. With remarkable agility, the intruders had vaulted back over the balcony wall and scattered through the grounds before they could be caught.

"I didn't imagine them." She was tired now. Yet surely she should feel more traumatized by her experience? Instead, her overriding emotion was disappointment that she wouldn't get to see Khan. "My bodyguards saw them, too."

The detective consulted his notes. "And these men made no attempt to hide their faces?"

"That's right. I've already given your colleague a description." Sarange resisted the temptation to sigh.

"Tall, muscular, medium brown hair, amber eyes, sharp features." His eyes probed her face. "That's your description...of all of them?"

"Yes." They had been through this. Several times. She knew how weird it sounded. "They could have been quadruplets."

Before he could say anything else, she heard a commotion. It sounded like it was downstairs, possibly in the entrance hall. Disturbances didn't happen in her house. In her life. She paid people to make sure of it. Now, twice in one day, her ordered existence was being tilted off course. But this time, she knew the reason. She could feel it...*him*. Khan was close by. She had no idea *how* she knew he was the source of the fire and fury taking place elsewhere in her home. She just did. This connection they had transcended normal rules.

Detective Kidd turned his head to look at the uniformed officer who was standing by the door. "Find out what's going on."

Before the police officer could move, Khan strode through the door, instantly filling her bedroom with his presence. Those hypnotic eyes, golden and fiery, fixed on Sarange as though there was no one else present. "They tried to stop me seeing you."

Sarange's head of security burst into the room behind Khan. His shirt was torn and a scratch on his face oozed blood. "I'm sorry. He was like a wild animal..."

"It's okay, Marco." And it was. Suddenly, it was as though she had been wrapped in a protective blanket. Without words, Khan had managed to do what the police and her bodyguards couldn't. Just by being there, he had reassured her that she was safe.

"Call me if you need anything." With obvious reluctance, Marco left the room.

Khan was about to cross to the bed when he appeared to notice Detective Kidd and his companion for the first time. "Why are these people here?"

"The detective wants to ask me some more questions."

"I think not." No one could do arrogant like Khan. As he turned that feline gaze on Detective Kidd, the words of protest died on the police officer's lips. Moving to the door, Khan held it open.

"There is something very strange about this incident. If you think of anything else, give me a call." Tossing a look of dislike in Khan's direction, the detective and his colleague left.

Sarange barely had an instant to wonder why Khan had come here. After taking so much trouble to show her he didn't want anything to do with her, why was he in her bedroom right now? And why was he gazing at her with *that* look in his eyes? Within a second or two of the door closing, he had crossed the room and dropped on one knee beside the bed, catching hold of her hand and raising it to his lips.

"I wasn't here to protect you. I will never forgive

myself for that." The antagonism was gone. His voice throbbed with genuine regret.

This should be weird. That was her first response to his words. She should run a mile from a man who spoke to her that way. She definitely shouldn't tangle her hands in his hair, or utter a sound that was midway between a laugh and a sob. This shouldn't feel like the best thing ever to happen to her. Yet, as she touched Khan, she could feel strength and heat flowing from him and into her body.

This is real. Whatever it is, this is happening.

"Who were they?" Khan lifted his head. "Did you know the men who broke in here?"

Sarange shook her head. "I've never seen them before. They didn't speak to me, so I don't know what they wanted. They were trying to drag me out of the house when I raised the alarm. Marco and my other bodyguards burst in. They called the police, but the intruders had already gone."

Khan raised a hand, his touch featherlight as he traced the bruise on her cheek. "They hurt you."

"Because I fought them."

There was a flash of fire in the depths of his eyes. She glimpsed something in him then, something raw and animal. It called to an answering part of her own character. A part she hadn't known existed until now.

"You are safe now. I'm here." His smile was pure insolence and undiluted mischief. "You no longer have to rely on second-rate protection."

"I get a rock star for a bodyguard?"

He got to his feet, and she looked up at him. He was breathtaking. "You get Khan." The words should have been conceited. Instead they comforted and scared her. Was it possible to feel those conflicting emotions at the same time? It seemed Khan could make her feel the impossible.

Khan pulled a chair over to the side of the bed and sat in it. Resting his feet on the mattress, he leaned back with his arms folded across his chest. Sarange turned on her side, drinking in the beauty of his profile. "You can't stay there all night."

"How else will I make sure you are safe?"

It was on the tip of her tongue to suggest he could join her, but she stopped short of saying the words. This wasn't a fling, or even the start of a brief relationship. This was beyond anything she had ever known. There was magic between them, but there were barriers as well. She still had no idea what this attraction was about. She suspected Khan knew and was fighting forces that went way beyond her comprehension.

She spent the night content to drift in and out of sleep, enjoying the deep contentment his presence brought. Strange snippets of dreams gripped her as slumber pulled her deeper into its embrace. Four men who all looked alike. Blue Fire. Great Tiger. Golden Eagle. The words meant nothing and everything. Each time she stirred and opened her eyes, Khan was there, watching over her.

Her life had just changed forever, and she didn't know whether fear or excitement was her strongest emotion. She only knew she had never felt either with such intensity.

Sleeping was one of Khan's favorite activities. Fortunately, he could do it pretty much anywhere. When he was on stage, he expended huge amounts of energy, and afterward his inner tiger took over to restore his energy. While on tour, he had been known to spend half the day sleeping. It wasn't considered unusual among his bandmates. Diablo and Dev were also werecats. No one flinched when Finglas bowed down before the full moon, Torque took to the skies or Ged disappeared into the forest for hours. There was mutual respect among the group for the diverse traits of the individual members.

So sleeping in a chair at Sarange's bedside shouldn't be a problem for him. Physically, it wasn't. He could curl his long limbs into a comfortable position and, catlike, be asleep in seconds. Even though they hadn't spoken about her attackers and their motivation, the possibility that they might return was at the back of Khan's mind. He wasn't afraid of that. They wouldn't sneak up on him while he slumbered. Khan didn't know who these people were, but he could go from sleeping to waking in an instant. The slightest sound, movement, scent, even a shift in the air would alert him to danger. His every sense would power up and be ready to take on the enemy. His fingers curled into the shape of claws as he looked forward to the prospect of confronting them.

No, it wasn't the physical practicalities of sleeping in a chair that bothered him. It was the problem of being so close to Sarange and not touching her. He had crossed a line tonight. Resistance had become acceptance. He had been fighting his attraction to her so hard that he had ignored another part of his role as a mate…protection. Alongside the admission that he had a duty to care for her, some of the barriers he had worked so hard to erect had come tumbling down. He couldn't remain antagonistic toward her when he needed to be at her side 24/7. He didn't know what the future had in store, but the present held a new rapport. Khan could snarl about the quirk of fate that had brought them here, but he was honest enough to admit he liked it. A little too much.

Although why watching Sarange sleep should bring him so much pleasure, he had no idea. She lay curled on her side in the huge bed, with one hand under her uninjured cheek. Her braid hung like a glossy rope over her shoulder, and the bedclothes had slipped down to reveal her pink pajama top. Her features were relaxed, her long lashes shadowing her cheeks, her lips slightly parted. And, alongside the fire in his blood, something softer bloomed within him.

He'd had enough torture. There was only so much nobility one person could stand. Slipping off his shoes, he leaned over Sarange and pulled the comforter up to her shoulders before lying down next to her. He was fully dressed. She was beneath the bedclothes. Resisting temptation would be a new experience, but he was prepared to try it.

Holding his breath in an attempt not to disturb Sarange, he settled his weight, turning on his side and mirroring her position. This was the problem with being a solitary being living among social creatures. Khan was used to doing what made him feel good without considering others. He stopped short of breaking the law and tried not to hurt anyone—either physically or emotionally—in the process. Even so, he had a lot in common with the ultimate hedonists who had colonized this human world. Like a domestic cat, Khan sought his pleasures, took them and only considered others as a means of getting what he wanted.

Right now his perfect pleasure was lying next to him...but he wasn't going to take her. His life had changed the moment he saw Sarange. The fabric of who he was comprised a unique pattern, woven by his experiences. It was ever-changing with old colors and textures fading and disappearing and new ones emerging. Even Khan had no idea how long he had been alive, or where his life had begun. Held in captivity in China, he had been in his tiger form when he was captured. The darkness, despair, hunger and weakness of his imprisonment had lasted many lifetimes. His captors had used silver to weaken him, but they couldn't kill him. He was unique, and that frustrated them. Now and then, he suspected his captors might have been werewolves, but he had no idea why they wanted him. A weretiger against a group of werewolves? It should have been no contest. That had been his last coherent memory of his capture until he was rescued by Ged.

Kept in a cage barely larger than a large dog kennel, deprived of natural light and half-starved, Khan had been close to death when Ged, acting on a story passed on by one of his informants, found him.

Ged was an enigma, even to his closest friends. A werebear of giant proportions, in his human form he poured his considerable talents into the day job. How he balanced managing one of the most successful rock bands in the world with his other persona was a mystery. Ged helped shifters who were injured, damaged or at risk of harm. Khan knew very little about his rescue work, only that Ged was the founder of an international team. *Like the Red Cross for shifters.*

Ged had always hoped that, once Khan was restored to full health and the trauma of his captivity had receded, his memory would return. It never had. There were snippets now and then. Of stalking deer along thicketed watercourses. Of vast, arid deserts. Of peering into shoreline bracken. Of crawling through a latticework of tangled low shrubs, emerging into willow and poplar forests. Nothing of himself, of who he was. *Who is Khan?* He had no idea.

Yet lying here, breathing in time with Sarange's rhythm, inhaling her sweet scent, he felt something stir inside him. Barely enough to call a memory, different to the bonds that bound him to her physically and emotionally. Certainty. That was what it felt like. A confidence that this woman was part of who he was. That pattern in the fabric of his life? The vibrant threads Khan didn't recognize had been woven by a different hand. *Hers.*

He didn't know how that could be so when Sarange believed herself to be human. She had no memory of herself as a shifter, let alone a shifter whose life had intersected his own. They both appeared to have a re-membrance short circuit. Now that they had met, was it possible they would trigger each other's memories?

On that optimistic note, Khan draped an arm over her waist and rubbed his cheek against the silken mass of her hair. Sarange murmured in her sleep and he smiled as he closed his eyes. This was the only pleasure he needed.

Sarange came awake abruptly, unsure what had alerted her to danger. Moonlight streamed in through the light drapes as her eyes searched the darkened corners of the room, seeking confirmation of what she already knew. Someone was in the room. No, not some-*one*, there was more than one person, standing just inside the balcony doors. Before she could do anything, the strong arm around her waist tightened its grip and a hand moved up to cover her mouth. Her first instinct was to struggle, but then she remembered.

Khan. He was signaling for her to stay silent. Sarange gave a slight nod to show she understood and he moved his hand away. Although his touch reassured her, she couldn't help being concerned. If the same men had returned, it would be four against one. Surely it would be better if she used her cell phone alarm and got security up here?

With a stealth that amazed her, Khan slid from the bed. Noiseless and unerring, he made his way across the room. His night vision must be incredible. A crash and a cry signaled that he had reached the intruders.

Sarange weighed her options. She could lie still and speculate about what was happening. Or she could find a way to go to Khan's aid. Switching on the lamp at the side of the bed, she froze in horror at the scene unfolding in her luxurious bedroom.

The four men who had tried to abduct her earlier were back. Even as fear kicked in and her heart rate soared, she took a moment to notice all over again the weirdness of their similarity to each other. She had fought them; she knew they weren't in disguise. They didn't just look alike. They were identical. Were they quadruplets? Clones? She swallowed hard. Was it possible that they weren't human?

Unsure where that last thought had come from, she snaked out a hand for the cell phone on her bedside table. Khan was going to need help after all.

"Don't call security." Khan's voice was like a whiplash. He was half-turned away from her, but he must have seen the movement out of the corner of his eye. "I've got this."

One of the men was already bleeding hard from a cut across his cheek. Did Khan have a knife? Sarange couldn't see anything in his hand. She remembered when Khan had burst into the house earlier. Marco had tried to stop him from seeing her and had suffered scratches to his face as a result. The wound on this intruder's face was too deep to have been caused by fingernails...

She slid from the bed, trying to scour the room for something she could use as a weapon while also keeping her eyes on Khan. The four men began to circle Khan, their manner predatory. She didn't like the matching smiles on their faces. It looked too much like they were snarling.

One of the men lunged and Khan was on him in a blur of movement, fighting like a wild animal. He didn't adopt a conventional style. Feet, fists, teeth and nails all went into the attack. His opponent went down fast under the onslaught.

The other intruders joined in, leaping on Khan. As incredible as it seemed, he kept going without pause. Swinging, slashing, powering into them. It was like watching a giant beast taking on a group of lesser creatures.

But something was happening. As if acting on an unseen signal, the four men were changing. It was swift and subtle. One second their human bodies were being tossed around by Khan as they attempted to bring him down onto the expensive cream-and-rose rug. The next, their facial features had elongated. In place of a nose, they each had a snout. Instead of a mouth, they had huge jaws with sharp snapping teeth. Their limbs stretched, becoming lithe and muscular. As they shook off the remains of their clothing, Sarange saw thick brown fur covering their bodies. A new scent pervaded the air. Like animal fur and carrion, it reminded her that she wasn't dreaming.

Wolves? Sarange shook her head in an attempt to

clear it. These were no ordinary wolves. *There are four werewolves in my bedroom.*

As if in confirmation of that thought, one of them threw back his head and gave a single, triumphant howl.

Even as she tried to process why four werewolves had come for her and tried to abduct her, Sarange's thoughts were on Khan. This took the danger to a whole new level. He might have been able to fight four men—although that must have taken some kind of superhuman strength—but this? Four sets of lethal canines trying to rip out his throat? Four sets of claws aimed at his belly?

Khan didn't seem concerned. On the contrary, he was smiling as he faced the werewolf pack.

And...oh, my goodness. This can't be happening.

Yet somehow she knew it was going to happen. The transformation was over in the blink of an eye. Khan's clothing burst apart. Beneath the remaining shreds there was brilliant orange fur slashed across with diagonal stripes, each as thick, black and straight as a hand-drawn charcoal line. In his place, a giant tiger reared on its hind legs, lips drawn back in a snarl that revealed white fangs almost as wide as Sarange's wrist.

The attitude of the werewolves changed in an instant from aggression to fear. Whimpering, they abased themselves, pressing their bellies into the floor and flattening their ears.

Khan dropped onto all fours. Even by the dim light provided by the moon and the lamp, Sarange could see the ripple of pure muscle beneath his thick pelt. *And why am I noticing his muscles when there is a tiger in my bedroom? A tiger in place of the man who had his arm around me minutes ago?*

The sound that filled the room was a soft, echoing rumble of pure menace. Originating in the depths of the tiger's deep chest, it shook every part of Sarange's body, even though she knew it wasn't intended for her.

How do I know that? How do I know he's not going to turn on me once he's finished with those werewolves?

The answer was simple. He was Khan. And he was hers.

At the sound of the tiger's growl, the wolves scrambled into action. Heading for the open doors, they couldn't scramble over the balcony rail fast enough. Khan followed them, his movements deceptive. That big body appeared to barely expend any energy, but he covered the space between him and the werewolves in double time, staying just behind them.

As Khan sprang from the balcony, Sarange ran to see what was going on. From her vantage point, she watched as the security lights below, triggered by movement, came on. The alarm remained silent, and she guessed the intruders must have disabled it and the security cameras before they broke in.

Below her, the elegant patio resembled a scene from a movie, as four werewolves crouched behind deck furniture to avoid the prowling tiger. Eventually, they broke free and headed across the lawn toward the pool. Khan was after them in a bound. The last view Sarange had was when he caught up with them on the extreme edge of her property.

With a shaky exhale, she turned on the lights and sat on the bed, waiting for his return. Because he would return. And when he did, he had some explaining to do.

Chapter 5

Khan knew the werewolves wouldn't be able to out-run him. He'd never come across another shifter that could match him for speed. The problem was, once the werewolves leaped over the perimeter wall surrounding Sarange's property, they did exactly what he expected them to. They split up and ran in four different directions.

Wolf instincts. He could never understand it. They would sacrifice one for the sake of the pack.

Khan's inner tiger was prompting him to kill, but his human senses were urging caution. He could catch one of the werewolves, but forcing the guy to shift back and start talking? That needed privacy and time. And a tiger in the heart of Beverly Hills didn't have the luxury of either of those things. He faced a choice. Risk bringing chaos and carnage into the heart of the human world, or let the werewolves go.

The two halves of his psyche went to war. While his tiger was pushing him to hunt and kill, his human was arguing for restraint. Because he was in tiger form, it would be easy to go with the voice of his inner animal. His tiger instincts were strong, but he fought them. Reluctantly. Now was not the time. This was definitely not the place.

The werewolves had been given a powerful warning. They knew what they were dealing with. They would be back—tenacity was one of wolves' strongest traits—but Khan would be ready for them.

With a feeling of resignation—a tiger always knew when to give up the hunt—he turned back toward Sarange's house. He should shift back before he was seen. That way, his only problem would be that he was a naked man in the heart of Beverly Hills. That, and the fact that he needed to talk to Sarange about what she had just witnessed. He had hoped to ease her in gently to his shifter status. The werewolves had taken that opportunity away from him.

Shifting back, he kept to the shadows. Even in his human form, he retained elements of his inner cat. They showed through in his strength, speed and agility. When he had fought the four men back in Sarange's bedroom, there was no hesitation. He had known he could take them on and beat them. Just as he knew now he could scale the wall surrounding her house. Nimble as his inner cat, he pulled himself up and over the wall, dropping into a crouch on the other side.

Khan's eyes scoured the darkened yard, his keen vision easily picking out the security cameras. Sarange had live-in security, but no one had been roused by the arrival of four intruders. The werewolves had somehow bypassed her security system. His protective instincts went into overdrive again, his hands curling into the shape of tiger claws. *If I hadn't been here...*

He forced his breathing back to a regular rhythm. He had been here. He *would* be here. But they still didn't know what the werewolves wanted from her. All they knew for sure was this wasn't a robbery. This was about Sarange.

Using the ornate shrubs and flowers as cover, he made his way across the yard. Stepping onto a patio table, he climbed from there onto the balcony. Swinging himself over the rail, he looked around for something to cover his nakedness. He couldn't see anything. Maybe that was because his gaze was immediately captured by an ice-blue stare.

Arms folded across her chest, Sarange was standing in the doorway, blocking his entrance to the room. "You can start talking now."

"I was hoping to shower first. Maybe find some clothes."

"You turned into a *tiger*." He wasn't sure whether the wobble in her voice was caused by anger or shock. It didn't matter. She kept going, coming toward him until he was pressed up against the balcony rail and she had to tilt her chin to look up at him. "I need to know what's going on."

He caught hold of her upper arms, and as soon as he touched her, she collapsed into his arms. The feel of her body against his drove every other thought out of Khan's mind, and a harsh groan of surrender was dragged from him. His whole body was entranced by her. His eyelids half closed as if weighted and he lowered his head, compelled by a force beyond his control to graze Sarange's lips with his.

I don't want to control this.

The instant his mouth touched hers, their ragged breathing united in a single rhythm. Sarange melted into him, nuzzling his lips with her own. He clutched her tighter to his wildly beating heart, deepening a kiss that left Khan reeling. Achingly tender, it should have been unique. So why the hell did it feel so familiar?

His body was on fire, his arousal in danger of reaching epic proportions. Khan needed to regain control of the situation. But he was naked, with a beautiful woman in his arms. Restraint, never easy for him, was getting harder by the second.

"I'm hungry." He murmured the words into her hair.

"I can tell." She glanced down at his erection. In the moonlight, he could see a blush staining her cheekbones.

Khan groaned as temptation almost got the better of him. He pressed his forehead to hers. "No, I really am hungry. For food. Shifting affects me that way."

"Shifting?" She wrinkled her brow. "Is that what you call it when you change?"

"Yes. I'm a shape-shifter."

She was silent for a moment. When she raised her eyes to his, the anger was gone. He wasn't sure he could name the emotions that replaced it. There was a healthy dose of understandable confusion, but he thought he could see acceptance. Of what, he wasn't sure. His shifter self? Or of *them*?

"Take a shower. The security guards have spare uniforms. I'll see if I can find something to fit you. Although—" there was that blush again "—you are very big. Then we'll go down to the kitchen. You can talk while you eat."

* * *

Khan had already eaten the remains of a cold chicken, a quiche and a bowl of potato salad. He had washed this feast down with a half quart of milk. Now he was prowling the kitchen, opening cupboards and regarding Sarange with a look of dismay. "No cookies?"

"I don't really eat sweet things."

"Let me guess." He pointed to the chicken carcass. "You'd rather eat the meat than the salad. You like your steak rare. No one ever quite cooks it bloody enough for you, am I right?"

She blinked at him, the hairs on the back of her neck prickling slightly. On one level, it didn't matter how she liked her steak. On another, it was scary that Khan could somehow get inside her head and know that much detail about her.

"Is your special tiger sense telling you that?" *What else is it telling you? Is it telling you who those men—those* werewolves—*are, and what they want with me?*

Khan came to sit on a stool next to her at the counter. "I'm not sure I have a special sense. Maybe it was a lucky guess."

She shook her head. "You're going to have to do better than that."

"I know."

He gazed into space, gathering his thoughts, and she took a moment to study him. The sweatpants and T-shirt she had found were stretched tight over his bulging muscles, and his hair was still damp from the shower. Now that she knew what she was looking for, she could see the tiger in the man. It was there in the tawny tint of his hair, the broad, arrogant nose, the fiery gold eyes. In the lines of his body, she could see the coiled strength of the mighty beast, the long, lithe sinews and the powerful muscles. Most of all, she could see it in his mannerisms. Khan *was* a cat. He was the ultimate rebel. His movements were all stealth and grace.

He was breathtaking, and yet…he was the opposite of everything she had believed she wanted in a man. In the past, she had never admired flashy good looks and strength. She'd have run a mile from a promiscuous narcissist like Khan. So why did it feel like everything, her whole life, her next breath—*who I am*—was wrapped up in this man?

Was that why she had accepted his shape-shifting, if not with ease, at least with composure? Although her mind was still struggling to make sense of what she had seen, she had felt no real surprise or skepticism. Instead there had been a sense of "So *that's* what this is all about."

Yet a man to whom she was attracted—more, this was so much more than straightforward attraction—had changed into a tiger before her eyes. She should be cowering in a corner at least. Probably there should be screaming involved. Sitting next to him, gazing at him as if her whole world hinged on his next breath, was possibly not the most sensible approach to how this night was unfolding.

Sarange had a feeling she had waved goodbye to sensibility around the time she first set eyes on Khan.

"I'm not an expert on the history of shape-shifters." When he turned back to face her, the smile in his eyes undid her. Took everything she was and unraveled it. Sarangerel Tsedev came apart and became…just his. "You would need to talk to Ged if you want an in-depth analysis."

"I want to know about you. Anyone else can wait.

Start by explaining what you meant when you said you are a shape-shifter."

"It means I can take on the physical form of an animal while maintaining my human consciousness." He regarded her warily, as though unsure of her reaction.

"Can you do it any time you want?"

Khan nodded.

"But you control it? It doesn't just happen without warning?"

Another nod.

"Can you become any animal you choose?"

"No, I'm a weretiger. My DNA is part human, part tiger." There was a note of pride in his voice. "With an extra shifter-something thrown in for good measure."

"Were you born this way?" She had so many questions, but no uncertainty. He was telling the truth. Even if she hadn't seen the evidence for herself, she would know it.

He pulled in a long, slow breath. "Most shifters are born with their abilities. Rarely, they are converts. That means they are turned by a bite. It can happen in conflict. If a shifter leaves a victim close to death but still alive, that person will himself become a shifter."

"Like the horror stories of werewolves?" Sarange thought of the movies that had scared her when she first came to America. Although nothing could have prepared her for the scene that had played out in her bedroom a few hours ago.

"Exactly. It's a big responsibility. But shifters living in the human world are peaceful. Conflict is rare. The other way a human can convert is voluntarily."

"Really?" Sarange couldn't imagine a situation in which that would happen. "Do you guys hold recruitment drives?"

He laughed. "No. When a human falls in love with a shifter, he, or she, might choose to take the bite of his mate." *Ah.* A little bit of electricity crackled through the air briefly. "But I believe I was born a shifter."

"You believe it? That sounds like you don't know."

"I don't." He was on his feet again. Restless, noiseless, stealthy. Opening the blinds to peer out at the darkened yard. Rearranging the utensils on the rack. Taking the knives from the block and testing their sharpness against his thumb. "I don't know anything about my early life."

Sarange slid from her perch on the high stool and went to him. Standing close, she reached up a hand and ran it through the thick mass of his almost-dry hair.

Khan ducked his head, pushing back against her touch, a smile curving his lips. "I know what you're doing."

"You do?" She hadn't thought about what she was doing. Had just acted on impulse to try and soothe him.

"You're stroking me."

"So I am." She continued the movement, pushing her fingers through his hair, watching in fascination as he visibly relaxed.

"Just so you know—" his voice was almost a purr "—catnip doesn't work."

She laughed. "I'm glad you told me." She looked into those incredible eyes. "Can you talk about it?"

He hunched a shoulder in a half shrug. "There isn't much to talk about. I was rescued from captivity by Ged about ten years ago. I can't remember anything before that. I don't even know exactly how I came to be captured."

As he spoke, every part of his body tensed once more. She could hear the pain in his words, felt each one being dragged out of him. "I know Ged is you manager, but what else does he do?"

Without knowing it, she had found the right question. At the mention of his manager's name, Khan relaxed. "Did you ever read the stories of the Scarlet Pimpernel?"

Sarange wasn't sure where this was going, but she nodded. "He was the fictional hero who rescued French aristocrats before they could be sent to the guillotine. He pretended to be a bumbling Englishman, but in reality, he was a quick-thinking escape artist."

"Ged is the shifter version of the Scarlet Pimpernel," Khan said. "By day he is long-suffering rock star manager Ged Taverner. By night he is a werebear who rescues shifters from danger."

Sarange shook her head in an attempt to clear it. "This night keeps getting stranger." There were still so many questions that needed answers. She decided to start with the obvious. "Those men who came into the house earlier? They were also shifters. Do you know who they are?"

"No. They are werewolves, but I've never seen them before. I didn't manage to catch up with them to find out why they were here, but they'll be back. It's the wolf way. Tenacity is in their blood. Once they have a mission, they won't give up." His eyes scanned her face as though seeking a response.

What do you want from me, Khan? I know nothing about werewolves, but you're looking at me as though I have the answer. I don't even know the question.

"And now that they know what they're up against, they'll reinforce the pack."

Sarange cast a scared look over her shoulder. "What

shall we do? They'll tear my human security guards apart."

Khan stretched his arms above his head. "Right now? We'll get some sleep. They'll need time to regroup. Wolves don't do anything spontaneously." His smile managed to reassure her and heat her blood at the same time. "Tomorrow we'll bring in a few reinforcements of our own."

While Sarange slept, Khan walked the house and grounds, learning the layout. Getting to know his territory. He had napped briefly, but he was conscious of danger nearby, threatening his mate.

Tigers don't mate for life.

It was an insistent little voice in his head, warning him to keep his distance. He didn't need any more warnings. This whole situation couldn't get any more screwed up. He was a shifter who couldn't remember anything prior to his rescue ten years ago. Sarange didn't even know she was a shifter. To make things worse, they were from different species. Just about as opposite as two beings could get. Unfortunately, no one had told their raging hormones about the obstacles. The instincts drawing them together were stronger than anything driving them apart. *As if we were free to mate and be together for life.* The thought caught him hard in the chest, knocking the breath from the lungs. It wasn't a good idea to indulge in *if only.* And at some point, he was going to have to tell Sarange that. How the hell he was going to begin *that* conversation, he had no idea.

Tigers don't mate for life, but shifters do.

That was the problem. Now that they'd found each other, he had a feeling there would never be anyone else. For either of them. How do you tell a werewolf, who doesn't know she's a werewolf, that she can't mate with a tiger? Those cute internet pictures of domestic cats and dogs snuggling up together? Not the same thing as lifelong mates. Lions and hyenas? Leopards and jackals? Tigers and wolves? It didn't happen.

Oh, hell. I need Ged here. This is a halfway-down-the-second-bottle conversation.

Luckily, Ged was on his way. When it came to reinforcements, there was only one group of people Khan trusted. Beast members bickered their way around the world. Their competing egos didn't allow for true friendship. Khan knew he was a big part of why that was true. Put a tiger at the center of any group and the grandest of the big cats was always going to stake his leadership claim. Khan shook his head. The idea that he would ever back down and let anyone else take his place was so ridiculous it wasn't worth considering.

There were other big, alpha male personalities in the band. The next fight was always only a snarl away. The peacekeepers—Ged and Torque—had their work cut out, particularly when Khan and Diablo clashed. But when it mattered? Khan would trust his bandmates with his life.

"Let me get this straight." Ged was used to getting "bail me out" calls from Khan at any hour of the day or night. Even so, his voice had been a sleepy rumble. "We were due to fly back to New York at noon. Now you want us to change our plans. Instead of working on the new album, we're going to move into Sarange's house and take an extended vacation while we do bodyguard duty."

"There are plenty of recording studios in Los Angeles," Khan had said. "We don't have to stop working."

Just as Khan had known he would, Ged had agreed.

Because that was how it worked. No questions, no explanations, no protests. His friends—because that was the closest word he could find to describe what they were—would have his back. And when the time came, Khan would do the same for them. When Ged brought Beast together, they had been a collection of lost and damaged souls. Each of them had a horrific story to tell. Joining the band had been their rehabilitation. Maybe it was their redemption.

As Khan walked through the grounds in the early morning light, the foul werewolf stench of the intruders lingered. It was strange how that worked. Khan hated the smell of werewolves. Even in their human form, he could barely stand to be in the same room with them. He had built up a sort of immunity to the scent of his bandmate Finglas. He could tolerate his aroma, without liking it. Almost as if the guy wore an obnoxious cologne. So why was it that Sarange smelled like the sweetest thing in the world? She was a werewolf. Khan should detest her scent. Instead, he couldn't get enough of her. He wanted to nuzzle her, sniff her skin, lick her all over...

He looked up at the balcony that led to her room, picturing her asleep in that big, ridiculously opulent bed. He couldn't help the leap of joy his heart gave every time he thought of her. Dogs and cats. Had there ever been a time in the past? Could the first time be now?

Those werewolves had come after Sarange for a reason. Why now? What was going on in her life right now that meant four werewolves wanted to abduct her? Diablo would sneer at Khan's first thought.

"The world does not revolve around you, Tiger Boy." It was Diablo's favorite phrase.

Diablo was wrong, of course. And Khan delighted in telling him so. "Try telling the world that."

Right now, when he was examining what was happening to Sarange, Khan's entry into her life was one thing that could have triggered the werewolf attack. Why? He had no idea. He was simply considering the possibilities.

The only other things he could think of were the Animals Alive campaign and Sarange's determination to save the blue wolves. Again, when it came to trying to establish a link between either of those things and the intruders, Khan came up with a big, fat nothing.

He was tired of thinking. It was still early. The world wasn't fully awake. There was only one place he wanted to be. Up close to Sarange. Pressed so tight against her even a sliver of light couldn't get between them. That sounded like a plan. Breaking into a loping run, he retraced his steps back to the house.

Chapter 6

Sarange had given orders to her housekeeper, Henry, about rooms and food, and requested that Marco liaise with the manager of the gated community about the tour bus. People always assumed that she was a loner, but that wasn't her choice. Sarange liked having others around her. Being alone was just the way her life had worked out.

Having Beast around? That was going to take some getting used to. It was like her cool, luxurious home had been turned into a snow globe. Shaken up, it was now a blur of noise and color. In addition to Khan, there were now five other big, muscular men taking up every corner of her space. They had been there half a day and she was already tripping over guitars, boots, jackets, empty take-out boxes and beer bottles. They didn't seek each other out to have a conversation. They yelled from one end of the house to the other. And they

spoke in a strange shorthand only they understood. One
minute they were snickering at jokes no one else was
part of. The next, they were exploding with rage over
an imagined slight.

"We are an acquired taste." Torque, the lead guitarist, smiled at her with sympathy in his unusual eyes.
Just when she thought they were dull and gray, they appeared to change color, reminding her of opals as they
shimmered with iridescent light.

"After what's happened over the last few days, I'm
happy to acquire it."

It was true. She'd take noise and mess if they brought
her safety…and Khan. Although she still wasn't sure
what benefits Beast brought over a team of security
guards. Khan had admitted that Ged was a shifter. Did
that mean…? She cast a sidelong glance in Torque's direction. If he was a shifter, she couldn't figure him out.
What was his alter ego? Something with quicksilver
movements and lightning reflexes.

"Dragon."

"Pardon?"

"That's what you were wondering, isn't it? I'm a
weredragon." Torque grinned at her dumbfounded expression. "But don't worry, I promise not to burn your
house down."

She was still wondering if he was joking when Khan
called the band together in the sitting room, outlining
why they were there. He turned to Finglas. "Have you
heard anything about these guys?"

Finglas gave a long-suffering sigh. "You say that as
though I hang out in werewolf bars, or I have wolf informants." Khan frowned and Finglas held up a hand
in a gesture of peace. "No, I don't know anything about
these guys. But werewolves who are prepared to draw

attention to themselves by going on the attack? That's not normal." He turned to Sarange. "And they all looked alike?"

"Identical. Their hair was a medium brown color, their eyes were light—sort of a golden brown—and they all had the same features. I got a good look at them. Both times."

"And they're not a pack you know?"

Sarange frowned at the strangeness of the question. A pack she knew? Just how many werewolves did he think she was familiar with? Being a lycanthrope himself, Finglas possibly thought everyone had shapeshifter acquaintances. Before she could answer, Khan took the conversation in a different direction.

"These guys didn't come here to rob or kill Sarange. They were trying to abduct her. Someone wants her. I brought you here to protect her, but I need to find out who that someone is."

"That's a dangerous move." Ged's deep, calm voice held a warning note. "If you want information, it means when they come back we have to keep at least one of them alive. Even then, getting a werewolf to betray his leader won't be easy. A wolf's loyalty is second only to its stubbornness."

"Ahem. Wolf in the room." Finglas quirked a brow in Sarange's direction. "Two wolves, actually."

Okay, this was getting seriously weird. She decided it was time to call him on the implication that she was a werewolf. "What do you mean by that?"

Finglas regarded her with something that looked a lot like amazement. Before he could speak, Ged's placid voice intervened. "Can we get back to the logistics?"

Ged's apologetic smile to Sarange took the heat out of the way he'd redirected the conversation away from her question. She supposed he was right. Keeping them out of danger was more important than her vague feeling of unease about Finglas's strange comments. Finglas was a werewolf. Maybe they were all eccentric. How would she know? He was the first one she had met.

"The werewolves have been here twice. Both times in a group of four. That's a small pack, but they were expecting to come up against only human bodyguards. Now they know there's a tiger waiting for them. They'll rethink their strategy, but they won't be deterred."

"They should be." Khan's lip curled.

Ged shook his head. "You know that's not the werewolf way. They will be wary of facing a tiger, but they won't back down. Werewolves will see their task through to the end. They will sacrifice a few foot soldiers for the sake of the mission."

"You mean they'll be happy to throw a few werewolves to Khan as a distraction while the others focus on Sarange?" Torque said.

"Exactly." Khan's golden gaze was fierce as he looked around the room at his bandmates. "I'm relying on you to make sure they don't get as far as Sarange."

Diablo yawned. "We can take a few werewolves."

The feeling that she had stepped into an alternate reality was growing stronger by the second. Her ordered world had become a place of danger and she had no idea how or why it had happened. Now her elegant sitting room was filled with shifters who were calmly discussing how to kill werewolves. *But let's not forget the importance of keeping at least one alive. You know, just so we can find out who is behind this plot to abduct me...*

Could she have somehow, in the last few days, drifted into a nightmare from which she hadn't woken? That was how this felt. That curious dream-state feel-

ing that everything was the same, yet *different*. That
she had changed. That dreaming Sarange and waking
Sarange inhabited the same body at the same time, but
had separate experiences. All the time, there was something important that was being hidden from both parts
of her psyche.

Right now she needed time to breathe and think…
and she needed the answer to one very important question.

"I need to talk to you." From Sarange's troubled expression, Khan could guess what this was about. *Damn.*
He should have known Finglas would say something. It
was his own fault for not warning the others in advance.

She left the room and he waited until the door closed
behind her. "This is going to sound strange, but she
doesn't know she's a werewolf."

Finglas choked on the soda he had been drinking.
"You're joking, right?"

Khan sighed. "No. She genuinely has no idea."

"We all know what trauma feels like. It affects every
shifter in a different way. Until we know Sarange's
story, we can't understand what made her this way."
Ged placed a hand on Khan's shoulder. "Just go easy
on her. Take it slow."

Khan's smile was rueful. "You think I can't do sensitive?"

"I think you're a tiger."

He found Sarange in her bedroom, pacing the length
of the patterned rug. She paused when he entered the
room, turning to face him, and he got the feeling she
wanted to throw herself into his arms. It was more than
a feeling. It was a certainty, based on a memory deep

in his heart and his muscles. He even braced himself
for the impact of her weight against him.

But she held back. "What's going on? Why does
Finglas think I'm a werewolf?"

Because you are. He took her hands in his, feeling
the quiver that ran through her body, and drew her down
to sit next to him on the bed. "I guess he's wondering
why you are being pursued by werewolves."

"That's a mighty big leap. I'm not in denial about
the existence of werewolves. I saw them with my own
eyes. But what you're suggesting doesn't make sense.
Werewolves are after me, so I must be one myself?"

"It makes more sense to a shifter."

She leaned her head against his shoulder, seeming
to take comfort from his nearness, and the depth of his
responsibility to her hit Khan full force. It was a new
sensation for him. New, but not unknown. How did that
work? He wasn't sure, he only knew it was tied into
his complex feelings for this woman. He was a loner.
He walked away from caring, but he would never walk
away from Sarange.

After a few minutes, she raised her head. Those
unusual eyes were so ice-chip light, they should have
appeared cold. Instead, they conveyed a strength of
emotion that swept him up and dragged him under.
"You can protect me physically, but I need the truth
from you."

"What do you want to know?"

"When we first met, you called me 'wolf girl.' Did
you think I was a werewolf?"

Go easy on her. Take it slow. Ged's words hadn't allowed for an out-and-out question. "Yes."

Her eyelids fluttered closed and he caught her tight
against him. To hell with cats and dogs. If there was

ever only one moment in his life that mattered, this was it. Holding Sarange in his arms as if he would never let her go. Showing her with his strength and his body how much he needed her. Encircling her. Keeping her warm and safe until the trembling in her limbs subsided.

"Why? What made you think that?" The whispered words left his heart raw and bleeding.

"Shifters know other shifters. We recognize each other."

"Could you be wrong?"

"There's always that chance."

She tilted her face up to look at him, her eyes widening. "You don't think you're wrong."

He didn't respond. Instead, he lay on the bed, drawing her down to lie next to him. "Tell me about your early life."

Sarange nestled into his side. "I don't talk about it when I give interviews because it sounds too much like a fairy tale. I was found by a shaman when I was a few days old, wrapped in a reindeer hide, miles from civilization."

"A shaman? Is that a wise man?"

"In this case a wise woman, a shamanka. In Mongolia, shamanism is widely practiced and known as Tengerism. The shaman are the intermediaries between the visible world and the hidden realm of the spirits. The shamanka who found me was a member of a nomadic tribe. She had left her people briefly to be alone and commune with the spirits."

Khan couldn't see her face, but he could hear the warmth in her voice.

"Her name, the closest you can get in Western words, was Golden Wing. I called her Grandmother. My childhood was spent as part of the tribe, traveling the snow-packed tundra, caring for the reindeer, goats and sheep."

"That's a long way from LA."

She laughed. "When I reached my teens, Golden Wing announced one day that she had family in California. Although emigration from Mongolia had become more common, and my grandmother had insisted on educating me, America was like a distant dream. But it was a dream that came true. While I was here, my American family recognized my singing ability and I auditioned for a TV talent show. The rest, as they say, is history."

"And your grandmother?"

Sarange was silent for a moment. "Golden Wing died not long after I came to America. I was heartbroken that I wasn't with her at the end. I'll always wonder if she knew she was ill and perhaps sent me here to start a new life. The relatives I was staying with adopted me. They were her relatives, not mine, of course. I have no idea who my birth family is." She seemed to shake off the introspective mood. "It doesn't matter. My aunt and uncle Tsedev are my *real* family."

"Have you been back to Mongolia?" She was right, it did sound a lot like a fairy tale.

"Only once. It felt different. Like I was going back as a tourist instead of as little Sarangerel, the girl who rose at dawn and milked the goats."

If she was a werewolf, she'd have been little Sarangerel, the girl who rose at dawn to *eat* the goats. Khan decided not to break the mood by mentioning that. "You should take a backpack. Do it the hard way."

She leaned her chin on his chest. "Like you would?" Her eyes were teasing. "Mr. Hedonism?"

He lifted her so she lay on top of him, wrapping

his arms tight around her waist as she squirmed in his hold. Letting her feel the aching length of his erection against the softness of her stomach. One slender thigh slipped between his, and she stilled, sensing the change in his mood.

A tiny gasp escaped her. "This is the reason you haven't made love to me."

Khan tangled his hand in her hair, tilting her head to his. "There are many reasons. None of them have anything to do with not wanting you."

Her lower lip trembled. "No matter how much you want me, you can't change who we are. If you're correct about me, I'm the last person in the world you should want. I'm not even the right species."

Khan muttered a curse, sliding a hand behind her head and bringing her lips down to his. "Who cares about right when wrong feels like it was meant to be?"

As soon as Khan kissed her, moving his big, warm hands beneath her T-shirt and up her spine, arousal slammed into Sarange with all the force of a freight train. It was a need unlike anything she had ever known, so powerful it should have scared her. Instead, it excited her. Made her picture experiences beyond her previous imaginings. That was what Khan had done to her. Flung her past the outer limits of her curiosity.

The images that filled her head were so incredibly explicit that it was hard to believe she had never been intimate with this man. It was as if she knew, in erotic detail, how it would be between them. As though her body and mind were working together with perfect sensual timing. Her nipples tightened and her sex heated as her inner muscles clenched in expectation.

When Khan lifted his head to study her face, his

golden eyes were glazed with lust and uncertainty. "This affinity between us… I've never felt anything like it before."

Sarange liked that she wasn't the only one feeling thrown off balance. His eyes burned into her, telling her everything she needed to know about his need for her. Her world had been tilted wildly off course, but clinging to Khan was what she wanted. His touch, his warmth, his kisses, they were the only things that made any sense. Emotion blossomed deep within her. Certainty came in its wake. This feeling. This knowledge that Khan was everything, that being with him was her whole life…it was a bone-deep commitment, stronger than a vow.

Passion was an electrical current in the air between them, in and around their bodies. Sarange raised her hands above her head, allowing Khan to pull her T-shirt over her head. "That's because your soul already knows me." The words resonated through them both. She had the strangest feeling of them lighting up time and space like a string of fairy lights illuminating a path to bring them together.

When he kissed her again, the connection tingled all over her body as if a spell was cast with each touch. Pulling him closer, she tasted his lips, his mouth and his tongue, wanting more each time.

As he removed her bra she squirmed, pressing her legs tight together to relieve the ache between them. Khan's hands roamed over her exposed flesh as his mouth swooped down on her nipple. It ignited a fire through her bloodstream.

"I want to make you feel so many things." His voice was hoarse as his lips moved to her other breast. He turned her so she lay on her back as his hands moved swiftly to undo her jeans. "So many different ways I want to make you scream." Her jeans were thrown to the floor with her underwear quickly following. "Would you like that, Sarange? Do you want me to make you scream?" He laughed as he lowered his head and nipped the sensitive flesh of her breast again. "Or howl?"

Even though the idea that she could be a werewolf hadn't fully taken hold in her mind, that single word made her surge against him. Still fully clothed, Khan inched down the bed.

"Open your legs for me."

Slowly, Sarange parted her knees. Khan moved into place between them, spreading her thighs farther apart with his broad shoulders. His fingers slid up and down her crease, opening her to his gaze.

"So pretty. Pink and wet. Just perfect" He lapped her center in a single lick. The slightly rough texture of his tongue was delicious, making her gasp and shudder.

Khan circled her opening with the tip of his tongue. "I already knew how you'd taste. The sweetest flavor in the world." He plunged deep and she cried out, grasping his hair in both hands.

Replacing his tongue with two fingers, he moved his mouth up to concentrate on her clit. With his other hand, he circled one hard nipple with a fingertip before squeezing the tight flesh in time with the thrust of his fingers.

Incoherent sounds escaped Sarange's lips as she clutched his hair tighter, shaking and thrusting her hips toward his mouth. Her inner muscles gripped him hard and her thighs began to tremble as her body sought its release. Khan nipped at her nub with his teeth as his fingers curled up, finding the sweet spot inside her and triggering spasms of pleasure that rippled out of control. The fire in her blood flared to new heights and her whole body began to vibrate.

"Khan…"

Her hands moved to his shoulders, clawing at his smooth flesh as every muscle tightened with shards of diamond-bright pleasure. And as she arched off the bed, the sound that left her lips *was* a lot like a howl. The climax that roared through her was the most exquisite torture she had ever experienced. And it went on and on as Khan kept his mouth on her, licking in time with the shudders that shook her, slowing gradually until she reached a standstill.

He moved to lie next to her, smoothing her hair back from her face.

Sarange sighed. "That was…"

"Amazing?" His grin was pure Khan. "Felt that way for me, too."

The look in his eyes started a slow burn deep in her core all over again. "Do you have a condom?" she asked.

"I'll be right back." He slid from the bed, going to where his luggage—delivered by his bandmates earlier—was stacked near the closet.

When he returned, he shrugged quickly out of his clothes. Sarange's breath caught in her throat. Khan was always magnificent, and she had glimpsed him naked when he returned from his pursuit of the wolves, but now…

She raised her arms to him. "Come to me, my tiger."

Khan lay on the bed next to Sarange. *Come to me, my tiger.* He wouldn't have believed it was possible to want her more. Yet, as soon as she uttered those words, they thrilled through him, spiking his desire even higher. As if they had a meaning beyond what she said. A code that spoke directly to his nerve endings. When Khan kissed her, it started out soft and persuasive. He parted her lips with his tongue, entering her mouth with gentle licks. When Sarange returned his caress, the slow start was soon transformed into plunging thrusts as their tongues met and twirled together.

"I need to touch you." Sarange's eyelids drooped as she studied him. "All over."

Her fingertips left surface-of-the-sun heat trails as they danced over the muscled ridges of his abdomen. Tracing up his biceps, over his shoulders, and around his back, she dropped around to run her hands over his taut ass. His muscles tightened and trembled as though shot through with electricity. The anticipation of her touch hadn't come close to the reality. His mind was shutting down, handing him over completely to sensation.

Returning to the front of his body, Sarange reached for his straining cock and ran a finger lightly around the head. Khan hissed. It was the only sound he was capable of making.

She moved her mouth to his collarbone, nipping lightly, seeming to know that was his most sensitive place. Encircling his shaft, she gripped the base before slowly stroking his length.

"Feels good." Khan managed to get the words out through gritted teeth.

"That's what I want. I want to make you feel good." Her eyes were on his face, watching his reaction to her touch.

How could he explain that "good" didn't come close to explaining how she made him feel? That everything else faded into nothingness in contrast to this? Even being on stage, the one thing in his life that had felt real and true, became meaningless compared to Sarange.

Her hand on him was too much, and he placed his own fingers over hers, stilling her movements.

"Condom," he explained hoarsely, glad he was still capable of rational thought.

When the protection was in place, he moved in position between her thighs. He studied Sarange's face, exulting in how she looked in that moment, eyes half-closed, cheeks flushed, lips parted. He rubbed himself against her, up and down, and her head fell back.

"Look at me." His words were slurred with desire.

Sarange lifted her head, giving him back the eye contact he needed. For an instant, he held her there. Their gazes caught and locked as if a pause button had been pressed on time and space.

Then Khan lowered his eyes and watched the point where their bodies met as he pushed into her. The sensations powering through him were extraordinary. Forget the legends. Nothing had prepared him for this. It was a bond like no other.

"Sarange." He threw his head back, feeling his connection to her in every part of him. Mind, body and soul.

Sarange was trembling all over. Her hands tightly grasped his upper arms, her teeth gripped her lower lip and her breath was coming in shallow gasps.

He paused, regarding her with concern. "Is this okay?"

"Don't stop." She lifted her hips, urging him to continue. "Please…"

He inched inside her a little more, halfway into her. He could feel her stretching to take him. His neck and shoulder muscles strained with the effort of holding back from pounding hard and fast. The feeling of driving slowly into tight heat was too delicious to rush. It was like a warm memory and he wanted to savor every second.

As his feelings threatened to overcome him, he took a couple of deep breaths. Looking back at where their bodies joined, he pushed forward once more. Sarange arched her back, surging up to meet him.

"You're so big."

With a final thrust, Khan seated himself all the way to the hilt. "Too big?" He growled...because growling seemed to be all he was capable of doing.

She tossed her head from side to side on the pillow. "Just perfect."

He tried to go slow, starting out by pumping in and out, adding a roll to his hips that had Sarange grinding her pelvis against him. But slow wouldn't quench the fire that was raging out of control between them. It was as though this need had been burning his whole life. He picked up the pace, thrusting deep, feeling her body clench around him.

Pulling his hips back, he drew his shaft through the tight grip of her inner muscles, paused a beat, then thrust hard once more. Sarange shook wildly. Her vaginal walls clasped him and her eyelids fluttered closed. He felt the moment her orgasm gripped her, held her suspended in time before tipping her over into violent, whole-body shaking pleasure.

Khan continued to thrust into her, taking her harder, using the aftershocks of her climax to increase her pleasure.

"Khan..." In that second, as he stared at her, something more than their gazes locked and something beyond their bodies connected. Two more deep, hard penetrations and fire streaked along his spine. He came so hard it felt like his heart was exploding. At the same time, a tightness inside him unfurled. The darkness that had been part of him for a very long time just got lighter.

He purred his pleasure deep in his throat, holding on to Sarange like he was never going to let her go. As he waited for the world to stop spinning, he wondered if he ever *could* find the strength to release her. Because finding Sarange had been like finding a missing part of himself. The image wasn't yet complete, but every second he spent with her added a tiny piece to the overall picture that was Khan.

Chapter 7

Sarange didn't recognize this version of herself. Letting another person into her life and her heart was a new experience, one that contrasted with everything that had gone before. She didn't know why the fear of loss was so strong inside her. Maybe it was because of her abandonment as a baby, although she questioned if that could be true. All she knew for sure was that she had always backed off from intimacy. It was a simple formula, one that had worked well until now. If she didn't let anyone get close, she couldn't get hurt.

There were other reasons why this was out of character. She had a house full of guests. That brought responsibility. Sarange was good at duty, organization, order. Yet she had abandoned all those things to lie in Khan's arms. Wrapped in their own world, here in her room, in her bed. The rest of the world had faded away. And she was *enjoying* it.

She didn't care that those people downstairs—his bandmates, her staff—would think of her as a horrible hostess. That they would raise their brows and exchange knowing glances about her and Khan. All that mattered was his chest beneath her cheek, his fingertips tracing her spine and the occasional rumble of his laughter when they spoke. They didn't speak much.

In between talking and touching, there was plenty of time for thinking, but her mind seemed to have been infused with the same soporific effects as her body. Her adrenaline levels should have been sky high. Right about now she should have been running for the hills, or calling the police. Not only did she have four werewolves on her tail, she also had a weretiger in her bed. And he was trying to convince her that she was a werewolf herself.

Surely the last thing she should be doing right now was indulging in delicious, toe-curling, sheet-ripping sex with the aforementioned big cat? The thought made her bite back a smile. What had Khan said? Right and wrong didn't matter when it was meant to be. It was crazy, but true. The wildest, most impossible series of events had brought her into his arms. Yet, in this instant, within the protective mantle of Khan's embrace was where she belonged.

Being with him seemed to have unleashed an inner self she hadn't known existed. There was a wild side to her that she didn't recognize, but it was one she definitely liked. And it was as if a cache of hidden memories was waiting just out of reach. *But why would I have hidden memories?* Unlike Khan, Sarange knew who she was. She remembered everything about her life.

This sense of not knowing herself, this new duality, bothered her more than the idea that she might be a werewolf. Or were the two things entwined? Was it possible that the perception of being two people was because she *was*? Without knowing it, could she be the person she had always known…and a werewolf?

Surely, I would know? I don't feel any burning desire to howl at the moon. I have never met anyone and longed to rip out their throat. I don't even like red meat…

And yet there was the affinity she felt to the blue wolves. It was overwhelming. From the first time she had heard about them, their plight touched her more than any other animal she had heard of. She even dreamed of them. Sarange was an animal rights campaigner. It was her life. Yet that remote wolf pack had called to something deep within her.

She sat up abruptly, hugging her knees up to her chin. "The blue wolves."

Khan frowned. Lazily, he tugged the comforter around his waist as he moved into a reclining position against the headboard. "You think that's who these werewolves are?"

"No." Sarange was thinking out loud, trying to clear her head of a jumble of thoughts that were only half-formed. "The blue wolves are a small pack, a subspecies of the Mongolian gray wolves. They are unusual because of their blue eyes. True wolves shouldn't have blue eyes. It's thought to be a genetic mutation unique to this pack." She turned her head to look at him. "There is no longer one single idea of what it means to have traditional Mongolian coloring, but in my tribe when I was growing up, I was considered unusual because of my blue eyes."

"You have blue eyes. So do they. It's a tenuous link at best."

"I agree…if that was all. But it's more about what I feel. Here." She pressed a fist to her chest. "When I heard that the blue wolves were in danger of dying out, it became an obsession with me to do something to save them. I've always felt strongly about helping endangered animals, probably because of Golden Wing and the tradition in which she raised me. Shamanism is animalistic. Her belief was that, in the spirit community, all beings are equal. Humans are not greater than other creatures."

"Who told you that the blue wolves were at risk?" Sarange had noticed that expression in Khan's eyes before. It was his tiger look. He appeared lazy and unconcerned, but there was razor-sharp concentration in those golden depths.

"My aunt Gerel. I think she has some shaman tendencies, although, having embraced a Western lifestyle, she keeps them hidden. When I was approached by Radin to make a wildlife documentary in Mongolia, naturally I wanted it to be about the blue wolves. You met him when we discussed the documentary. He owns Real Planet, the production company that came up with the original proposal. Radin is the creative brain behind the operation. As I told you, he changed his mind and wanted you and me to work on the program together when the rumors started about our relationship. Getting us together was a money spinner."

"It seems to me we need to find out more about the blue wolves."

"We need to speak to my uncle Bek." Although the man who had adopted her when Golden Wing died had lived in America for most of his adult life, he was an expert on the history and culture of his home country. "Right now."

Khan's hand on her wrist stopped her from jumping up there and then. When Sarange raised a questioning brow, he nodded toward the open balcony door. The light was already fading. "The werewolves will come back under the cover of darkness."

"If I'm a werewolf, I should be able to fight alongside you." Sarange's expression was stubborn as she faced Khan. Wolf determination was etched in every line of her body. It shook him all over again that she could have reached adulthood not knowing who she was.

They had eaten dinner with the rest of the band. Ignoring Marco's objections, Sarange had given her human security team the night off. Khan didn't want any witnesses to what was about to happen. Now he was organizing where everyone should be in readiness for the inevitable werewolf attack. The only problem was Sarange. She had decided she didn't want to return to her bedroom and wait there while Khan and his bandmates confronted the intruders.

"That argument is flawed on so many levels." He tried not to sound patronizing. This was her house. She was the person in danger. He didn't want to take the decision-making away from her. Okay, that wasn't true. He *did* want to take over. He wanted to wrap her up and keep her safe from harm. Forever. But he already knew Sarange well enough to be aware that a display of alpha-maleness from him wouldn't go down well with her. "You've only just discovered you may be a werewolf. You aren't even half convinced it's true. Suppose it is. You have no idea how to shift into your wolf form, do you?"

She drew herself up to her full height, opening her

mouth as she appeared about to voice a protest. Under his probing gaze, she subsided. "No."

"Take the whole thing to the extreme. Imagine what would happen if you did face a pack of experienced werewolf fighters alongside an experienced group of shifters. Even supposing at the last minute you discovered your own ability to shift, do you believe you would also find a hidden talent for fighting to the death at the same time?"

Sarange huffed out a breath. "Well, when you put it like that…"

He gripped her shoulders, drawing her closer. "I know how hard it is for you to hand this over to others."

"Do you? How is that?" Her gaze scanned his face, and there was a tremor of fear in her voice. "It's true, but how do you understand me so well, Khan? And how do I know you like I know myself?"

He wasn't sure telling her what he knew would be helpful. After a brief debate with himself, he decided *not* telling her would be unfair. "There is a belief in shifter legend that there is one mate for each of us. That we are fated to meet that person and be together for life."

"You think that's what has happened to us?" Her brow wrinkled. "But how could that be true of us? You are a weretiger. If you're right about me, I'm a werewolf. I may be new to your world, but I'm guessing that puts us at opposite ends of your shifter spectrum. We can't be together forever. We may not be at elephant and mice incompatibility levels, but we're not far from it."

Khan started to laugh. "Elephants and mice?"

"You're picturing it, aren't you?"

Sarange was trying to keep her voice stern, but he could see the smile in her eyes.

"Admit it. It would be quite a love story," he said.

She allowed a chuckle to escape, but shook her head. "I need you to focus your cat attention span back on us. What you said about mates would explain the attraction we feel. It wouldn't explain the other things."

She was right, of course. He knew what she was going to say, but he couldn't give her any answers. He could probably throw a whole load of more questions back at her.

"When I touch you, it's electric. But why do I feel like it's happened a hundred times before? When I look at you, my pulse races. But why do I feel like you're the missing part of me I never knew I'd lost? My lips say the words. *We shouldn't be together. You're a tiger. I'm a wolf...*apparently. But my heart doesn't listen, because my soul knows different."

What she was saying resonated deep inside him. Khan didn't want to leave her and go into a fight. His mind and body were still reeling from the effects of their lovemaking, of a connection that had taken them beyond anything physical. He had known the moment he first saw Sarange that they had a unique bond, but sex had elevated it to a whole new level. And she was right. There was a mysterious sense of *knowing*. Could they have been together before in another life? He was a shifter. He had to open his mind to the mysteries of the universe, but that idea took some getting used to. And there were other problems to deal with right now. Problems that had teeth, claws and came in a pack.

He pressed his lips to her temple. "I don't know. All I know is I feel the same. And maybe when these werewolves come back, we'll get some answers." He tilted her chin up so he could scan her face. "Promise me you'll stay here. That way I can focus on them without worrying about your safety."

She nodded. "How lucky was I that you came into my life at just the right time? When these werewolves appeared and attacked me, I had you here to protect me."

"Or we could look at it another way." Her brow furrowed in confusion as he voiced the thought that had been troubling him. "Just after I came into your life, a group of werewolves turned up and tried to abduct you. Was it a lucky chance that I arrived in time to take care of you? Or was I the trigger for their attack?"

Sarange might have agreed to stay in her room, but Khan hadn't said anything about not watching the action. From her balcony, she had a good view of most of the grounds at the rear of the house. If the werewolves wanted her, this was the way they would have to approach her suite.

When she had bought this property, it felt like a dream come true. And yet...part of her still missed the wide-open spaces and freedom of her childhood. A land where everything, as far as the eye could see, was untouched. Living in a gated community with bodyguards, alarms and security cameras often felt alien and restrictive. It closed her down from friendships and even acquaintances. Sarange liked people—*is that because I'm a werewolf, a pack animal?*—and being a celebrity could be a lonely life. She had her aunt and uncle, of course. They were more than her family, they were her link with Mongolia and her past life.

For the first time, she wondered how much of her fairy-tale life had happened by chance. Could Golden Wing have foreseen this future for her? Even arranged it? The thought was foolish. How could a lone shamanka, all those thousands of miles away, have so much influence that she could shape the future? Sarange was growing fanciful, her mind making connections that didn't exist. There were enough strange things happening without the need to invent more.

In the moonlight below her, Khan was a shadowy figure prowling the darkened yard. The security lights, triggered to activate at the first sign of movement, had been disabled. She knew the other members of Beast were deployed at strategic points around the gardens.

"Let the werewolves get in, surround them, trap them." Khan's instructions had been delivered in a cold, precise voice. There was no trace of the frivolous rock star. He had been a general directing his troops. How did she know he had done that before? *Because I was there.*

More than a military leader directing his men, he was a tiger ordering his dragon, wolf, bear, panther and leopard. The knowledge of who they were was still sinking in. It was surreal. This was Beast, one of the best known bands in the world. Now she knew why they protected their privacy so fiercely, why biographical details about them were so bland. They were hell raisers, but no one knew much about where they went after they partied hard. All that legendary raw energy they brought to a performance? Sarange was seeing for herself, up close, where it came from. On stage, they were five uncaged animals. The effect was eye-watering.

It was a still night, and sound traveled. She could hear traffic in the distance, and a faint breeze rustled the trees. Her hearing had always been good. Did that mean...? *Oh, dear Lord, can I please stop taking every thought back to whether I'm a werewolf?*

Her annoyance spiked and took a sudden nosedive

as a new sound caught her attention. Faint, stealthy, unmistakable. Someone—more than one someone—was climbing the outer wall. Her gaze went to Khan as he dropped to a crouch in the shadows below the balcony.

Sarange's eyes strained to count the figures making their way over the manicured lawn. Definitely eight. Possibly ten. Already in wolf form. *Too many.* There were only six people protecting her. Khan had underestimated the opposition.

As the werewolves neared the balcony, the yard beneath her erupted into life. The lack of light meant it was like watching a flickering black-and-white movie, but she could see enough. In addition to the tiger just below her vantage point, she watched two other big cats burst from the shelter of the ornate trees at the far side of the yard. She registered that the muscular black panther who aligned himself with Khan must be Diablo. Silent as a ghost, Dev, now in the form of a huge snow leopard, sharp and white in contrast to the shadows around him, moved into place at Khan's other side.

She couldn't focus on the trio of big cats for long. Not when, from the opposite corner of the house, Torque strode into view, still in human form. Raising his hands, he unleashed a series of explosions in his path. As he walked, he grew in size until he towered over the werewolves and big cats. Even in the darkness, Sarange could see his eyes were bright red, the color filling the entire surface. The pupils had become vertical black slits. He blinked, his top and bottom lids moving in reptilian manner to meet each other.

As Torque broke into a run, the clothes tore from his body. His arm and leg muscles thickened, and he dropped onto all fours, enormous claws the size of a mechanical digger churning up the lawn. Giant wings unfurled, and a spiked tail flicked out before he opened his mouth to shoot a stream of blue-white flame in the direction of the werewolves. Transfixed, Sarange watched as Torque, the most mild-mannered band member, became a fearsome, beautiful dragon. He rose and hovered, his wings spanning most of the house.

Maybe six will be enough. The thought had barely formed when Finglas, a lithe werewolf, and Ged, a huge, majestic bear, appeared. They closed off any avenue of escape. Khan's plan had worked. The werewolves were surrounded.

Some deep-seated instinct told Sarange the werewolves would not retreat. Even when faced with such fearsome opponents, they had a mission, and they would see it through. She could understand that tenacity. It was part of her own makeup.

The moonlit scene quickly became all action. The three big cats bounded forward in one fluid movement of bared teeth and lethal claws. The werewolves, caught unawares, attempted to scatter across the lawn. They weren't fast enough and Khan, Diablo and Dev each caught a werewolf in his mouth or between his paws.

Sarange had expected to be horrified by the brutality of their attack. Maybe it was the unreality of the shadowy scene. Possibly it was because it happened mercifully fast. Blood appeared black as it sprayed up from the throats of the captured werewolves. Movement ceased. The big cats flung the lifeless bodies aside and moved on. She watched it, if not with indifference, with acceptance. With a sense that this was how it had to be. This was the shifter world. It was brutal, but necessary.

Throwing off one of the smaller werewolves as it leaped onto his back, Finglas sank his teeth into the attacker's belly. His victory howl was muted. No need to alert the neighbors.

Surprisingly graceful for such a large animal, Ged bounded into the center of the action, throwing himself into the fray. Landing on the back of one of the startled werewolves, the mighty bear used its lethal claws to tear a chunk of flesh from its victim's neck. The whole time, Torque hovered over the scene, shooting jets of fire at any werewolves who were not directly involved in the fight.

The werewolves rallied. Targeting Khan as though sensing he was in charge, two of them brought him crashing to the ground. With a roar of fury, the huge tiger rose on his hind legs, attempting to shake them off. A swift white streak came to his aid as Dev hurled himself on one of the werewolves, sinking his teeth into its neck and prying it loose from its hold on Khan. Diablo hooked his claws into the other attacker and seconds later the werewolf lay twitching on the patio below where Sarange was standing.

The fight didn't last long. As she watched the conflict unfold, Sarange wondered how she had ever thought the werewolves would win. They were hopelessly outclassed by the superior fighting powers of their opponents. Before long, her beautiful yard was littered with discarded werewolf bodies. It was carnage.

Dropping into a crouch with his teeth bared, Khan patrolled the area. *Keep one of them alive.* That was what he had said. They needed to be able to question one of the werewolves.

Obedient to his leader's command, Finglas dropped one of the werewolves at Khan's feet. Although injured, the werewolf snarled at the huge tiger standing over him. Sarange felt a flicker of unexpected emotion. Was it respect? A sense of pride that a werewolf would dare show defiance to a big cat? It was a fleeting sensation. That werewolf had been sent to abduct her. She might admire his courage, but she couldn't feel any sympathy for him.

Khan subdued the werewolf by placing one huge paw on its back. The fight was over. He shifted back and signaled for his companions to do the same. Six naked men gathered around the injured werewolf.

"Ged and I will take this guy inside and persuade him to shift back."

Even in the moonlight, Sarange could see the way Khan's lips drew back in a snarl to show his gleaming teeth.

"Then I want to talk to him. The rest of you need to clean up out here. Don't leave any trace."

"Do you think we might be able to get dressed before we start?" Dev's cool tones brought a hint of normality to the surreal situation.

Khan gave a snort of laughter. "I guess I can permit that."

Sarange pressed her hands to her cheeks as she stepped back inside the bedroom. The fact that she'd just been watching six magnificent naked men without embarrassment probably wasn't the strangest aspect of this situation. It was simply a measure of how much her life had changed.

stayed in his animal form, it would be an effective way of not answering questions.

"He will." Khan's expression was grim. And determined.

He and Ged wore sweatpants. The other members of the band had also slipped on the same garments and boots or sneakers before returning to the yard for the cleanup operation. Sarange didn't want to inquire too closely about what that would entail. Memories of horror stories and movies came back to her. Could werewolves truly be considered dead without silver bullets or knives? Wasn't beheading or fire necessary? It was probably best if she kept her attention right here in the kitchen and didn't speculate on what might be going on outside.

Using the toes of one bare foot, Khan rolled the werewolf over onto his back. He lay still, regarding Khan with wary eyes. Crouching, Khan gripped the shifter's throat. "You have thirty seconds to shift back, my friend, or I'll rip off your balls and make you wear them as a necklace."

Sarange gulped. This wasn't the laid-back Khan she had gotten to know. She didn't know if the werewolf believed him...but she did.

"I'd do as he says." Leaning over Khan's shoulder, Ged spoke directly to the werewolf. "I've seen him do it. Wearing your own balls? Not the look any guy wants to go for."

The words weren't needed. The werewolf had shifted back into human form before Ged finished speaking.

"Wise choice." Khan got to his feet. "Now talk. Who do you work for?"

The man rubbed his throat and sat up slowly. It was easy to see his thought processes as he looked at the

Chapter 8

"Are you okay?" Khan moved closer to Sarange, speaking quietly so only she could hear.

"I'm fine." Although she tried to sound convincing, her teeth were doing their best to chatter and her eyes seemed to be open too wide. Surely it was understandable? It wasn't every day there was a bloodstained werewolf lying on the expensive marble tiles of her kitchen floor. "What are you going to do with him?"

Khan glanced down at the werewolf. "He's going to tell us who he's working for."

The werewolf whimpered and flattened his ears, abasing himself on the floor. His show of defiance was over. Sarange knew about animal behavior. He was getting as low as he could in an attempt to show Khan he was no longer a threat.

"What if he doesn't shift back?" If the werewolf

two large men standing over him and appeared to measure the distance between them and the door. He clearly decided quickly that escape was out of the question.

"I don't know his full name." His voice came out as a croak.

"I'll get him some water and something to cover himself." Sarange went to the fridge to get a bottle of water. When she handed it to the werewolf, he gulped down half its contents in one long swallow.

As she left the room to go to the nearby bathroom in search of a towel, Khan was speaking again. "Okay, we'll go along with the story that you don't know the name of your leader. For now. Where are you from?"

Sarange returned moments later and handed the towel to the werewolf who wrapped it around his waist. He looked bewildered. "I don't understand."

"It's a simple question." Khan's voice was impatient. "Do you come from Los Angeles, or are you from somewhere else?"

Sarange could see why he was asking the question. The werewolf had what she thought of as traditional Mongolian features. Although those stereotypes were becoming outdated as the world changed, she herself was an example of what her own people would consider a typical Mongolian. This man's eyes were a curious light green color and hers were blue, but his appearance was otherwise similar to her own. One thing was certain. He was not one of the four men who had broken into her house on the previous night.

"I am from Ulaanbaatar." Clearly terrified, the young werewolf cast another longing glance in the direction of the door.

"It's the capital city of Mongolia," Sarange said in answer to Khan's raised brows.

"You're a very long way from home." Khan's impatience appeared to be fading. Sarange was glad. This werewolf was barely more than a teenager. Quivering all over, with deep scratch marks to his side and back, he was pathetic rather than threatening. "You'd better tell us how you came to be here. Start by telling us your name."

"I am Jirandai. Known as Jiran. Although I'm a werewolf, I lead a normal, human life in my home country. I am a student at the National University of Mongolia and I came to America on an exchange visit. I have been studying at Berkeley for the last three months."

An uncomfortable prickle ran up Sarange's spine. "Who is your professor at Berkeley?"

Jiran turned his attention to her. "Bek Tsedev."

"Why does this matter?" Khan asked. His eyes probed her face. The connection between them was so strong that she could tell he already knew it *did* matter. Knew Jiran's response to her question had thrown her off balance.

"Bek Tsedev is my uncle, the man who adopted me when I came to America. He is a professor in the Department of East Asian Languages and Cultures at University of California, Berkeley."

"Did you know this?" Khan swung back to face Jiran so rapidly that the young werewolf scurried backward across the floor, only stopping when his back collided with a cabinet. "Were you aware of the connection?"

"No! I swear…" He covered his face with his hands. "I don't know how it happened. I don't understand any of this."

Ged placed a hand on Khan's arm. "Let me try."

He knelt on the tiles beside the cowering werewolf.

"How did you meet the other werewolves who came here tonight?"

Sarange was surprised at the gentleness in the big man's voice. It had an immediate soothing effect on Jiran, who turned toward Ged in relief. "I went to a nightclub last night with a group of friends. We were approached by a man who talked as though he knew us. We tried to explain that he was mistaken. Then we realized he knew our secret—" Jiran drew in a shuddering breath "—he knew we were werewolves."

"How did he know that?" Ged asked.

Jiran shook his head. "I don't know how he could. Even at home in Mongolia, my friends and I have always been careful about our anonymity. Our pack is small and we don't draw attention to ourselves. Here in America, none of us had even shifted. But this man, Bora, seemed to know everything about us. And it was like—" he shook his head "—it didn't matter. It was okay that he knew all about us. I think he must have given us something powerful to drink."

"Were you drinking a lot?" Ged's voice remained calm and quiet. Sarange sensed he was sympathetic toward the young man, who was clearly confused and frightened.

"I didn't think so at the time, but I can't think of any other explanation for how I felt then or why I can't clearly recall what happened." Jiran shivered. "Because the next thing I remember, we were here. I lost a whole twenty-four hours. Then my friends and I were caught up in a fight with you and I don't know how, or why."

Ged got to his feet and Khan drew him to one side. "Do you believe that?" Khan's voice was skeptical.

"I think I do." Ged studied the forlorn figure on the floor. "If he's lying, he's good."

"I believe him." Sarange didn't know why, but the young werewolf's story tugged at her heart. Her intuition told her his story was real. "Do you think he was drugged?"

"Either that or hypnotized," Ged said. "Possibly bewitched."

Khan still appeared unconvinced, although Sarange could see he was wavering. She had a sudden awareness of a powerful difference between them. He didn't have the same sort of empathy she did. It wasn't because he was hard or cold, it was simply his tiger DNA. He wasn't a pack animal. Reading others wasn't a strong part of his experience. *So what does that say about me? Does it mean I am a pack animal?* That wasn't the important part of her flash of insight. What mattered was that she and Khan complemented each other. They had focused on the tiger-wolf, cat-dog thing as though it was bad. As though it should drive them apart. Yes, they were opposites. *But we complete each other. Together, we are whole.*

There was only time for that brief thought before she turned back to Jiran and his plight.

Ged, of course, was part bear. He routinely distinguished between threatening and nonthreatening behavior in other animals. His driving traits were intelligence, empathy and the desire to protect. Khan seemed to relax when he knew Ged was prepared to trust what Jiran was telling him.

"This Bora, was he one of the werewolves who was with you tonight?" Khan asked.

"No." Jiran shook his head. "I only saw him in the nightclub. I didn't see him again after that."

"How did you get from San Francisco to Los Angeles?"

"I don't know." The young werewolf became distressed again. "All I know was I was in that club talking to Bora, and then I was here in the middle of a fight."

"Did you know the other werewolves who were here?" Khan ran a hand through his hair. "Other than your friends?"

"No, but there were a few minutes just before we shifted when I was able to get a look at them in human form. There were four of them. They were older than us and they looked exactly alike." Jiran choked back a sob. "And my friends...now they're all dead, aren't they?"

That was one of the hardest things to accept. From what Jiran was saying, a group of innocent young men had been sent by someone—*Who? Why?*—to their deaths tonight. Sarange could feel her own sorrow reflected back at her from Khan and Ged. They had done the killing, but they would never have deliberately harmed those innocent young men.

"Who is your pack?" She placed a hand on Jiran's shoulder as she spoke and he regarded her with wide, troubled eyes. Why did she need to know? How did she know it mattered?

"Although I am a gray werewolf, my mother was a blue werewolf—" he ducked his head in a gesture of submission "—and I bow to you, blue werewolf leader."

Khan and Sarange discussed the possibility that they could be recognized. Theirs were two of the most famous faces in the world. They had also recently been subject to intense media speculation about their relationship. In the end, they wore beanies and oversize shades and checked in separately for the flight from Los Angeles to San Francisco. Sarange disguised her slender figure beneath baggy sweatpants and a man's sweater. Khan still thought she was the hottest thing he had ever seen.

Sarange had relaxed once she knew Beast would be guarding her house. They also decided that Jiran should remain in Ged's care for the time being.

"We don't know what this guy, Bora, will do when he finds out how the attack went down. Once he knows Jiran survived and can identify him…" Khan had left the sentence hanging.

"I'm not sure I could identify him. The conversation I had with him is a blur." Some of Jiran's composure had been restored after he took a shower and Finglas, the smallest member of the band, had lent him some clothes.

"He may not know that." Khan's words had driven the color from the young werewolf's face.

Now Khan gripped Sarange's hand as they exited the airport building and made their way to the rental car complex. She had been quiet ever since Jiran's strange vow of allegiance to her as the blue werewolf leader. She also looked tired. It was close to dawn and they hadn't slept. Once they had made the decision to come to San Francisco, Ged booked them onto the next available flight.

"What makes you so sure your uncle will have the answers to your questions?"

Even though her eyes were hidden by her shades, he could tell she had been lost in thought. "I don't know. Not for sure. But Bek was in touch with Golden Wing before she died, so he's the only person who knows anything about my early life. And he's an expert on Mongolian history and culture."

"What about your aunt?"

Sarange smiled. "My aunt Gerel is the sweetest, kindest woman you will ever meet. She often reminds me of Golden Wing. Perhaps she would know about my link to the blue wolves, but I think she is sometimes a little afraid of her shaman powers. Her health is poor. That's why I don't want to descend on them unexpectedly at their house. I'd rather visit my uncle at the university to ask my questions, then go see my aunt for a social call."

"So the plan is to check into a hotel and get a few hours' sleep before we drive out to Berkeley?"

Sarange rolled her shoulders wearily. "That sounds like the best plan ever. And maybe when we wake up it will all have been a dream."

"Not all of it." His voice was husky as he gazed down at her.

Her fingers gripped his tighter. "Except us. I will never wish that away."

After they'd completed the rental car formalities, the drive into the city passed in an early morning blur. Khan took the wheel while Sarange used her cell phone to check them into a discreet hotel she had used before. They both knew the score. Anywhere they went, they took a chance on being recognized. This was the life they had chosen. Complaining about it would be hypocritical. But there were times when anonymity was needed, and there were things they could do to minimize the chances of being identified.

When they reached the hotel, Khan drove straight into the underground parking lot. From there, they took an elevator directly to reception, where the clerk had their room key ready for them.

"My kind of place," Khan said as they took a second elevator up to the second floor.

"In case anyone asks, we are Mr. and Mrs. Wolf."

He grinned. "Is that an invitation for me to unleash the beast within?"

Although she laughed as she stepped into the room, when she removed the shades her expression was serious. "I'd rather you held me."

Khan dropped their bags to the floor. "I can do that… For as long as you want me to."

How about forever? The thought was unprompted, but, for the first time, it wasn't unwelcome. He wished he could explore it. Wished there wasn't this strangeness pressing down on them. A man called Bora had sent a group of young men to Sarange's house a few hours ago alongside the four werewolves who had tried to abduct her the previous night. Apart from Jiran, all of those werewolves had died. Either Bora thought his werewolves would succeed in capturing Sarange, or he knew they would die. Both thoughts were too horrible to contemplate. Could he have knowingly sent them to their deaths? Had the mysterious Bora used Beast as a murder weapon? And why?

Sarange moved into the circle of his arms, pressing her cheek to his chest. They stood that way for long, still minutes until he felt her breathing settle into the same rhythm as his. Her heartbeat slowed. He sensed her relaxing. There was nothing about the situation they were in that was okay. Except this. In the midst of madness, they had found each other, and there was a world of rightness about that. He didn't understand it, but he was happy to accept it. More than happy. She was the best thing that had ever happened to him. Even though he knew nothing about a huge chunk of his life, he knew that.

Sarange raised her head. "I have no idea what's going on."

"Nor have I. For now, let's concentrate on getting some sleep." He kissed the top of her head. "Then we'll go in search of answers."

This dream was the most vivid Sarange had ever had. The night sky was lit with sacred fire. Chanting voices rose and fell in time with the steady drumming of fingertips on taut animal skin. The blue-eyed watchers stood on the snowy peaks, observing the human ritual. Sarange felt their approval. Their spirits touched hers. Human, wolf, tiger, shifter. In that instant, it mattered not. They were as one.

The shamanka's voice rose above the others, high-pitched and nasal, as she raised their joined hands aloft for all to see. Sarange held her breath. This was the moment. She turned to the man at her side, saw the love in his eyes, felt the acceptance of their people. They were united…

A flash of movement on the periphery of her dreaming vision caught her attention as the golden eyes of the gray wolf gleamed. He was gone almost as soon as she locked her gaze on his, but his presence unsettled her. The shamanka continued to chant while the tribe sang and drummed and the blue wolves looked on, but the gray wolf's presence had interrupted the spirits. It was an omen.

Sarange woke, shivering at the intensity of the emotions the dream had provoked in her. It was as if she had been watching a movie. No, it was more than that. *It was as if I was there.*

She sat up, checking the clock on the table next to the bed. Even though it felt like she had slept for hours, it was still only noon. A warm hand closed over her wrist and she turned to look into Khan's sleepy gold eyes.

"Something is troubling you."

She settled back down, lying on her side so her face was only inches from his. "Just a dream."

He cupped her cheek with one hand, pressing his lips to the pulse at the base of her throat. "Tell me."

"It was very vivid. Some sort of tribal celebration. I think, from the dream I just had, that it was to do with a marriage. The spirits came together to celebrate. Wolves, humans—" she laughed "—there was even a tiger in the background somewhere. Although I suspect anyone trying to interpret my dreams wouldn't have far to look for the source of *that* part of it."

Khan smiled. "Can I help it if I'm unforgettable… even when you're asleep?"

Even though she returned the smile, the remembered sense of unease returned. "There was something there in the background. A feeling of menace. The dream was clear enough for me to see the source. It was a gray wolf, lurking in the shadows, watching the celebration."

"Is it possible you dreamed about a gray wolf because of what Jiran said?"

"It's not only possible, it's likely. But that doesn't alter the feeling of the dream. Until the gray wolf appeared, the spirits were aligned and the portents were positive." She felt that shiver again, like a cold hand running gleeful fingers down her spine. "The gray wolf unbalanced that, and turned it into a nightmare."

Khan pulled her closer. "That's all it was. And, considering everything that's been happening to you, I'm surprised it wasn't a whole lot worse."

"Maybe it would have been…if you weren't here."

One of his hands slid down her back to her bottom while the other curled around the nape of her neck.

"Sarange." His voice was barely a whisper against her hair. "You are so beautiful you take my breath away."

He traced the seam of her lips with his, coaxing them to part. When his tongue met hers, everything but the feel, taste and scent of Khan vanished. Need coursed through her as his tongue danced with hers in sweet, languorous passes and deep thrusts. Only breaking the kiss for seconds, they stripped away the few clothes they had worn to sleep in.

Using the heel of her hand on his shoulder, Sarange pushed Khan onto his back, skating gentle kisses down his abdomen. He huffed out her name on a breath.

"Shh." She looked up at him with a smile. "I'm busy."

Flicking out her tongue, she licked her way down the length of his erection.

"Damn." Khan pressed his head into the pillow, arching his back and jerking his hips upward.

Placing her lips to his tip, she kissed all the way around the sensitive head of his cock. Taking his groan as a sign of approval, she curled her fingers around the base of his shaft, sliding her hand up and down, while engulfing him in her mouth. Khan muttered a curse as he tangled his fingers in her hair.

Plunging down hard, she took him deep, letting him strike the back of her throat. Khan pumped his hips in time with her movements. Reaching for her hips, he swung her lower body around until it was in line with his face.

Once she was in the position he wanted, Khan parted her folds with his fingers. Opening her to his gaze, he buried his face in her sex, thrusting his tongue into her, over and over. He set her on fire, driving her into a frenzy within seconds. Sarange moaned, bobbing her head up and down faster over his straining erection.

When her legs started to tremble, Khan grabbed her by the waist and tipped her onto her back.

"Need to be inside you when you come." He scrabbled on the floor for the jeans he had abandoned earlier.

Locating a condom in his pocket, he had it on in record time. Sarange reached up, cupping a hand to the back of his head and pulling him down into a kiss. Every touch heated her blood until she was lost in him. Lost *to* him. Their tongues met as his hands moved down her sides and over her hips, lifting her to him. She raised her pelvis and opened her legs, unable to wait another second.

Khan lined himself up with her entrance and drove right in. Sarange gasped, her back arching at an extreme angle, pressing her body tight to his. From hip to shoulder, there wasn't a part of them that wasn't touching. Yet she needed more. Needed to press closer, to claim him. To mark him as hers. Trailing openmouthed kisses along his jaw and neck, she dug her nails into his shoulders and writhed against him. Craving more, even though it was already too much.

As soon as she drew a breath, Khan moved. "I love how you tighten around me." He lifted himself with his elbows on either side of her head, watching her face as he pushed into her. "Love the feel of those hot muscles taking me deeper."

Sarange tried to say his name, but the only sound that left her lips was a strangled cry. The noise seemed to spur Khan to move faster and harder. Slamming into her, never letting up on the delicious, relentless thrusts, he gripped her chin, keeping his gaze fixed on hers.

"Let me hear that sweet sound again, Sarange. Show me how it feels when I'm inside you."

Desperately, she cried out his name and raked her nails down his back.

"I need to come, Sarange, but not without you. Never without you."

"Together." She managed to gasp out the word as the first spasms hit.

Pleasure exploded, sending a million tiny shards through her nerve endings as her body stiffened beneath him.

"Always—" Khan pounded harder, his pelvis hitting her clit with each movement, pushing her further over the edge. "Always together from now on."

Her orgasm crashed through her at full force, taking away the ability to even scream, and she clung to him, shuddering wildly. Khan dropped his head to her shoulder, pumping in short, shallow thrusts as she felt him jerk and tremble with his own release.

Chapter 9

"Always together from now on?" Sarange stood on the tips of her toes to press a kiss to Khan's lips.

Her long plait was still damp from the shower and she smelled delicious. Soapy clean and fresh with her own unique underlying scent. She was seriously testing his ability to concentrate.

"Pardon?"

"That was what you said." She blushed. "When we were having sex. You said, 'always together from now on.' That's quite an ambition. I know it's a fantasy, but it's quite unrealistic to expect that we could always climax together…"

Khan caught hold of her waist. "Is that what you thought I meant?"

Her brow furrowed. "What else could you mean?"

He dropped a kiss on the end of her nose. "If we stay

here and discuss it, we might not catch your uncle at the end of his classes."

Sarange pulled on her hat and shades. "I suppose you think you just neatly sidestepped that conversation."

He laughed. "I have enough experience of wolves to know I didn't."

"Now you're being cryptic." She followed him out of the room. "Wolves may have taken up a big part of our time lately, but what do they have to do with it?"

He waited until they were alone in the elevator before he answered, "You, my beautiful werewolf, are as tenacious as your brothers and sisters in the wild. Which means I'm sure you will bring the subject up again."

She appeared to give the matter some thought. "We don't know for certain than I *am* a werewolf."

"I think we do."

Sarange sighed. "If that's the case, why don't I feel something when you say I'm a werewolf?" They passed through the hotel reception and made their way to the underground parking lot. When they were in the car, she elaborated. "I have no wolf feelings at all. No desire to shift. No idea how to do it if I did. There is no part of me that feels wolf-like."

"I wonder if you ever did? Is it possible you once knew you were a werewolf, but like the werewolves who came to your house last night, you've been hypnotized, drugged or bewitched into some kind of memory loss?"

"That's a scary thought." Sarange slumped down in her seat, watching the buildings pass by. "I don't understand why anyone would want to do that to me. And for a plot like that to be successful, it would need the collusion of my family. If I was born a werewolf, Golden Wing must have known. When she found me, I was too young to hide who I was from her."

"We're heading to the right place." Khan rested a hand on her knee. "Let's hope your uncle can answer some of your questions."

Sarange didn't look reassured. "I was already in my teens when I came to America. Bek may be able to tell us about Mongolia and what he knows about the blue wolves, but I'm not sure how much information Golden Wing gave him about me and my early years."

Khan could sense her frustration. It matched something inside him. The feeling that part of his life was missing and that no amount of pushing or pulling either inside himself or externally was going to get it back. There was always that sense of incompleteness. Too many what-ifs and whys. At least Khan knew *what* he was even if he didn't have all the details of his story. Sarange didn't even have that. It was no good other people telling her. She would have to find her inner wolf for herself.

They drove in silence through slow-moving traffic, reaching the Department of East Asian Studies at Berkeley just over half an hour later. Sarange smiled as she indicated an ancient yellow Citroën. "Bek is still here. That's his car."

Khan found a parking space close by. "Sarange, have you ever considered using some of your millions to buy your uncle a better car?"

She laughed. "I have offered. Many times. He won't hear of it. Don't let Bek hear you criticize his beloved Chinggis."

Sarange clearly knew her way. Leading Khan from the parking lot into the building, she removed her shades before approaching the clerk at the reception desk. The woman smiled as she recognized her. "It's nice to see you again, Ms. Tsedev. The professor was just talking about you the other day. He's still in his office. Go on up."

"Do you come here regularly?" Khan asked as they mounted the stairs.

"Not as often as I'd like. If I can get away, I try to come and see my aunt and uncle." They reached the second floor and turned a corner onto a corridor. "Since Bek spends so much time here, I have to pry him away from his desk if I want to take him for lunch."

She knocked once on a door and, hearing a voice from within, entered. The man seated behind the desk looked up with a hint of impatience. The expression vanished when he saw who his visitor was. A broad smile lit up his features and he rose to his feet, enfolding Sarange in a hug.

"Now, this is a good way to end a bad day."

"You wouldn't have bad days if you didn't work so hard." Sarange's voice was affectionate, and Khan stood back, content to observe the exchange.

Bek shook his head. "Nothing to do with work. This is about a group of missing exchange students."

Sarange cast a brief glance in Khan's direction. Should they tell Bek what they knew? Jiran would be returning, but the other werewolves who had gone to her house were all dead. She decided to wait and see how the visit went. Introducing the subject of werewolves to her gentle, but conventional, uncle would not be easy.

"Are you going to introduce me?" Bek's question put an end to any immediate thoughts of the Bora problem.

Sarange reached out a hand. "This is Khan."

Bek smiled. "A very distinguished name."

"Of course." Sarange frowned. "Why didn't I make the connection?"

Khan looked from one to the other with a touch of bemusement. "You've lost me."

Bek pointed to a picture on the wall. It was a portrait Khan had seen before. This was a copy of an original that had clearly been painted centuries earlier. It depicted a black-eyed, white-robed man with a scant gray beard. The image was compelling. The painter had managed to convey great energy in that seemingly blank stare.

"You share your name with a Mongolian hero. His personal name was Temujjn, but he was given the title Chinggis Khan, the closest translation of which is 'Supreme Ruler.' You may have heard the western pronunciation of his title... Genghis."

"Like everyone else, I have of him," Khan said. The dark gaze of the man in the picture caught and held him. "But I didn't know he was considered a hero. I thought he was a bloodthirsty despot."

"Chinggis Khan was the founder of our nation," Bek said. "A mighty warrior who led his army to carve out an empire stretching from the Caspian to the Pacific. But you are right. Historians calculate that he was responsible for the deaths of about forty million people during the Mongol conquests."

"Golden Wing used to tell me stories of Chinggis Khan's birth," Sarange said. "About how he was descended from the wolves."

Bek nodded. "The wolf plays an important role in Mongolian culture. Wolves are respected for their power, stealth and tenacity. Because the Mongols are traditionally herders and hunters, we have great respect for the wolf as a powerful and skilled hunter. It is believed that Chinggis Khan was the spiritual descendant of a very particular wolf."

His words stirred memories to life inside Khan like a stick causing the embers of a dying fire to flare. "The blue wolf."

How did he know that? He knew nothing of Mongolia or the blue wolves, yet something came to life within him at the words. Something powerful and primal. It was almost a memory. How could he have known Chinggis Khan was supposed to have been descended from the blue wolves? Sarange had talked about the wolf pack many times and he had felt no connection to them. Yet the link to Mongolia's great leader triggered a pull, a certainty, inside him. It was like the words he had just spoken were drawn from deep inside his very soul.

"It was the union of the wolf and the tiger." Sarange looked around her as though seeking the source of the words she had just uttered. As though they couldn't have come from her own lips. Khan knew how she felt. It was as if they were both under the same spell.

Bek looked surprised. "Although it is now suggested that the importance of wolves in Mongolian history and culture has been overplayed, that is a little known fact about the starting point of the legend. There is a story about how, almost a thousand years ago, a great Caspian tiger came to the aid of Chinua, the female leader of the blue werewolves, to defeat a rival gray werewolf pack. Their romance led to the birth of a great shapeshifter dynasty. Although Chinggis Khan was human, it is believed that theirs was the family from which the great leader was descended."

"A tiger and a wolf?" It was the union his heart craved, but Khan couldn't contain his skepticism. "Even in a legend, that's asking for a stretch of the imagination."

Bek smiled. "It is one of the greatest love stories ever told, enduring throughout the centuries until the tiger was taken from the wolf by enemies who wished to destroy their dynasty. Chinua vowed to search for her lover forever, but her body grew weak and faded away. Her spirit is said to roam our great country, seeking her lost love. Since then, the conflict between the blue and gray werewolves has raged unchecked. Now it is said that the gray werewolves are on the rise and a sure sign that the blue werewolves are losing the fight is the fact that the wild blue wolves are dying out."

"I don't understand." Sarange frowned. "These are just legends. But even if they were true, how could something that was happening in the werewolf sphere affect the natural world?"

"There is an affinity between the blue werewolves and their wild counterparts."

"Perhaps a Caspian tiger will come again to save them?" Khan kept his tone light, signaling his continuing incredulity. He hadn't come here to listen to a fairy tale.

"The Caspian tiger is extinct. Although we speak of folklore, I do not believe, even in the world of shapeshifters, that it is possible for a long-dead creature to rise again." Bek roused himself from the sadness that had gripped him as he spoke of the ancient legend. "But you didn't come here to listen to old stories of my homeland." He gestured to a large, well-worn sofa and indicated the coffeemaker.

Khan and Sarange sat down, but declined the offer of refreshments. "I hope my aunt Gerel is well? I'm looking forward to visiting her when we leave here."

Bek nodded. "You know she is always happy to see you."

He pulled forward the chair from behind his desk and sat opposite them, tenting his fingers beneath his chin. Khan decided he wouldn't want to be a troublesome student on Bek's program. The mild-mannered professor had a quiet, perceptive stare that indicated he knew they weren't here for a social call. He was biding his time, waiting for them to tell them the real reason for the visit.

"There have been some strange events taking place in my life." Sarange had obviously decided to get straight to the point. "Things that may be linked to my childhood in Mongolia. I wondered how much Golden Wing told you about me before she died."

Bek was silent for long moments. "We didn't know Golden Wing well before she sent you to us. She was distantly related to Gerel. When she wrote to Gerel asking if you could visit, it was the first time we had heard from her in many years. Although we came to live in America when we first married, the pull of shamanism was still strong for us. Golden Wing said she wanted you to experience a world beyond the tribe, even beyond Mongolia. She said the spirits told her you were destined for greatness."

"I never knew that." Sarange looked and sounded surprised.

"So Golden Wing knew Sarange would become famous?" Khan said. "Do you think that's why she wanted to send her to America? To give her the opportunity to appear on the TV talent show?"

"No." Bek infused the word with a meaning Khan couldn't grasp. "Golden Wing was a powerful shamanka. Her ability to reach the spirits was possibly the strongest of any ever known. There were some within the shamanic tradition who questioned why she didn't take her healing arts and teachings to a wider audience. But she chose to live simply within a nomadic tribe. Her message that Sarange would achieve greatness was not about fame or fortune. Those things would have been meaningless to Golden Wing."

"So what did it mean?" Sarange asked.

Bek shrugged. "I have no more idea now than I did then. Gerel and I agreed to your visit to please Golden Wing." He smiled. "But once you were here, we didn't need any incentive other than the pleasure of your company. Gerel's health has never been good and we couldn't have children of our own. When Golden Wing died, we didn't adopt you out of duty or pity. We did it because we loved you."

Sarange's eyes were filled with tears. "I know that. I have been very blessed. I don't know what happened to my birth parents, but I found love…first with Golden Wing and then with you and my aunt Gerel."

Bek leaned forward and clasped her hand warmly. "I'm glad we showed you how much you mean to us."

"Could the greatness in Sarange's destiny be about the work she does to save endangered animals?" Khan asked.

Sarange's brow cleared. "That must be what Golden Wing intended. By sending me here to you, she set in motion a chain of events that meant I would have the money and influence to do something to help animals that are at risk of extinction. No matter what I do, it's never enough to save them all, but that must be the greatness my grandmother talked of. The spirits intended for me to do this."

"It's hard to know what else she could have meant." Although Bek smiled, Khan had a curious feeling that he remained unconvinced. "But you said strange things had been going on. That worries me. What has been happening?"

Sarange reached out a hand and placed it in Khan's. There were two men in the room, one of whom she had known and loved for many years. Yet her instinct had been to reach for Khan. His heart gave a glad little bound at the message of trust behind the gesture.

"This is going to sound very odd—"

"Sarange, this has been one of the strangest weeks of my life." Bek ran a hand through his thick black hair. "It started with a visit from a man who attempted to persuade me to drop everything and give a talk to a political party in Mongolia. He was most persistent, offering a large donation to the faculty and an all-expenses-paid vacation for me and Gerel after I had delivered the talk. Even though I explained that this was the busiest part of the semester, he was most reluctant to let it go." There was a faint look of distaste on Bek's face. "Even if I had been able to get away, I would not have accepted his invitation."

"Why?" Khan was diverted by Bek's obvious hostility toward the idea.

"The Chanco Party is a relatively new, but increasingly powerful, political movement in Mongolia. Let's just say I disagree with every policy they have," Bek said. "Moving on to the rest of my week, I am now dealing with the problem of a group of five missing exchange students. What I'm trying to say is, I don't think anything you can say will add to the strangeness."

"I'm not so sure." That odd, uncomfortable feeling of certainty gripped Khan again. "What was the name of the man who wanted you to drop everything and go to Mongolia?"

"Bora."

* * *

Bek was still shaking his head in disbelief as they exited the building and crossed the parking lot. "Humans transforming into animals is an integral shamanic belief. I grew up hearing stories of werewolves and other shape-shifters. But this story is incredible. The world I live in today is not the one of my childhood. I can't believe those missing students are werewolves."

"Sadly, for four of them, we have to say they *were* werewolves," Sarange said. The sense of horror and incredulity still lingered when she thought about it. "Only Jiran survived."

"And the man called Bora was behind this?" They had reached Bek's car, and he halted beside it. "He recruited, or tricked, these students, into going to your house? Why would he do that?"

"I have a horrible feeling it was to test our strength." Khan put forward the first theory he had.

Sarange shivered, wrapping her arms around her body as though protecting herself from a chill. "You mean he sent those young men to their deaths simply so he could find out how strong you and your friends were?"

His second theory wasn't any better. "Or he was showing us just how evil he can be."

She raised a hand to her lips. "Do you think he was observing the fight?"

Khan nodded. "I'm sure of it."

"That's horrible. He watched them die in some sort of experiment."

"Why would this man want to get me to go to Mongolia?" Bek asked. "I have no influence over these students beyond what happens on the program. I'm not a werewolf." He gave a shaky laugh. "I can't quite believe

I just said those words out loud. The talk he wanted me to deliver was routine, the sort of thing I do regularly. I don't understand my place in his plans."

"It's possible he didn't know how much the exchange students had confided in you. He clearly knew you were an expert in shamanism. Maybe he wanted you out of the way. Sending you to Mongolia was one way of achieving that." Khan paused. "Or he wanted to use you to influence Sarange. If he had you in his power, she would be more likely to do what he wanted."

Bek looked dubious. "A visit to another country wouldn't have happened fast. Even if I'd been able to re-schedule classes and leave within a few days, it wouldn't have been soon enough."

"I've got a feeling we'll be hearing more from the mysterious Bora, so we may discover more about his motives soon." Khan moved toward the rental car. "We'll meet you at your house."

Sarange settled into the passenger seat. "Do you think Bora knows we're here?" She cast a glance over her shoulder, unable to shake the fear that a malignant presence was pursuing them. "That he could be watching us?"

Khan had been about to start the engine, but he paused. Turning his body toward her, he placed his hands on her shoulders, drawing her to him. "If he is, he'll soon find out he made a mistake. I told you I'm going to keep you safe. That hasn't changed."

Sarange gave a sigh as she nestled her cheek into the curve of his neck. His touch instantly soothed her. "I believe you. I just wish I understood *why* you have to keep me safe. Why does someone I don't know want to harm me?"

Khan kissed her before releasing her. "We will find out what this is all about. I promise you."

Bek and Gerel lived in a small, cozy house overlooking Muir Beach. Bek had called ahead, and when they arrived, Gerel was waiting on the doorstep to greet them. Sarange always experienced a rush of affection for the woman who had been like a mother to her since she was fourteen, but it was stronger than ever this time. As she embraced Gerel, concern hit her hard. Her aunt looked even more frail than usual. It was as if her health had rapidly declined since Sarange last saw her.

Gerel was tiny and she had to tilt her head right back to look up at Khan. "You are not what I expected."

His lips curved into an amused smile. "Can I take it from that statement that you are not a fan of rock music, Mrs. Tsedev?"

Sarange had never seen Gerel become flustered. Usually she was the most serene person Sarange knew. Now, as she twisted her hands together and studied the top step, her expression was agitated. "I meant you are not the sort of person I expected Sarange to become involved with."

Bek stepped out from the house and slid a hand under his wife's elbow. "You are not making this any better, my love." His voice was mildly amused. "But I don't suppose Khan will be offended."

Khan laughed. "Far from it. I'm not the sort of person *I'd* expect Sarange to get involved with—" he lowered his voice as he followed Sarange into the house "—but my reasons for saying that might surprise you."

"Now is not the time to mention your tiger tendencies." Sarange's warning whisper was for his ears alone.

"Don't worry. I won't disgrace you by showing my stripes while we're having dinner."

She shook her head at him, half amused and half outraged at his audacity. How boring her life had been before Khan swaggered into it! Even though the past few days had been a blur of danger, this time spent with him had been a precious gift. She hadn't changed how she saw herself, but he had made her see another side to her being. The problem was... Khan was the other side to her. *He is the other half of me. The tiger to my wolf.*

It was not the best time for such a momentous revelation. She was finally prepared to open her mind and heart to the idea that she was a werewolf. But now she was taking a step further. She was also accepting that, just like that legendary leader of the blue werewolves, she needed a tiger to complete her. There was a reason why opposites attracted. It was that Khan brought with him all the things Sarange lacked.

She shone a spotlight on herself. And she saw a wolf. She liked order, hated when her routine was disrupted. Bek and Gerel were her only family, but they meant everything to her. If she gave her friendship, it was a precious gift, not lightly bestowed. She was fiercely loyal to the few friends she had. Khan had called her stubborn. She smiled. A dog with a bone? Once she got her teeth into something, she refused to let it go.

Sarange liked rules. She liked to know where she was meant to be and what she was supposed to do when she got there. She had a reputation for being the least demanding person in the music industry. The ultimate professional. *Or am I just obedient?* Doing the right thing because, in a pack, there was no place for a maverick.

She glanced across at where Khan was standing in her aunt and uncle's kitchen, admiring the view while Gerel fixed him a drink. The ultimate maverick. He had brought chaos into her ordered life. Brought all the things Sarange would have said she hated. Spontaneity. Disruption. Defiance. Rules? To Khan they existed only to be flouted. Authority? It was there to be challenged. In Khan's world, other people bowed down before him. He did nothing to please them. He was bold, loud and beautiful. A tiger who already owned more of her wolf heart than she cared to admit.

"Put the drinks on hold, Gerel." Khan turned away from the window, his eyes flashing a golden warning. "We've got company."

Chapter 10

The yard at the rear of the house sloped down and had an ocean view. The light had almost gone, but the prospect of the neat garden with the distant water beyond was stunning. Khan, whose eyesight was as good in the darkness as it was in the daylight, had been admiring this through the full-length window when his keen gaze caught the first movement.

"Bek, I'm guessing most of your visitors use the front door?" He kept his eyes fixed on the shrubs, where he had seen the activity. There it was again, so slight only a tiger would catch it.

"Yes." There was a nervous quiver in the older man's voice. "Shall I call the police?"

"No. Get Sarange and Gerel upstairs. I'll take care of this."

"But—"

"Do as he says, Bek." Gerel's voice was surprisingly

calm as she interrupted her husband's protest. "We can trust Khan."

Khan didn't have time to examine the strangeness of her words. He was too intent on what was going on beyond the window. Over to his left. There were four. This opponent liked that number. So did Khan. Four posed no problem for his inner tiger.

Unfortunately, he reckoned there were another four over to his right.

"What's going on?" Sarange was standing just behind him.

He frowned but kept his gaze on the darkened yard. "You are supposed to be upstairs."

"I decided to try being rebellious for once in my life."

"It doesn't work that way." He risked a glance over his shoulder and caught a flash of understanding from her blue eyes. "I do the rebelling. You're the one who holds me back."

He looked back at the yard and Sarange moved closer, resting her chin on his shoulder. He felt her sigh reverberate through him. "You feel it as well? We are opposite halves of the same whole? That's how we work."

"I feel it. I sure as hell don't understand it."

"You don't need to understand it. If you accept it, you know you need me here next to you. Completing you."

He flicked another glance her way. "I don't want you in danger."

"I'm not. I'm getting you out of it."

"Stop being such a stubborn she-wolf."

She laughed. "Only if you stop being such an overbearing alpha tiger."

Even in the face of a looming threat, the exchange felt easy. Like they had teased each other the same way a hundred times. And wasn't it time to face up to the truth? To admit that they *had* done these things that felt so familiar. He didn't know enough about how the cosmos worked, but he was a shape-shifter. He wasn't going to question the intricacies and mysteries of the universe. Somehow, some way, he had known Sarange before. She had played an important role in his life. More than that. Without knowing it, she held the key to who he was.

Now was possibly a bad time for soul searching. No matter how many intruders were out there in the shadows, his mate was in danger and Khan would defend her with his life. And that vow worked both ways. He sensed a new determination in Sarange. A change had taken place, and with it there had come a new steadfastness and courage. Hiding away wasn't an option. She was going to face her adversaries no matter where the confrontation might lead her.

Just the way she always did.

"Stay close to me." He had no real expectation that she would listen to him. His instincts told him she would go her own way. They also told him to trust her. Sarange wasn't weak and helpless. She wasn't a tiger, but the bravery and vitality that flowed through her veins were strong enough to move mountains.

"Khan." Her breath brushed his cheek and he turned his head. "I may not know what is going on, but I know one thing with absolute certainty. You are talking to the person who taught you everything you know about werewolf warfare."

Was that true? No matter what he thought, Sarange believed it and it was too late now to do anything other than trust her judgment. The shadows on the edge of the garden were closing in. Men were emerging from the shrubs. Their enemies were encircling them.

Khan slid the window open just wide enough so that he could step through the gap. The breeze carried the first chill of nightfall and the salty tang of the ocean. Sarange pressed close up behind him.

"Werewolves." Her voice was barely a whisper. "I can smell them."

"You're getting good at this." He drew her with him to one side of the small deck area, crouching low as he scanned the yard. "You're almost a shifter."

"Now I just have to find a way to shift."

"Do you think you can do it?" As he looked her way, her face was a pale blur in the darkness.

"There's only one way to find out."

As she shrugged out of her clothes, the night air caressed Sarange's skin, leaving shivery pinpricks in its wake. *I want this.* The thought surprised her with its passion. She had hidden behind her cool, professional persona for so long. Now the desire to reach inside herself and find her inner wolf was overwhelming in its intensity. *Let's get on with it.* The real Sarange had been hidden for too long. It was time to release her. To meet her. Again.

There was just one problem. Shifting. What was it? How did it happen? Before she had met Khan, it was something that happened in books and movies. It was fiction. Like fairies and phantoms. She had never paid any attention to the logistics, because it wasn't something she would need. *Why the hell didn't I take notes in those horror movies instead of covering my face with my hands?*

"There is more magic than science in being a shifter." Khan's voice was softly persuasive, almost as if he could read her mind. "You need to think your way

into your inner wolf. She's there, deep inside you. You
have to find a way to set her free."

I have a wolf inside me. The thought should have
been scary. Instead, it was curiously liberating, as
though everything finally made sense. *She* made sense.
Instead of skimming the surface of who she was, she
was shining a light into the darkest recesses of her soul.
It was something she had never wanted to do. She had
never wanted to inquire too closely into the darkest
corners of her psyche. What if she didn't like what she
found? What if, instead of order and calm, she found
chaos? Now she was seeking a part of herself that was
wild. She wanted to set the untamed part of herself
free. Wanted to know what it would be like to break
free from the restraints of her human self and find the
animal within. Sarange the wolf. She was looking forward to unleashing her.

Deep inside her body, something stirred. In a part
of herself she had shut off and never examined, a surge
of something unexpected and primal made her utter a
soft cry. She stifled it instantly, pressing a hand to her
chest and breathing hard.

"Do you feel her?" Khan kept his voice low. Sarange nodded, unable to speak as the feelings continued to surge and grow. "Let it happen. Let your inner
wolf take over."

Let it happen? She couldn't stop it. That newly discovered part of herself was in control now. Her inner
wolf was taking over. Sarange curled tightly into a ball.
A moan—a sound close to a howl—left her lips as she
gave herself up to the feeling of shifting. The first sensation was of her body tightening as her limbs stretched
and changed shape. *There is no pain.* The thought was
clear and sharp, taking her by surprise. Her jaw length-

ened and her features altered. Her canines grew into
fangs, her fingernails sharpened and became claws.
Shifting was the right word. It was over quickly. It was
part of who she was. Sarange the human wasn't gone.
For now, she was the one who was hidden. There was
no conflict in the exchange. She was both human and
wolf. They were equal. Both valued. Both unique.

She liked Sarange the wolf. The feel of thick fur covering her body was like being wrapped in silver-colored
velvet. Her wolf stance was confident, the lines of her
body lithe and strong. Her movements were effortlessly
fluid. Teeth, claws and muscles were in perfect condi-
tion. This wolf knew how to take care of herself, knew
how to take the lead. She was in charge…and even
Khan knew it. As he removed his clothes and shifted
into his tiger form, she could see it in his eyes. Respect,
recognition and joy combined.

Sarange didn't know the details of their story, but she
knew enough. Khan had once walked at her side. With
every step, he had shouldered her burdens and listened
to her problems. He had been her mate, her friend and
her protector. But Sarange had been his leader. He had
bowed his head to her along with her werewolf pack.

The werewolves moving toward them out of the
darkness were not her pack. Having shifted, she felt her
senses become supercharged. Her heightened awareness
of smell and her sensitive hearing brought every tiny
movement to her. She sniffed the air and tilted her head,
knowing that Khan would be relying on his own dominant sense—his sight—to fill in what she couldn't see.

His restless head movement was the signal they both
recognized. Moving side by side, they left the deck
and launched into a surprise attack. The night breeze
whipped against Sarange's face, bringing the aroma of

the night to life. This wasn't her homeland, but some of the elements of her world were here. She relished the dank scent of earth and the feel of wet grass beneath her paws. The moon hung three-quarters full over the ocean and she took a moment to appreciate its magical beauty.

The memories came flooding back. Similar fights, always at Khan's side. Invading werewolf packs that wanted to destroy her dynasty, to bring her down as leader. Stories abounded about the tiger and the wolf, but even the legends couldn't do them justice. *We are an invincible team.* Bound by a mystical bond, they were stronger together than the sum of their parts.

Sarange crouched low, baring her teeth in readiness for the attack as the snarls and howls of the invading werewolves rent the night air. It seemed they already knew who they were facing. Blue Wolf. Great Tiger. A legend born centuries ago beneath an Asian sky was coming back to life…and these attackers didn't want to be caught up in its might.

Khan launched into the attack. He fought like a demon. With a furious snarl, he lunged at the nearest werewolf. They rolled together across the grass. It was an uneven fight. Khan's huge claws ripped into the tender skin of the werewolf's abdomen, causing the creature to yelp as sharp talons sliced through fur and flesh. When he had finished with him, Khan flung his opponent across the yard.

Lightning fast, Khan lunged, throwing himself on top of another intruder. The werewolf tried to fight back. It was a futile attempt. Khan pushed down hard on the werewolf's rib cage. The sound of bones crunching under pressure was sickening. The werewolf drew back its teeth and a howl of rage echoed through the night sky.

Khan gave a warning growl. It was a message. Back off. He would allow the injured werewolf to live if it stayed out of the rest of the fight. The werewolf snarled a defiant response.

Under that ancient sky, the blue wolf and the great tiger had learned not to give second chances. Lowering his snout, Khan bared his giant canines. Using his teeth like knives to tear into the exposed flesh of the werewolf's throat, he ripped into muscle. Blood flew in a dark arc. Another of their enemies was down.

Sarange experienced a surge of energy. A bloody battle wasn't something she relished, but she wasn't afraid of it. The recollection of past conflicts came back to her and she moved toward the werewolves. One of them made a break toward the low wall that bordered the property and she set off in pursuit. *You came here to intimidate me. Let's see how that works out for you.*

The werewolf's agonized whine sliced through the air as Sarange caught up to him and her long talons dug into his side. He thrashed about, in an attempt to throw her off. Sarange swiped at him, slashing down his face. Blood spewed out of the werewolf's open mouth. A ripple of triumph swept through Sarange as she saw fear flicker in the depths of her opponent's eyes. She used it to her advantage, gouging again.

With a surge of strength, the other werewolf pulled himself up on his hind legs, drawing Sarange with him in a deadly embrace. Teeth snapped and claws slashed as they writhed together, both determined to gain the upper hand. Fighting to keep his fangs from closing on her neck, Sarange let out a yelp of agony as sharp claws caught the soft flesh of her belly.

On the periphery of her vision, she was aware of Khan catching an attacker in midair. There was a sickening snap as his teeth closed on its neck. He cast the werewolf's body aside like a limp rag doll and moved on to the next.

Spurred on by his success, Sarange raised a paw and swiped it once again across her opponent's face. Blood welled in a line down the center of his snout, spraying across both their faces. Seizing her chance, Sarange drove the other werewolf to the ground, pinning him down on his back.

Canines bared, she struck fast, tearing deep into the flesh of his throat. The warm coppery flavor of his blood flooded her mouth. Her human wanted to recoil, but her wolf was in charge. The werewolf beneath her struggled and thrashed. Sarange followed her instincts. Shaking her head violently, she heard the crack of his neck breaking. When she lifted her head, her jaw dripped blood and the other werewolf lay lifeless at her feet.

Bounding to Khan's side, she worked with him. They harried the remaining opponents, confusing them until they didn't know where the next snap of teeth or swipe of claws was coming from. Khan caught a retreating werewolf by the hind leg and dragged it across the grass before sinking his giant fangs into its neck. Another werewolf landed on Sarange's back and she shook it off with a furious growl. Before she could wrestle it to the ground, the animal took off and cleared the wall in a single leap. She weighed whether to follow and decided against it. This was not the raw wilderness of Mongolia. A werewolf fight in the streets of San Francisco? It was unlikely to go unnoticed and she didn't want to be part of the ensuing news story.

She moved back to stand beside Khan, reaching up to rest her muzzle on his broad shoulder. Feeling the

thick expanse of his fur and his powerful tiger muscles
sent a renewed thrill through her body. She tilted her
head back, seeking the low-slung moon. A soft, triumphant cry left her lips.

I have found you at last, my tiger.

"I may only know about these things from legends
and movies, but I believe a werewolf can only truly be
killed by beheading?" Bek used the flashlight he carried to illuminate the scene of carnage that had once
been his elegant yard. He looked pale but was quite calm
considering what he had just witnessed from his bedroom window. "And that a silver sword must be used?"

Khan had shifted back and pulled on the jeans he
had discarded before he shifted. "That's right. The bodies of these werewolves have been brutalized, but they
are not truly dead. To leave them this way would be the
ultimate cruelty. Their injuries will condemn them to
a half life. They will be unable to resume their place in
either the human or the shifter worlds."

"What do you propose we do with them?"

Khan ran a hand through his hair. It was a good
question. There was an unwritten shifter code. Fight
with honor. Die with dignity. No trace of conflict must
remain for the forces of human law and order to find.
There was also a responsibility to the enemy. He and
Sarange owed these werewolves a shifter's death. There
was just one problem. He didn't have access to the
means to provide it.

Sarange reappeared, having showered away the
blood from her skin and hair. She had changed into
sweatpants, T-shirt and sneakers. Khan guessed she
must keep spare clothing here at her aunt and uncle's
house. Gerel was at her side. Khan wasn't sure how Sa-

range's quiet, gentle aunt was going to cope with the sight of the broken and bloody werewolf bodies littering her lawn.

Gerel surveyed the scene silently for a few moments. "I guess you're going to need a silver sword?" She might have been asking if he wanted cream in his coffee.

"Um—" Khan didn't often find himself at a loss for words, but this was one of those rare occasions "—that would be useful."

"I'll be right back." Gerel returned to the house.

Bek watched her with an expression of disbelief. "I have no idea what that's all about."

Sarange placed her hand on Khan's shoulder and rose on the tips of her toes to kiss him. "I have wolf blood on me," he warned.

"Wouldn't be the first time I've kissed you bloody." Her voice was husky.

"You remember that?" He studied her face in the light that spilled out from the window. She had been amazing in that fight. Stylish, graceful...deadly.

Sarange shook her head. "Not properly. Not fully formed memories. I just know we were together in the past."

He nodded, returning the gentle pressure of her lips. "We have some gaps in our relationship timeline."

Gerel interrupted any further conversation. She stepped through the open window, carrying a gleaming silver sword.

Bek swallowed so hard Khan heard the click in his throat from several feet away. "Where did you get that?"

Gerel's smile was gentle. "I keep it in the loft." She handed the sword to Khan.

"Are you able to hold that?" Bek asked. "Isn't silver poison to a shifter?"

"I'm unique. I don't know how, or why, but I can't be killed by silver…which means I can't be killed." He looked at the sword in his hand. "This stuff is a toxin to me. It leaves me weak, but it doesn't overpower me the way it does with other shifters." He smiled at Gerel. "I see you have bound the handle of this in leather. That greatly reduces the impact."

She nodded. "That's what I'd heard. How about you dispose of these bodies? Burying them in the woods is going to take some time. Bek, you will need to get a couple of spades from the garage and some of the tarp we use when we go camping. Wrap the bodies in it before you put them in the trailer. I don't want to have to clean up blood." She smiled. "While the three of you get my yard back to normal, I'll organize dinner. We can talk while we eat."

Even Khan, who had just met her, was shocked at the transformation from kindly, middle-aged lady, to werewolf disposal expert. Sarange and Bek appeared frozen in shock. Gerel hummed quietly to herself as she went back into the house.

Khan approached the first werewolf body. "I'm glad there isn't any other property close by."

"Why?" Bek looked like a man who had to rouse himself from a trance to ask the question.

"This is not something we want to risk the neighbors catching sight of." Khan gripped the leather-bound handle of the sword with both hands and raised it above his head.

"I'll go and get the things we need from the garage." Bek scurried away before Khan brought the blade down on the werewolf's neck.

It was messy and unpleasant, but Khan knew the task was a duty. He was a loner. He didn't get involved in other people's fights or politics, whether human or shifter. But he knew the basics of his kind. On the whole, shifters lived peaceful, anonymous lives. It hadn't always been so. This was a point they had reached over time. Centuries ago, bitter fighting within and between different shifter species had threatened to spill over and disturb the peace of the human domain. Tearing down the veil that existed between worlds couldn't be allowed.

To humans, shifters should only exist in legend. Along with other creatures of the otherworld—vampires, phantoms, dryads, elves…to name a few—interactions between werewolves and mortals must be prevented.

When the worlds did collide, there was an obligation to protect humanity from the truth of what lay beyond the veil. Since his rescue from captivity, Khan had been involved in a few shifter skirmishes, none of which had necessitated this sort of cleanup operation. Even so, as he strode around the yard in the moonlight with Sarange at his side, performing the final act of kindness on the broken werewolf bodies, he knew he had done this many times before.

"We fought many battles for our homeland." He was breathing hard when he lowered the sword for the final time.

"They were determined to take it from us." Her voice had a dreamy quality to it as though she was with him, but talking about something just beyond him.

"Who were *they*, Sarange? The gray werewolves?"

When she spoke, he picked up on her frustration. "I don't know all of it. Not yet. When I do, we'll know why they have come after us again. Then we will be able to crush them once more."

Her voice resonated through him. Strong and decisive. Khan would follow wherever she chose to lead.

But for now, he decided they needed to take some immediate action. "Let's get these bodies into the woods and start digging. I'm dirty, smelly and hungry…and I want to know why your aunt had a silver sword hidden in the loft."

Chapter 11

The thought hit at the same time that Khan carried the last werewolf body to the edge of the grave. What if an overly vigilant paparazzo had managed to find their location? The fans who longed for pictures of Sarange and Khan together would be stunned if they could see them now. If a long-distance lens captured images of what they were doing among the redwoods... The image caused Sarange to utter a snort of laughter.

Khan glanced up from his task. By the light of Bek's powerful flashlight, his torso was shiny with sweat and streaked with dirt. "Is something wrong?"

"I was picturing tomorrow's headlines if there happened to be a photographer hidden in the trees."

He grinned. "Kha-range? Celebrity wolf killers?"

Bek shuffled his feet impatiently. "You two might find this situation amusing, but I'd prefer to get on with it and get out of here."

"A few more spadesful of earth should do it." Khan's strength was phenomenal. After digging a deep pit, he had hauled the tarp-wrapped remains of the werewolves into it. Now the grave was almost completely filled in.

Once he had finished, Sarange stepped back and surveyed the burial site. "We need to cover the grave with branches and leaves."

Bek had driven toward Muir Woods. Instead of following the tourist trails, they had carried the werewolf bodies into the dense, lesser used parts of the forest. Once Khan was satisfied they were deep enough in the woods, they had chosen this site. It was unlikely even the hardiest hiker would stray this far from the park trails, but Sarange wanted to make sure the grave remained hidden.

Once they had disguised the area to Sarange's satisfaction, they made their way back to Bek's car with its attached trailer. "The tarp protected the trailer from bloodstains, but we can clean and disinfect it properly later," Khan said as he climbed into the back seat.

They completed the return journey in silence. As Bek pulled into the drive, he turned to look at Sarange. "When you said there had been some strange events taking place in your life, perhaps I should have asked you to elaborate. Although nothing could have prepared me for the reality of what you were talking about."

"I would not place you and Gerel in danger for anything." Her voice trembled with emotion.

Bek placed a hand on her knee. "This is your home. Where else would you come when you need help?"

Where else indeed? As she covered his hand gratefully with her own, she had a crystal-clear image of a sky so dark it was like velvet scattered with diamond stars. Of pristine lakes; empty, rolling steppes and majestic mountains. Of Khan at her side and her pack running with them. The blue werewolves of shifter legend were the nomadic people of her past. *Where else would I go? Maybe to my home. To the land that is now called Mongolia.*

Inside the house, the delicious aroma of Gerel's home-cooked chili greeted them. Sarange led Khan up the stairs in the direction of the room that was still "her" bedroom. It was the room she slept in when she stayed here. Warm, cozy, filled with the remnants of her past. She felt comfortable here in the place that had been her sanctuary for so many years.

Gerel had carried their bags up here and laid clean clothes on the bed for Khan. He examined them in surprise. "Did your aunt iron these?"

"Probably." Sarange smiled. "Gerel is a homemaker in the true sense of the word. It matters to her that the people around her feel comfortable."

"She clearly doesn't know I spend most of my time on tour with a group of other men. I usually pick my clothes up off the floor. That's if Diablo hasn't kicked them halfway down the bus in a temper."

"I know enough about your relationship with Diablo to guess that happens when you provoke him." Sarange held open the bathroom door. "Everything you need is in here. I'll wait for you downstairs."

His eyes flashed gold fire, scorching her skin with a blaze of passion. "You're not joining me?"

"As tempting as that offer is, I wasn't the one doing the dirty work…and I need to talk to my aunt and uncle." It was true, but she wasn't sure where she would start. How was she going to explain something she didn't understand herself?

Khan's expression softened. "They are good people and they love you. Just tell them what you know."

Her brow furrowed so hard it hurt. "What do I know? Every time I think I see something in my past—*our* past—it feels like I get sand thrown in my eyes all over again."

"They may be able to help you see things more clearly."

Sarange wasn't hopeful, but she left him to shower and went back downstairs feeling vaguely embarrassed. It was as though she had let Bek and Gerel down by being caught out in a teenage misdemeanor. How did she begin to tell the two people she loved most in the world about an undiscovered past, a secret identity, about which she was only just learning? Bringing a bloody werewolf battle into the backyard of their quiet home was hardly on the same level as teenage misbehavior like staying out past her curfew, or trying a sneaky cigarette.

It seemed harder because this was the closest thing she had to a home. Her own luxurious house in Los Angeles was part of her celebrity persona, but this was where she felt at ease. Settling into a chair at the scrubbed pine table, she felt as if she had never been away. When Gerel placed a basket of her home-baked corn bread in the center of the table, Sarange surprised her aunt, and herself, by bursting into tears.

I'm supposed to be some mighty werewolf leader? I can't even smell my aunt's home-cooking without crying.

It was some time, and several tissues, before she was able to speak. "I don't know what's happening to me."

"This is your destiny." Gerel drew Sarange's head onto her shoulder the way she used to when she was younger and she needed her aunt's soothing presence. "This is the greatness of which Golden Wing spoke."

"You don't mind that I'm a werewolf?"

Gerel laughed. "I have been waiting for this day for a very long time."

"You have?" Bek selected a bottle of his favorite wine from the rack. Bringing it, a corkscrew and glasses to the table, he joined them. "Was there any point at which you considered enlightening me about that? Or about the sword you had tucked away in the loft?"

Gerel patted his hand. "You knew when you married me that I had the same powers as all the women in my family. I have the ability to enter the spirit realm."

"Are you a shamanka?" Sarange asked. She had always suspected her aunt had the same powers as Golden Wing, perhaps in a lesser degree. It was a relief to hear her finally admit it.

"I do not practice shamanism day to day. When we left Mongolia, I left that part of my life behind me," Gerel said. "But I can communicate with the spirits. I have some influence over the natural world."

"Did you know I was a werewolf?" It hurt Sarange to ask the question. Until Khan had entered her life she had trusted Gerel and Bek more than anyone. If she discovered now that Gerel had kept such a momentous secret from her, the knowledge would tilt her life even farther off course.

Her whole world had already been tipped upside down. Losing sight of what mattered to her, what grounded her... No, she couldn't bear that as well. Gerel's next words left her light-headed with relief.

"I would never have kept such an important piece of your story from you." Gerel drew a breath as she took hold of Sarange's hand. "But I would be lying if I didn't confess that I always knew there was something different about you. Something more than the talent that carried you to the top of your profession."

"The stubbornness and inability to let go of an argument didn't give you a clue that she's a wolf?" Khan entered the kitchen and slid into the seat next to Sarange, his teasing smile taking the sting out of the words.

His presence instantly warmed her. In the midst of all this chaos, there was *him*. And as crazy as it seemed, she would happily take everything that was thrown at her in return for Khan. For how he made her feel. She had been half alive before she met him, believing she was content and secure in the life she had. One look at Khan had blown that myth apart. It scared her now that she might have continued on that steady course and never have discovered these feelings. Might never have known this restless, burning hunger. This pure, perfect peace.

What frightened her even more was the thought of what the future held for them. Khan had no memory of his past before his captivity. Sarange, thrust into a new reality over which she had no control, had snippets of memories that lacked detail. The only certainty was that their past lives were somehow entwined. They needed to unravel the mystery of their shared story if they were to vanquish this faceless enemy who was so determined to destroy them. But what would they uncover? Once this fight was over, would the past set them free? And what sort of future, if any, would that freedom grant them? Because, although he had only been in her life a short time—*he has been* back *in my life a short time*—a future without Khan was one she didn't want to contemplate.

Gerel served dinner and Sarange was amazed at how

hungry she was. "Does shifting always make you feel as though you are half starved?" she asked after she had demolished her second bowl of chili.

Khan, who was embarking on his third helping, nodded. "It's the same for every shifter I know. Changing into your animal form, and back again, seems easy, but it uses a huge amount of energy."

Gerel nodded. "You are replenishing the physical strength your transformation has used with food. But shifting also requires a great deal of psychic energy. You must take care of your entire being."

"How do I do that?" Sarange asked. "I'm still in shock about this whole thing. I don't understand how I can be a werewolf, how Jiran can have believed I was the leader of the blue werewolves, and how I can remember being a leader of an ancient dynasty with Khan at my side. Am I remembering my werewolf self?" She frowned. "It doesn't seem that way."

"You are trying too hard to force your memories," Gerel said. "Relax, and they will come to you. Behind the reality we see, there is a web of life. It is a network of invisible links that connect the spirits and living things, the past and the present. The truth is simple. The blue wolf is your guardian, Sarange, the animal with which you most closely identify. But you are not a wolf. You are a shifter—part wolf, part human. Both parts of your being are equal."

"So I am not the leader of the actual blue wolves? The wild animals who are now endangered?" It seemed strange to be asking her aunt these questions. To accept that Gerel, the quiet, unassuming woman who had devoted so much of her life to bringing up Sarange, suddenly seemed different. She had an inner glow, a new energy. Her strength seemed to be returning by the minute. A wave of emotion washed over Sarange. In that instant, Gerel reminded her more than ever of Golden Wing.

"No, but their plight may be linked to what is happening with you." Gerel frowned. "If you are the leader of the blue werewolves, there is a bond between you and the wild wolves. When you are in danger it will impact them."

Sarange reached for the glass of wine that Bek had poured and swallowed some of the rich ruby liquid. "How can I be leader? I write songs and campaign for animals." She leaned her head against Khan's upper arm.

"This is about the past as well as the present," Gerel said. "Time is like a silken thread. It can be stretched to its fullest length, or it can be twisted back on itself. When that happens, past and present can touch and the strands of time can cross. Sometimes it can happen briefly and we get that strange feeling of déjà vu. Sometimes it goes on for longer and we hear stories of reincarnation."

"Is that what has happened to Khan and me? Are we reincarnated souls who loved each other in the past?" Saying it out loud no longer felt strange. It made sense. It was their story. Their truth.

Khan took hold of her hand, twining his fingers with hers. "I think we already know the answer to that question."

She was amazed at the depth of emotion in his voice. His golden gaze locked on hers, drawing her in. Giving her a glimpse of his soul. The tenderness was intoxicating. This was Khan. Bold, strutting, loud, arrogant. A tiger in every sense. Except with her. With Sarange he wasn't afraid to show this side of himself. And every time she looked into his eyes she was drawn deeper into enchantment.

"But we don't know all of it." She could hear the frustration in her own voice. "It's like a puzzle with half the pieces missing."

"This all kicked off when we met. It feels like someone doesn't want us to be together." Khan looked at Gerel for confirmation and she nodded. "Around the time we met, we had the offer from Radin to go to Mongolia and make his documentary about the blue wolves."

Sarange quirked a smile at him. "I seem to remember you were less than enthusiastic about that suggestion."

Khan had a range of smiles. From the one that made fans swoon to the one that was just for Sarange and melted her heart. This one held a mix of mischief and sheepishness. "That was when I was still fighting how attracted I was to you."

"Fighting it by pretending you hated me?" She couldn't resist trying to make him squirm just a little bit.

She should have known better. Khan didn't do squirming. The smile intensified, heating every part of her. He raised her hand to his lips, pressing a kiss into the center of her palm. "I don't like losing, but this one time? It felt good."

"It seems like going to Mongolia to make that documentary might be a good idea." Bek's words brought their focus back to the problems facing them. "It would take you to the heart of the blue wolf territory. Perhaps that's what you need to jolt your memories."

Khan raised a brow at Sarange. "What do you think?"

She nodded. "It's a good idea. The plans went on hold when you refused to take part. Radin was determined. At first, he just wanted me to make the documentary, but then he changed focus and insisted he wanted us both."

"I think we should pay Radin a visit in the morning."

"So tired." Sarange's gaze slid toward the bed as she closed the bedroom door behind them.

"Really?" Khan placed a hand on either side of her waist, pulling her toward him. "Because I had a few plans…and all of them require you to be conscious."

Warmth blossomed in the lightness of her eyes. "I guess I could be persuaded to stay awake a little longer."

Khan was close to exhaustion himself, but as soon as he got close to Sarange his body fired up with a new energy. All he wanted to do was hold her. To let his hands roam over her curves, to hear the soft sounds she made when he touched her. He flipped the long braid back from her shoulder and trailed his thumb along her collarbone, delighting in the way her breathing instantly hitched up a notch.

She wanted him as much as he wanted her. He could see it in her eyes every time he looked her way. With the slightest touch, they both went up in flames. Just the way the shifter legends predicted it would be. She was his mate. This was how it would always be for them. He would always want to kiss those perfect lips, to tear her clothes from her body, to run his tongue over every inch of her skin, to make her scream his name as she came so hard she saw stars.

He trailed a line of kisses along the graceful curve of her neck, the contact lighting white fires throughout his nerve endings.

"Khan." Sarange shivered as she murmured his name. He loved the way her body instantly responded to him. Her eyelids fluttered closed as her hands reached for his shoulders. Her nipples were already diamond hard against the thin cotton of her tank top.

Tipping her chin back, he kissed her. Slow and gentle. The sound she made was midway between a gasp and a murmur. Quiet and pleading. Her hands moved to the hem of his T-shirt, pushing it up over his torso. Khan raised his arms above his head, assisting her, and the garment was quickly flung aside. Featherlight, Sarange's fingertips traced the muscles of his abdomen and he sucked in a breath. That instant response worked both ways. Her touch was like a brand, leaving fiery tendrils in its wake.

Khan began to move, not breaking contact with Sarange. When he reached the bed, he pulled her down with him. She moved to straddle his hips and Khan gripped the round globes of her ass, rocking his pelvis against hers.

After lifting her tank top over her head, he covered her breasts with his hands. They were perfect, warm, soft and full against his palms. Bringing her closer to him, he drew one nipple into his mouth. Sarange cried out, her fingers sliding into his hair. Flicking his tongue over the hard nub, Khan watched her face as she arched her back, tiny gasps escaping her lips.

He flipped her over onto her back, bending his head to lavish attention over each breast in turn until she was moaning and writhing under him. When she reached out a hand for the button on his jeans, he caught hold of her fingertips.

"Not yet. After the evening we've just had, you need to relax. Let me make you feel good." He watched her face as he spoke. "I'm going to make you come. That's what you need right now."

Sarange murmured his name as he moved down her

body, kissing the space between her breasts, then across her rib cage, before sliding down the elasticized waist of her sweatpants. He kissed the skin he exposed as he removed her sweatpants and underwear. Parting her thighs, he bent his head and ran his tongue along the glistening length of her slit.

"So wet for me already."

He could feel tension in every line of her body. Even through her arousal, he could sense the damage done by the extraordinary events of the last few hours, and he was determined to erase them. Using gentle strokes of his fingers and tongue, he explored her, teasing and tantalizing her. Almost immediately she was digging her nails into his shoulders, rocking her hips against him and pleading for more. Khan had wanted this to be slow, but she was at the brink so fast he could already feel her muscles stiffening.

He slid two fingers deep inside her as he massaged her clit with his tongue, driving her over the edge. Sarange shattered, her body shaking hard as she turned her head and smothered her cry with the pillow. Khan withdrew his fingers and kissed his way up her stomach. When he moved back up to kiss her lips again, she held him like she was never going to let him go. Which suited Khan just fine, since his own arousal had reached volcanic proportions.

The kiss heated up so fast Sarange gasped. Khan removed the remaining items of his clothing and returned to press close against her. Sarange's warm sex pressed against his rock-hard cock, inflaming him further. He skimmed his hands over her hips, lifting her tight to him, letting her feel him press into her.

"Condom." The word came out on a gasp as she squirmed against him.

"We can use one if you want, but we don't need to." She met his gaze, her brow furrowing in confusion. "Now that we know for sure that you are a werewolf, you have the same cycle as a female wolf. You are only fertile during the mating season. All that remains is for you to trust me when I tell you I'm clean."

He wasn't sure how she would take that piece of information. Was now a good time to mention it, or was it a mood killer? She was still and silent for a moment, then the flare of passion in her eyes intensified.

"I want to feel you inside me with nothing between us…my tiger."

Khan growled as he parted her knees and sank deep into her. Sarange writhed under him, scoring his back with her long nails, rocking her hips as she matched his thrusts. At the same time, she murmured his name over and over, encouraging him.

Nothing had ever felt like this; he knew it with a certainty that made his mind go blank. This connection between them was so right, so natural. Everything about Sarange—her smell, her taste, her skin, her lips—had been designed to fit him. Chemistry, trust, bonding. He guessed it was all true. Mate-sex really was the best sex.

He rolled them over, lifting her on top of him. Sarange straddled him again with her knees either side of his hips. Her long braid flopped forward and her breasts bounced teasingly close to his face. Gripping her waist, he drove his hips up in time with her movements. She tipped her head back, her expression one of pure concentration as she focused on riding him.

"Khan." Her tongue flicked out and his eyes were drawn to the sheen it left on her plump lower lip. "I'm going to…"

"Yes." He lifted her almost all the way off him,

bringing her down hard and fast onto his cock, rocking his pelvis against hers. "Come for me, Sarange. Come with me."

Her whole body went rigid as she called out his name. He turned her onto her back again, driving into her deeper and tighter until they both cried out at the intensity of the sensation. Shuddering, Sarange clung to him as her climax stormed through her.

With her internal muscles clenching around him, Khan arched into her with long strokes. His vision went dark as he followed her into the abyss. There was only Sarange, his mate, this moment, this pleasure, this intensity. He gave himself up to it before collapsing beside her, holding her close, and fighting to regain his breath.

After several long, silent minutes, Khan drew the comforter over them. "Sleep."

Sarange's eyes were already closed as she nestled closer to him. "Despite everything that's happened, with your arms around me, I think I can."

Chapter 12

The following morning, Khan called Ged, who told him everything had been quiet at Sarange's house since they had left. That information appeared to confirm Khan's suspicions that Bora was watching Sarange. If she was the target, there was no need to attack her Beverly Hills home when she wasn't there. The thought chilled him. *Step out of the shadows and fight me.*

When Sarange called her manager, she was greeted as though she had dropped off the face of the earth instead of having been out of touch for a day. Grimacing at Khan, she did her best to explain her absence without going into detail.

"I'm on my way to see Radin. Khan has decided to do the documentary on the blue wolves." Since their faceless enemy wanted them in Mongolia, they had decided to call his bluff.

She ended the call sometime later. It was incredible

how much her life had changed in such a short time. In the past, a call with her manager would have her making notes, firing questions, giving instructions. Now she wanted to hurry the conversation along so she could end the call and get back to what was important. The whole time the single thought *I'm a werewolf* persisted, pushing everything else to the back of her mind.

Almost everything. There was just the little matter of the vicious werewolves on her tail…and the man at her side. Both dominated her thoughts, but for very different reasons.

They had left Bek and Gerel's house before it was light, not even pausing to grab a cup of coffee before setting off. Khan had decided to drive rather than fly, reasoning that, if Bora was watching them, it would be harder for him to track their whereabouts. Now, almost six hours later, having stopped for breakfast on the way, they were approaching Los Angeles.

"When Ged freed you from captivity, where exactly were you being held?" Sarange studied the noble lines of Khan's profile as she asked the question.

"China." She could feel the tension coming off him in waves. "In the Xinjiang region."

Sarange knew of Xinjiang, China's largest province. Situated in the northwest of the country, it was a vast region of deserts and mountains that bordered her own homeland, Mongolia.

"Is that where you are from?"

"I don't know where I'm from." Although Khan's voice was devoid of emotion, she sensed how much it hurt him to talk of his past.

She was reluctant to push him further, but she knew the mystery of their shared past could hold the key to what was happening to them right now. Through her work with Animals Alive, she had learned about tigers in the wild. The ultimate symbol of an endangered species, the raw beauty of the tiger was captivating, its story tragic. She trawled through her memory for some understanding of the remaining habitat of the tiger. Khan, of course, was not really a tiger. He was a shifter. Just as with her and a wolf, there were similarities, but also differences between him and the wild animal.

"When you shift, you look like a cross between a Siberian and a Bengal tiger, but you are bigger than either of them."

Khan hunched a shoulder. "Since I don't know my parents, I can't ask them about that." He flicked a glance at her, the look in his eyes softening. "I'm sorry. I don't know how to talk about myself because I don't know who I am. I call myself a Bengal, but you're right. I don't look a hundred percent like any tiger alive today."

Sarange frowned. "Do you think you could be a tiger who is no longer alive?"

"I felt pretty much alive last night…and again in the shower this morning." He quirked a brow in her direction and Sarange felt a blush heat her cheeks.

The memory of his hands on her body, of his tongue exploring every hidden part of her, of him inside her, made her squirm with renewed desire. "You know that's not what I meant." She forced herself to concentrate on the conversation instead of on the way he could take her to heights of pleasure she had never even dreamed of. "There are some species of tiger that are already extinct. If you have been alive for a very long time, your animal self may be one of those."

Khan's lips turned down in an expression of distaste. "I'm not sure I like the idea of being extinct."

She decided on one more probe. "Is Khan your real name, or is that something else you don't know?"

"When Ged found me—when he dragged me from the cage where I'd been imprisoned—I was close to death." His voice when he said the words stirred something in her, a pain so sharp it made her want to cry out. Instead, she gripped the sides of the seat hard and let him continue. "I could barely speak, but I said one word. *Khan*." He shrugged. "Ged assumed it was my name and that's what I've been called ever since."

"Although Khan is a common name across the world now, it was originally Mongolian," Sarange said. "It means 'leader' or 'ruler.'"

"In that case, it was a useful name for the lead singer of a group of misfit shifters." Khan's reluctance to continue the conversation was evident.

They completed the remainder of the journey in silence. Real Planet Productions was located in a large gleaming office block in West Hollywood. Occupying an entire floor, Radin's small but successful production company was gaining recognition as the creative force behind several powerful wildlife films and documentaries.

Sarange looked up at the facade of the building with the sun reflecting off the windows. "If Bora is following us, aren't we exposing Radin to danger? Should we warn him?"

"If Bora turns up, we'll deal with him." Khan paused at the entrance to the building, catching hold of Sarange's forearm and halting her before she walked inside. He surveyed the revolving door for a moment or two before taking her hand and walking in at her side.

Sarange had called ahead and spoken to Radin's personal assistant. She and Khan had discussed the potential hazards involved in the move. On the one hand, by making an appointment, they were giving the enemy a heads-up about their whereabouts. On the other, they needed to be sure that Radin would be available to see them. In the end, they had decided that arranging to see Radin was the best option. The mysterious Bora seemed to know their every move anyway. One phone call wasn't going to make any difference to whether he had a welcome party waiting at Radin's office or not.

Now they were here and it appeared to be a regular working day in a prestigious office block. There was no pack of snarling werewolves awaiting them in the black marble and mirrored lobby. They were able to take the elevator to the tenth floor without being accosted. Once there, they were greeted by Radin's personal assistant, Maria, a coolly efficient young woman who pretended not to notice that the story the world had been waiting for was standing in her reception area. Khan and Sarange were holding hands right in front of her.

"Radin had an unexpected visitor, but he asked me to let you know he won't keep you waiting more than a few minutes." She gestured to the office just behind her desk. "Can I get you anything to drink?"

They both declined and went to stand near the window, looking out at an uninspiring view of similar buildings.

"We will get through this. Together." Khan's voice was low enough so that only Sarange could hear. It felt like there had been other times when they had stood this way, just the two of them, facing a very different view. And he had made the same promise.

"But then they took you from me."

"Pardon?"

She shook her head, unsure where the words had

come from, experiencing a sensation of utter desolation. It felt as if Khan had been torn from her side by hostile hands. Was that what had happened to them? Back in the mists of time? She thought of the shifter love story Bek had told. Of how, against the odds, the Caspian tiger and Chinua, the leader of the blue werewolves, had come together and created their own unique dynasty. When he was taken from her the blue werewolf had vowed to search for him forever, but her body had grown weak and finally faded away.

Had Chinua been reborn? The thought was like a thunderbolt of realization. More than that. It was one of certainty. Sarange tilted her head back, gazing up at Khan as she saw it all. Or most of it. The day she found Sarange, Golden Wing had left her tribe for a reason. But it was not the one she claimed. The shamanka had not gone to commune with nature in solitude. She had gone in search of the werewolf child she knew she would find on the vast, frozen tundra. And, having discovered Sarange, she had taken her back to the tribe and raised her as a human child. *Without ever telling me who I was.*

Why was that? Why had Golden Wing allowed her to grow up never knowing the truth about herself? Not only that she was a werewolf, but that she was the reincarnation of the great blue wolf leader of Mongolian legend? There were so many unanswered questions chasing around in Sarange's mind. How had her werewolf instincts remained subdued for so long? Why had Golden Wing insisted on sending her to America when her destiny was clearly tied up in her home country of Mongolia? Why was *this* time in her life the tipping point for so many momentous changes?

"You are a Caspian tiger." In her work with Animals Alive Foundation, she had heard of the largest tigers ever known. There was an ambitious conservation plan under way to bring them back to their natural Central Asia habitat.

"You sound very sure." Khan cast a glance over at the desk where Maria had her head bent over some papers.

"Not just any Caspian tiger. You are *the* Caspian tiger." Emotion made Sarange's voice husky. "My Caspian tiger."

He stared down at her, realization and acceptance dawning in the golden depths of his eyes. "And you are my blue wolf. My Chinua."

Tears pricked the back of her eyelids. "Do you remember?"

"Some of it. Enough to know it's true." He ran a hand through his hair. "As crazy as it sounds, I remember us."

She laughed. "So do I. A little. It's still blurred, like I'm looking at it through cracked glass, but—" she lifted a hand and touched his cheek "—my God, Khan. The story Bek described as one of the greatest love stories ever told…that was us, wasn't it?"

Before he could reply, there was a shout and a crash from Radin's office. Without pausing, Khan leaped across the reception desk and flung open the door. Sarange was just behind him. The sight that met her eyes as she entered the office brought them both to an instant halt.

Radin was lying on the floor, apparently unconscious. The room looked as though a struggle had recently taken place. Papers spilled from the desk onto the floor, and a chair had been tipped over. There was no one else in the room.

"How did he get out of here?" Khan barked out the

question to Maria while Sarange dropped to her knees beside Radin, checking his pulse.

"I don't know." Maria's face was white as she looked at her boss. "This is the only door."

Radin opened his eyes, blinking at Sarange and wincing as he lifted a hand to the back of his head. "What the hell...? He hit me with my own award." His hand shook as he pointed to a bronze statuette lying on the floor. He sat up slowly, his gaze wandering around the room before fixing on the desk. "And my laptop is gone."

"Gone where?" Khan was standing by the open door, his expression thunderous. "I still don't see how he— whoever he is—got away."

Sarange sat back on her heels, her head spinning. She guessed she already knew the answer to her next question, but she felt obliged to ask it anyway. "Who was in here with you?"

"A guy I've been working with on an outline for a new film. Today was the first time we've met."

"And his name is Bora." Khan's face was grim as he spoke.

"How did you know?" Radin frowned, whether in surprise at Khan's words or in pain, Sarange couldn't be sure.

"Call it a lucky guess."

At Khan's insistence, they moved fast. "I'm supposed to be recording a new album," he said, overriding Radin's protests about scheduling. "We do this now, or we don't do it at all."

Radin, having waved aside Sarange's suggestion that he should seek medical help, was seated at his desk, his fingers tented beneath his chin as he studied them. "What made you change your mind?"

Khan flapped a dismissive hand. "Let's get down to business. Sarange and I will be on our way to Mongolia later today. You can email us the details of when and where your team will meet us. Unless the documentary is no longer an option now that you've lost your laptop?"

Radin bristled slightly. "Everything is backed up. It's an inconvenience, nothing more."

Khan couldn't get rid of the twitchy feeling that something was wrong. He almost laughed out loud. Something was already very wrong. His instincts were telling him that something *more* was wrong. It must be Bora's lingering scent, or the knowledge that his enemy had been close.

He prowled the room, his gaze going to the full-length window and the street below. How the hell had Bora gotten out of here after he attacked Radin?

"And you'd never met this guy before today?" He swung back around to face Radin.

"I already told you that." Radin was starting to sound slightly irritable. "Twice."

"To be fair—" Sarange's calm voice cut across the exchange "—Radin has just been hit across the head."

Her gaze locked on Khan's. It had been quite a day already. There had been the revelation that they were the legendary lovers of Mongolian wolf-lore, then the realization that Bora had been in the building—just feet away—and had somehow eluded them. Khan wasn't good at appreciating the feelings of others, but he could read the message in Sarange's eyes. She wanted him to go easy on Radin. He supposed it was only fair. The guy was human, injured and shaken.

With a sigh, he took the seat next to Sarange on the

opposite side of the desk to Radin. His protective instincts were on high alert, pushing everything else to the back of his mind. His focus was Sarange. Always Sarange. But he didn't like Radin. There was nothing he could pinpoint about the other man to justify that feeling. It was possibly based on a certain warmth he detected in Radin's eyes when they rested on Sarange, a widening of his smile when he looked at her. His expression was… Khan struggled to find the right word. Awed? She was one of the most famous women on the planet, for God's sake. Millions of people looked at her that way.

"What was on your laptop?" Sarange asked.

"Everything. My whole life." Radin gave a snort of laughter. "But I back my work up, so, although the guy who took it has details of everything I've done, I have copies."

"Why would he want to steal your work?" Sarange frowned. "I'm sorry if this sounds ignorant, but has he taken anything of value?"

"Yes. He's taken my original ideas, and those of my clients." Radin shuffled one of the piles of papers on his desk as though attempting to get them back into some sort of order.

"We all know that's not what this is about." Khan had hidden his impatience for long enough. "This is about the documentary you want to make with Sarange. I take it all the details were stored on your laptop?"

Radin nodded. "Everything was finalized. Location, script ideas, timings. We have an experienced wildlife camera crew who have worked with wolf packs in other parts of the world. We were ready to go when, or should I say *if* you were?"

"You must have been confident I'd change my mind," Khan said.

His intention had been to make Radin squirm, but, although the other man appeared to have trouble maintaining eye contact, he didn't back down. "I'd worked hard on the planning. If you weren't going to do it, I was going to get someone else."

Radin was lying. It was coming off him in waves. He wanted Sarange for this because of her Mongolian heritage and because of who she was. She would light up the screen with her beauty and she was an animal ambassador. Her passion for endangered species would shine through. Put her in his documentary and Radin was guaranteed a success. Then he'd seen her and Khan together onstage and the dollar signs had appeared before his eyes. He wanted to use the chemistry between them and the rumors about their relationship to make money from his venture. On one level, Khan admired his astuteness. On another, he remembered that this was supposed to be about a species of wolf that was threatened with extinction. *What the hell happened to ethics?*

So what if this guy was a little sleazy? The end result was the same. He and Sarange were going to Mongolia anyway. They believed that the answers to what was happening lay there, just as they felt that the blue wolves were at the heart of the issue. Sarange would get her documentary. The profile of the blue wolves would be raised. And Radin? It was possible he had turned up with his documentary suggestion at the wrong time. That it was all a coincidence. Khan didn't believe any of that. He had every confidence that Bora, Radin and the blue wolves were all tied in to what they would find in Mongolia.

But what he couldn't define, or begin to express, was

the feeling that had gripped him ever since Sarange said those words. *You are* the *Caspian tiger. My Caspian tiger.* He knew she was right. Before his captivity, he had been the Great Tiger of Mongolian legend. He had fought, lived and loved at Sarange's side. So why was there a feeling of dread in his heart at the thought of returning to Mongolia? What had happened in his past to make him view a return to that land with trepidation?

It didn't matter. This was about Sarange and he would walk through the gates of hell for her.

Sarange was experiencing the strangest feeling. It was as if the tiredness induced by the long journey was going into reverse as they got closer to the Mongolian capital of Ulaanbaatar. At the same time, the curious tingling feeling of unseen eyes watching her was increasing. Flying from Los Angeles to Beijing felt like it had taken forever. Now, after a lengthy layover, they were almost there. Just her, Khan…and Jiran.

"Take me with you."

They had returned to her house, and as she had been throwing clothes into a backpack, Jiran's plea had made her pause.

"This will not be a vacation." She had tried to let him down gently. He still appeared to be in shock. It was hardly surprising. Having come here to study, he had been thrust into a nightmare. "If you want to go home to Mongolia, I can arrange that."

"No." He shook his head. "I want to help find the man who killed my friends. I want justice…and I can be your guide."

She had considered that, eventually taking the suggestion to Khan. "It's all very well being the Blue Wolf and Great Tiger of ancient lore, but Mongolia is a vast, empty country. I don't know where to begin the search for our past. Maybe having a guide wouldn't be a bad thing."

"I agree, but I'd prefer someone other than a traumatized boy."

"You and I have the teeth, claws and muscles. Jiran may be from a rival gray werewolf pack, but he knows the Altai Mountains. That's the only area where blue wolves still survive. It is also the place where legend says Chinua had her stronghold in a time before the land was called Mongolia." She had placed a hand on his arm. "Let Jiran do this. It will restore his lost confidence."

His golden eyes had looked beyond her words and into her soul. "This is about more than restoring his pride, isn't it, my *koke gal*?"

The words shook her. "That's what you used to call me. *Koke gal*. Blue fire." She didn't know how she understood his meaning, since she wasn't sure what language he was speaking. Although it resembled modern day Mongolian, the dialect was different.

"Flashes of this language keep coming to me. It's driving me crazy because I only get snippets of it now and then, never a whole sentence or anything I can make sense of. Just odd words. But that one I'm sure of. Blue fire." Khan shook his head as though trying to clear it. "How did you know what it meant?"

"Bek has ancient texts on the wall of his study, and your words reminded me of those. But the main reason I knew what you were saying was that I have heard those words from you before. Many times and in another life."

That was why Jiran was with them now. Because of the blue fire in Sarange's veins. That extra sense that told her they needed him. Never mind why. The part of her that was Chinua knew they would require the young gray werewolf's help. Perhaps it would be when they reached the Altai Mountains. The formidable, beautiful range extended through China, Mongolia, Russia and Kazakhstan, the jagged mountain ridges deriving their name from the word *altan*, meaning "golden."

Once they landed, the interior of the airport was like any other. It was only when they stepped outside that Sarange was reminded that she had made the dramatic transition from Los Angeles to Mongolia. Cabdrivers immediately clamored for their business, but Jiran led them toward the bus station.

"Anyone with a vehicle can provide a cab service in Mongolia. There's a good chance we'll get ripped off."

Sarange was about to point out that money didn't matter. So what if a Mongolian cabdriver cashed in on their journey? She could afford to pay more than the going rate. Then she realized how that sounded. It made her appear like the worst kind of spoiled celebrity. She remembered Khan's comments about seeing her country as a backpacker and decided that was the way to enjoy it. And possibly the best way to stay under Bora's radar.

The bus was full and Sarange was squashed tight up against Khan for the duration of the journey. It wasn't a hardship. He placed an arm around her to keep her safe and she leaned in close to the hard muscles of his chest. They passed a variety of methods of transport including different vehicles, carts, yaks and the occasional camel.

"Can you feel it?" He murmured the words into her hair.

"Yes." She tilted her head back to look up at him. "We are being watched."

He looked over the top of her head, his gaze roaming around the crowded space. The other passengers were mostly tourists. Although they were a mix of ages, they were predominantly backpackers. A few signaled their relative affluence with suitcases.

"Can't see anyone here who fits the profile," Khan sighed. "It's a pity we don't know what the profile is."

"Jiran does," Sarange reminded him. "He has met Bora."

"Another good reason to bring him along." He leaned closer to Jiran. "Do you see anyone here who looks like the guy who approached you in the nightclub?"

Jiran's complexion paled as his gaze skittered around the vehicle. "No. Absolutely not."

Sarange shivered slightly, pressing closer to Khan. "Invisible eyes on us?"

A soft growl started somewhere deep in his chest. "I don't care whether he's invisible or not. If Bora thinks he can intimidate me, he can think again."

Chapter 13

As they exited the bus, Khan studied the slightly depressing Soviet-style architecture all around him. It came as a shock. It was an enormous, pulsating city with wild traffic, sinful nightlife and a bohemian culture. It was chaotic, ever-changing, yet traditional, hinting at adventure and excitement. This was not the Mongolia he had been expecting.

Sarange and Jiran competed to explain that the concrete ugliness of Ulaanbaatar's buildings wasn't typical of the whole country.

"Once we leave the city, it is all open space," Jiran said.

"There are vast deserts, rolling sand dunes, mountains and parklands...this is the most beautiful country in the world. Right now all I want to do is get clean and sleep. I don't care if we are supposed to be doing this on a budget." Sarange's face wore an expression that wasn't going to tolerate any argument. "I want a suite with a huge bed and a bath big enough to swim in." She pointed across the square where they were standing to a large building with flags waving above its impressive entrance. "That place will do."

Beast had played a series of gigs in Moscow about eighteen months earlier, and the lobby of the Mongolia Palace reminded Khan of the grandeur of the Russian hotels the band had stayed in. Since Sarange was hugely famous in her own country, her face featuring on billboards around the capital city, she resorted to her beanie-and-shades disguise once more while Khan checked them in.

"Once I've caught up on some sleep, I'm going to visit my family," Jiran said as he left them to make his way to his own room. He bowed his head to Sarange. "If that's okay?"

It surprised Khan that Jiran had slipped so easily into a subservient role with Sarange. He didn't know much about wolf hierarchy, but he knew enough. In the wild, the alpha male ruled his pack with the alpha female at his side. But Sarange and Jiran were from different shifter packs, groups that had traditionally been at war. He was male and she was female. It made no sense for Jiran to bow down to her.

Sarange nodded. "Just be careful. I think Bora already knows we are here."

That was another thing that bothered Khan. *Another thing?* There were so many competing claims on his attention it was getting hard to focus. And his DNA was half cat. Concentration wasn't his shifter strong point. It was just as well his human senses were supercharged when it came to looking out for Sarange.

"*Bora.* That means gray, doesn't it?"

Both Sarange and Jiran regarded him in surprise. "No," Sarange said. "In Mongolian we say *saaral* for gray."

"Now you would. But in the past it was *bora*." Snippets of that ancient language kept returning to him and he was sure of it. "If your animal guardian is the gray wolf and Sarange's is the blue wolf, shouldn't you be enemies? In fact—" Khan kept his gaze fixed on Jiran's face "—if Bora is linked to the gray werewolves, shouldn't your allegiance be to him?"

Jiran paled. "You don't believe that, do you?" His pleading eyes traveled from Khan's face to Sarange's. "Bora tried to kill me...he killed my friends..."

Sarange placed a hand on his arm. "I trust you."

He visibly relaxed. "Thank you." Casting a scared look in Khan's direction, he scurried away.

"Is that wise?" As Sarange inserted the key card into the door of their room, Khan watched Jiran's retreating figure.

"Right now I'm going with my instincts. I haven't seen or felt anything from him to make me think he's double-crossing us." She stepped into the room and shrugged off her backpack with a sigh of relief. "But if he tries, I'll know how to deal with him."

He closed the door, leaning against it and drawing her to him. "I remember now. You can be a scary werewolf leader."

"Only when I need to." Her smile made his heart lighter. "You know what I want to do now?"

"You already said. Bathe, then sleep."

"Even before that." She ran her hands up his arms, her touch, even through his clothing, making his flesh tingle. "I'm still coming to terms with all this. You and me. The past. Being a werewolf. Being in charge. I want to get out of the city. Find somewhere we can be alone. Somewhere I can shift and run free." The smile became mischievous. "Let's take my wolf for a test drive."

Khan laughed. "That's the most un-wolflike thing I've ever heard you say."

Sarange grabbed his hand, pulling him back out the door toward the elevator. "I know a tiger who's a bad influence."

The Zaisan Memorial was a huge structure set high on a hill south of the city. "If we head in that direction, there are surrounding hills nearby where we can be alone," Sarange explained, using the towering monument as a guide.

As darkness fell, the busy capital city was coming alive. Bars, clubs and restaurants were teeming with people all determined to enjoy themselves. Khan's shifter shared their urges, but with a different purpose. His inner tiger cried out for freedom.

Ever since his release from captivity, he had suppressed his shifter instincts, pouring his energy into the band. He had focused on Khan the rock star, preferring to forget Khan the tiger. Not knowing who he was, how he had ended up in that tiny cage, emaciated, humiliated, disconnected from either human or shifter reality…he hadn't wanted to think about that time. It still hurt him to recall it now.

But his mind-set had recently undergone a change, and he didn't have far to look for the reason. She was right here at his side, holding his hand, her long stride matching his. Everything about her matching him. He hadn't wanted Sarange in his life, had fought strenuously to keep her out. Nevertheless, she was here. And now that she was in it, his life was different. The past had caught up with him and he was glad.

He didn't know it all. He had no idea where he had been born. His childhood, family, all those details about what had shaped him…they still remained a mystery. But he knew he had loved Sarange, or Chinua, as she had been at that time. At some point in his life, the impossible had happened. The tiger had fallen in love with the wolf. And side by side they had created their great dynasty.

"I would never have willingly left you, my *koke gal*." The fierceness of the emotion that seized him as he said the words almost brought him to his knees.

"I know. That's why I searched for you." Her grip tightened on his hand, her fingers fitting the spaces between his perfectly. *Completing me.* "I couldn't live without you."

There was no self-pity in the words, no drama. It was a simple statement of fact. One Khan understood absolutely. Before the great Chinggis Khan united the warring tribes and founded the Mongol Empire, Chinua had been one of the most powerful leaders in the region. Her enemies had tried, and failed, to destroy her by force. They had resorted to the only thing that could damage her. They had taken away her reason for living.

Khan had been Chinua's mate, her love, her constant companion. When they captured Khan, Chinua's reign had been ended. She had been devastated. Her personal decline had been followed by a deterioration in her clan. The mighty werewolf leader ceased to function without her tiger. And Khan knew it was the same for him. He had never known how long he was imprisoned. Years? Decades? He had no sense of the passage of time in that hell. Now he knew it had been centuries. Almost ten of them. A thousand years of pining for Sarange.

"Why now?" he asked. "After all this time, why has fate brought us back together now?" Khan couldn't believe it was all coincidence. Ten years ago, Ged had been given information that led him to Khan. He had found him and brought him back from the brink of death. Not only that, he had given him a new life as a rock star. In a parallel story, Chinua, her body and spirit destroyed by the search for her lost love, had been reborn as Sarange. Who also happened to be a famous singer...

"Maybe we had to meet again now because we are needed."

The thought chilled Khan. He wasn't sure he was ready to be needed. He could accept that his past self had been a responsible warrior who had stood shoulder to shoulder with the woman he loved and fought for what he believed. But now he lived a different life. His jokes about hedonism were partly true. He didn't want to be shaken out of his comfort zone. It was a self-preservation mechanism. The thought of captivity filled him with dread. *I don't know if I could do it again.*

Sarange looked up at him, her face an accurate reflection of his own thoughts. "Does that frighten you?"

He considered lying to her, being the strutting alpha male the world saw on stage. But this was Sarange. She deserved better than the act he gave everyone else. "Yes."

Her mouth tightened into a line. "It terrifies me."

He halted his stride, catching hold of both her hands so she swung around to face him. "No matter how much it scares me, I will never let you down. You are my *koke*

gal. My blue fire. Almost a thousand years have passed
since I first held you in my arms, but you mean as much
to me now as you did then. We will do this side by side,
the way we always did."

"The way we always did." She nodded, her expression changing, becoming determined. "I could always
count on you, my tiger."

They skirted the monument that was a tourist desti-
nation in daylight, heading instead for the surrounding
forest. As they progressed deeper into the trees, Khan
was reminded of the enchanted forests in a child's fairy
tale. This one beckoned them deeper into its darkness.
Its pulsing heart called to them and he could sense Sarange's restlessness growing to match his own. The
moon was high and bright. A wolf moon. It illuminated
the groves. Coils of vaporous mist lingered, writhing
around their ankles like the smoke effects of a Beast
concert, sensual and illusory. Most of the time a haunting silence hung over the ground. Nothing stirred. Now
and then, the flute-like piping of a lingering songbird
rent the silence high above them.

Mahogany brown tree trunks soared heavenward like
ancient sentinels guarding the path. Khan's sharp eyes
saw gems of amber clinging to their crusty exteriors.
His sharp ears picked up the metallic, tinkling sound
of a stream and he caught a glimpse of its bright silver
ribbon through the lace of leaves.

Once they were deep enough into this nighttime par-
adise, Sarange turned to face him. "This is where I
want to shift."

At the words, he felt something stir in the space
between them. Something dark and irresistible. The
weight of his past, of everything he'd denied for so long,
was there in the icy blue of Sarange's eyes, and Khan's

tiger leaped in response. She overloaded his senses and it was intoxicating. He could feel his shifter self rippling in the depths of his muscles, and simmering in his bloodstream. The call of his tiger was beating in time with his heart.

They stripped off their clothes and left them at the base of a tree. Khan reached out his hands and Sarange took them. She gazed into his eyes as he shifted. It was quick, quiet and natural. His human features changed, his golden eyes widened, his powerful body elongated as his muscles grew. Within seconds, the man was gone and Khan's tiger was before her. He knew he was a magnificent animal, standing almost eight feet tall on his hind legs. He dropped onto all fours and Sarange ran a hand through the thick orange fur of his neck. Khan rubbed his whiskery cheek against her thigh, maintaining eye contact. Waiting.

Slowly, Sarange lowered her head, studying the forest floor. He could tell what she was thinking. She was new to this. She wanted to savor it. Last time it had been a necessity, this time…she wanted to think about it. He could see the moment when she surrendered to the emotions coursing through her and gave herself up to her wolf. It was the most perfect, natural shift from human to animal, a harmonious exchange between the two beings who resided within her. She was a shifter, she felt the power of her other self surging through her veins.

Dropping onto all fours beside Khan, Sarange's wolf threw back her head and gave a single, triumphant howl.

Side by side, the tiger and the wolf ran through the forest, moving in time with each other. Khan was conscious of his power and speed compared to her lighter, slenderer frame. He was protective of her, shortening his long strides to match hers, pausing if he thought she was tiring. High on a ridge overlooking the river, they paused, their body language warm and loving. She rubbed her face along his neck and he growled long and low in appreciation.

They moved together and apart, challenging and inviting, in a timeless dance of mating. When they came together for the final time, she rolled onto her back, trusting him completely, a wolf presenting her unprotected belly to a tiger. He stood over her, baring his teeth as if he was about to rip out her tender throat. Two creatures who should never come together except in anger, tied by bonds of tenderness. When he released her, the female scampered to her feet, running from him toward the forest once more. With his long stride, he easily caught up to her and they ran together again, shifting back as they reached the cover of the trees.

Khan pushed Sarange up against the trunk of a tree, holding her naked body in place with his own. He was fire and she was ice, but when they came together, the ice infused the fire with a gentler passion that melted them both. The taste of him was seductive and potent, reminding her of their past and sending a hit of euphoria straight to her sex. Hunger, pure, clamoring and fiery, invaded her body.

After their run through the forest, she needed him right there and then. She plowed her hands into the thick, dark gold mass of his hair, her fingers tugging on the silken strands, pulling him closer as she took his tongue into her mouth, relishing the taste and feel of him.

A shudder tore through her as his big, warm hands stroked her bare back. His touch sent so many sensations, swift and brutal, rushing through her, striking at her core, making her gasp with instant longing.

Cold air prickled over her heated flesh as the breeze caught her. It added a momentary relief from the red-hot flames burning her flesh.

Khan's hand tugged on her braid as the fingers of the other reached upward, cupping one breast. Sarange sucked in a desperate breath at the heat of his hand burning her. It was like he was imprinting himself into her bloodstream. Her body was a riot of sensation and she didn't know where one feeling ended and the next one began. All that mattered was Khan, his touch and those brilliant gold eyes blazing into her.

He bent his head and the sharp edge of his teeth grazed sweet ecstasy along the sensitive skin of her collarbone. It was just the right side of too much.

"I need you." She barely recognized her own voice. "Always."

His fingers moved to her nipple, tightening as his teeth nipped a path lower. Capturing the hard, sensitive bud between his thumb and finger, he rolled it, making her senses reel out of control with pleasure.

Her arousal spiked until her clit was throbbing with erotic pain. Gripping his hair tighter, she drew his lips back to hers. His tongue licked, his teeth nipped, his lips devoured. Sarange was left breathless and moaning as she arched closer to him.

She stared up at him, at the strong, harshly carved features, and her heart short-circuited. There was so much strength and hunger in his expression. His eyes appeared neon bright in the moonlight. Intense and glowing with hunger. His expression was tight with lust, his lips even more full than usual from their kisses. But there was more than desire on his face. Mates loved.

They had loved. Loved each other with an intensity that had destroyed them.

Khan returned to take her lips once more and she felt the world fall away. She lost everything in the pleasure of his touch and the deep, probing intensity of his kiss. Her nails dug into his arm as a soft moan left her lips. She wanted him now, under the moon that called to her inner wolf.

She wanted to unleash this big, powerful male here alongside her memories of him. Here in the outdoors. Wanted them both panting and wild. Wanted to make up for the years apart, the times she had wandered this land alone, searching for him, wishing, wanting, aching…unable to function without his touch.

Pushed hard against the tree trunk, she could read Khan's thoughts. Knew with breathless certainty, as his gaze caught and held hers, that he wanted the same thing.

"Sweet Sarange." His voice rumbled through her, stirring her emotions into a frenzy. With him her strength dissolved. With him she could allow herself to feel, to be vulnerable.

His hand flattened on her stomach, sliding lower, his fingers trailing a heated path of desire in their wake as he cupped her sex. With a soft cry, Sarange lifted herself on the tips of her toes, pressing closer into his probing fingers. It was too much. His touch scorched her. She almost exploded with pleasure as he rubbed against the swollen nub of her clitoris.

"You smell perfect." His teeth raked along her jawline. "You smell like mine."

His words exerted as much power over her as his touch.

"You are so beautiful." His hands returned to cup

her breasts, his fingers tormenting her nipples into even harder peaks. "All those years. I thought I'd forgotten, but I couldn't erase your memory from my mind. I thought you were a dream. Now I know you were a memory."

Her heart almost broke at the words and the look in his eyes as he stared down at the rapid rise and fall of her breasts. Then her mind went blank as Khan wrapped his lips around one agonizingly tender tip.

The white-hot feel of his mouth tugging on her nipple sent a lightning bolt of pleasure through her. Her back arched away from the tree trunk and she gave a strangled cry of rapture.

Moving down her body, he pressed a series of kisses from her breasts, down her stomach, across her abdomen and along both hipbones.

The world was spinning out of control. As she tilted her head back, Sarange could see the stars whirling across the velvet darkness. The harsh trunk of the tree pressed into the flesh of her back, hurting her while the pine needles stung her bare feet. Cold damp air prickled over her bare flesh. None of it mattered. Her only sensations were caught up in the man kneeling at her feet. His fingers parting her legs, his lips pressing kisses on her inner thighs, his hot, hungry tongue stroking along her seam.

She arched toward him, her fingers gripping his shoulders, nails biting into his flesh as he licked and sucked, tipping her over the edge into an abyss of trembling arousal. Distantly, she was aware of the half snarl, half growl that left Khan's lips the instant before they covered her throbbing folds and he sucked her swollen clit into his mouth.

His tongue flickered back and forth over the tortured

little nub while his fingers probed her tight entrance. Sarange was shaking so hard she could barely stand. Pleasure tore through her, leaving her weak and trembling with the need to climax.

"Khan…" She was close to screaming as he pressed two fingers inside her, stretching her flesh as he caressed her. Calloused fingers worked deep inside, stroking her inner muscles until she was writhing and close to sobbing.

The first vibrations were building inside her, tightening her muscles, sending her nerve endings into a frenzy. Khan continued to lick and suck, driving his fingers in and out of her, slow and steady, then fast and hard, then slowing the pace again. Sarange's breathing was so erratic she couldn't even beg him for more.

Then the explosion hit, breaking over her with such fury she couldn't do anything except cling to Khan and ride the waves of a climax so intense she thought it might break her in two. Khan kept going, that masterful tongue and those skillful fingers driving her onward, until every last shred of pleasure had been wrung out of her and she hung limp in his arms.

When she finally lifted her head, she was breathing hard. Khan's lips were tender on hers and she raised her hands, holding them on either side of his face for a moment or two.

Watching him as he stood naked before her in the moonlight was one of the most erotic things she had ever done. Coming up close to her, Khan swung her around so she was facing the tree. Grasping her wrists, he pinned them above her head, holding them in place against the trunk with one of his hands. His feet moved her legs apart as he pressed up behind her, fitting his body to hers. His chest hair rasped the smooth flesh of her back. The front of his thighs were hard and strong as they pushed up against the back of hers, his pelvis thrust tight into her buttocks.

And then…he was pushing his cock into her still spasming vagina with long, slow, deliberate thrusts. His teeth gripped her shoulder, and his free hand grasped her waist. He rocked his hips, sending heated darts of pain-pleasure ricocheting through her. Sarange cried out, tilting her head back. She was on fire, inside and out. Her overstimulated internal muscles drew him in, every stroke of his rock-hard shaft over her sensitive flesh taking her to new heights.

"I'm coming again." She could hear the note of disbelief in her own voice as she pushed back against his thrusts, keeping time with the demands of his rhythm.

It was too much, not enough. Too fast, yet she needed him to speed up. Too hard, but she wanted him deeper. His pelvis slammed into her as her muscles clamped onto his cock. Khan's powerful pounding filled her, stroked her until she came apart again. This time she clenched around him, heightening every feeling. Ecstasy stormed through her as her second orgasm hit and she bucked and writhed against him.

She felt Khan's thrusts increase as the first wave tore through her. He growled and his bite pierced her shoulder. The pain intensified the aftershocks, sending her wild with renewed delight. Deep inside her, she felt him pulse and jerk.

His head lowered onto her shoulder as his whole body stiffened. She felt him join her in an ecstasy as deep, dark and exquisite as the night that surrounded them.

"This." It seemed like hours had gone by instead of minutes when Khan withdrew from her and turned her to face him, cradling her in his arms. "This is everything. You. The night. The forest."

Sarange nodded against his chest. "But we have to fight for it."

The growl rose from somewhere so deep within him she thought it must have started in his soul. "Always. But we will win." His arms tightened around her. "I don't care who stands in our way."

She tipped her head back to look at him. "Maybe before we do any fighting we should try to remember where we left our clothes?"

Chapter 14

"There is someone I think you should meet." Jiran eyed Khan warily as he said the words. It was his standard expression when he looked Khan's way.

Khan wasn't in the best of moods. He didn't like mornings, although the quality of the breakfast buffet had gone a long way to restoring his equanimity. They were leaving Ulaanbaatar later that day for the Altai Mountain region and Sarange wanted to pay a visit to the political offices of the Chanco Party first. Bora's suggestion that Bek should travel to Mongolia to give a talk at the headquarters of the political group might have been an excuse to get Sarange's uncle here. The Chanco Party might have no links to the gray werewolves.

An internet search had elaborated on what Bek had told them. The Chanco Party was a relatively new political force. Rising remarkably rapidly, predictions were that members would do well in the country's forthcoming elections. The trajectory of their increase in popularity was stunning. There were rumors of vote rigging, even voter intimidation, which was dismissed by the Chanco Party leadership as jealousy from their opposition.

Sarange's plan was to go to their headquarters and politely request a meeting. Khan was more in favor of kicking doors down and a confrontation. They had been debating the options in the hotel dining room when Jiran joined them.

"Who do you think we should meet?" Khan hoped Jiran wasn't about to invite a group of autograph hunters along.

"My father," Jiran said. "Like me, he is a werewolf, one of the gray werewolf pack." Khan was about to refuse, but Jiran's next words made him pause. "He knows something about the Chanco Party."

"Do we have time for this?" Khan asked Sarange. He half hoped she would respond in the negative. Action, not conversation, was what he wanted.

"Why not?" She smiled at Jiran. "Can your father come here this morning?"

He nodded eagerly. "He is waiting in the coffee shop across the road. I will go and get him." He gave them an apologetic look. "My father doesn't use a cell phone."

Khan watched him go. "Still sure you trust him?"

"Still giving him the benefit of the doubt." She frowned. "We have nothing to link Bora to the Chanco Party except the offer to Bek. It's very tenuous."

"Without that we have nothing." Khan tossed back the last of his coffee. "For now, let's see where tenuous takes us."

When Jiran returned, he was accompanied by a man

who was an older version of himself. "This is my father, Houlun. He speaks English."

Khan indicated the empty seats at their table, and the two men joined them. They didn't talk until a waiter had served coffee.

"I take it Jiran has told you what brought us here?" Sarange said.

Houlun's expression was serious. "I was shocked to learn of what had happened in California. How this man named Bora manipulated a group of young werewolves into fighting the way he did. I am a werewolf. I'm used to the way our lives can become violent. Although I mourn for his friends, I'm glad Jiran survived. But if Bora is the man I think he is, his actions are predictable. At least, they are to one who knows the motives of the Chanco Party."

Khan sat up straighter. "You think you know who Bora is?"

"Possibly. Maybe I should start by explaining my involvement with the Chanco Party?" He looked from Sarange to Khan and they both nodded. "The tribal loyalties of the Mongol werewolves go back into the mists of time. Among the werewolf community here, there is a saying that the gray wolf cannot thrive while the blue wolf lives. The Chanco Party is the modern day, political face of the gray werewolves. Although they present themselves as human—and they have attracted many human followers with their policies—they are remnants of the gray werewolf tribe. And one of their aims is to wipe out any remaining trace of the blue werewolves, who are a minority group."

"Does that mean this is a cultural thing?" Sarange asked. "The Chanco Party is hiding behind its true policy, one of genocide against the blue werewolves?"

Houlun nodded. "As the Chanco Party has risen in prominence, attacks on blue werewolves by gray werewolves have been increasing throughout the country. And because blue wolves in the wild are the guardians of the blue werewolves, they are dying out."

"You are a gray werewolf." Khan fixed his gaze on Houlun. "Why are you telling us this?"

"Because what is happening is wrong." The other man's quiet dignity was convincing. "Just because I belong to a different group doesn't mean I believe in persecuting a minority. Not all gray werewolves agree with what the Chanco Party is doing." His voice became quieter. "And my wife, Jiran's mother, was a blue werewolf."

"You said you had some involvement with the Chanco Party?" Sarange said.

"To my shame, I have to admit that I was once a member." Houlun lowered his gaze as he sipped his coffee. "They are very good at recruiting gray werewolves with promises of improved lifestyles. It was only once I was on the inside that I realized what they were covering up. I left when I knew how deep the viciousness and corruption went. That was several years ago. Things have gotten worse since then."

"Tell them the rest," Jiran urged.

"I have friends who are still members of the party. They tell me the leadership is excited about something big happening. Something that will take down the blue werewolves forever." Houlun cast an apologetic glance in Sarange's direction. "They say it will make the destruction of Chinua and her tiger mate look like nothing. The gray werewolves still see that as their glorious victory."

Khan clenched his fist tight against his thigh. "And this man, Bora, is he a member of the Chanco Party?"

"If he is the man I'm thinking of, he uses many disguises and different names," Houlun said. "But I think I have heard him referred to as Bora."

"Can you recall any of his other aliases?" Khan asked.

"No." Houlun shook his head regretfully. "I'm sorry."

"We're going to the offices of the Chanco Party this morning," Sarange said. "Will you come with us?"

Houlun looked alarmed. "I would not advise it. They will know you are a blue werewolf."

"What will they do? Kill me in broad daylight?" Sarange's words were joking, but Khan felt the anger begin to rise deep within him at the suggestion. That was what these people wanted. They wanted to kill her. The thought made it difficult for him to focus on anything beyond his rage.

"I cannot stress how dangerous these people are." Houlun persisted in his attempt to dissuade her. "Especially to you."

"Then they won't be expecting me to come calling, will they?"

Houlun turned his attention to Khan. "You should talk her out of this."

"Have you heard the stories of Chinua, the blue werewolf leader?" Khan asked.

Houlun looked slightly confused. "Yes."

Khan indicated Sarange. "You're looking at her. And you should know that nobody talks her out of anything."

The Chanco Party headquarters were housed in a nondescript office building. It made Sarange think of government offices with lengthy queues and filling out of forms. Houlun had overcome his reluctance and agreed to accompany them. He seemed determined to protect her from any harm that might be awaiting her inside. Such concern from a man she had only just met—a *gray werewolf* she had only just met—touched her. Perhaps there was hope for peace between the warring werewolf factions after all.

Sarange had abandoned her disguise. She wanted the leadership of the Chanco Party to know she was in Mongolia and she was coming for them. Khan had also tucked his shades into his top pocket. When they entered the building, a bored-looking receptionist looked up at their approach. Her eyes widened as she studied them. Two of the most famous celebrities in the world had just strolled in and interrupted her mundane day.

"I'd like to see the person in charge." Sarange spoke in Mongolian, while giving the woman the benefit of her front-of-camera smile.

"I'm not sure…" The receptionist regained a little of her composure. "Do you have an appointment?"

"No, and I'm only in town for a few hours. I'd appreciate half an hour of his, or her, time."

"Um…if you'll take a seat, I'll see what I can do." The receptionist indicated a group of plastic chairs. Houlun and Jiran obediently sat, while Khan and Sarange remained standing. The woman behind the desk picked up the phone and began speaking urgently into it.

"What's she saying?" Khan asked.

"Exactly what you'd expect. She's trying to explain to the person she's calling that Sarange—yes, *the* Sarange—has just walked in here with a famous rock star. She can't remember your name, but she's describing you." Sarange bit back a smile. "It seems whoever she is talking to is a Beast fan. Although I'm not sure he, or she, believes her."

Khan did an impatient circuit of the lobby. When he returned, he jerked his head in the direction of a poster at the side of the reception desk. "My grip on your language isn't great, but it looks to me like the Chanco Party is planning a celebration."

Sarange read the details. "They're holding a gala dinner here next week." She grimaced. "I guess you wouldn't want to be the blue werewolf who accidentally gate-crashed *that* occasion."

A few minutes later a tall, thin man emerged from an office to the right of the reception desk. Sarange's newfound instincts kicked in. Yes, he was a gray werewolf. He was frowning impatiently, until he saw Sarange and Khan. Then the frown melted away and became an expression of incredulity.

"I am Damdid Gandi, Secretary of the Chanco Party. We weren't expecting you."

Sarange introduced her companions. "Do you speak English? Khan doesn't speak Mongolian." They had already established that her words weren't strictly true. As Khan's memory was gradually returning, it became clear he did speak a form of Mongolian. Unfortunately, it was outdated and he found it difficult to follow the modern dialect.

Damdid nodded, switching languages easily. "I spent a year studying in London. Please, come through to my office."

They followed him into a large room that was furnished in a more comfortable style than the lobby. Damdid spent a minute or two organizing chairs for everyone. Sarange got the impression he was using the distraction to collect his thoughts.

"This is an unexpected honor." Unexpected, yes. Honor? Sarange wasn't so sure a gray werewolf would voluntarily describe her presence in quite that way. She decided she didn't like Damdid Gandi. It had nothing to do with the fact that he was a gray werewolf and everything to do with the fact that he was an unpleasant man. Both her wolf and human senses were telling her that clearly. She didn't need Houlun's prior information to tell her Damdid was a bully who would prey on the weak…or on a downtrodden minority. Her wolf instincts were onto it immediately. *Not an alpha, but wouldn't you love to be one, Mr. Gandi?* "We weren't expecting this visit."

"I wasn't planning on making it." She kept her voice light and conversational. "But I am passing through Ulaanbaatar on my way to the Altai Mountains. Having heard about the work you do, I thought there was an opportunity for us to collaborate."

"You did?"

Damdid's polite mask slipped for an instant. She saw incredulity and something more in his expression. She didn't like the something more. It was feral and nasty.

"We all know the ancient legends about the feud between the blue wolves and the gray wolves. We also know how damaging those stories can be to modern day allegiances in our country." She waited for some acknowledgment and Damdid inclined his head. "You may have heard of my work with the Animals Alive nonprofit organization? I'm here in Mongolia to make a documentary about the threat to the blue wolf pack. It's heartbreaking to think that one of our iconic creatures faces extinction."

"I'm not sure how this affects the Chanco Party."

She noticed how Damdid's face hardened. Her work

with the blue wolves was directly contrary to the aims of his party. If the guardians of the blue werewolves died out, the werewolves themselves would be damaged beyond repair.

"I'm offering you a public relations opportunity." *One I'm fairly sure you won't take.* Sarange's only reason for coming here today had been to look someone from this organization in the eye and find out if her suspicions were true. Were they linked to Bora? Every instinct told her they were. Anything she said was just an excuse for getting through the door. "If the Chanco Party works with me on my efforts to save the blue wolves, you can redress some of the bad publicity you've been getting."

Damdid bristled. "I'm not sure what you mean."

She was tired of the game. "I'll be blunt with you, Mr. Gandi. There are rumors that your party is responsible for inciting violence toward those who are perceived to be ancestors of the blue werewolves—"

Damdid made a sudden movement, and Khan was out of his seat like lightning. "Stay where you are."

"You can't come in here and threaten me." Damdid's complexion took on a sickly hue.

Khan placed both hands on the desk, leaning forward so his face was inches from the other man's. "Just did."

Damdid gave a shaky laugh. "Try telling the world out there your story about werewolves."

"I don't need to," Sarange said. "And nor do you. You have a public face and you maintain it well. But within this room, we all know the truth. We know what the Chanco Party is about. You have one policy…the annihilation of the blue werewolves and anyone descended from them."

His smile resembled a snarl. "Since we are being honest, let me assure you we will succeed."

"Who is Bora?" Khan asked.

"Your worst nightmare."

The words had only just left Damdid's lips when Khan lifted him by the front of his shirt and hurled him across the room. Damdid hit the wall opposite his desk with a thud and slid down it. He was still shaking his head in shock when Khan's fist connected with his face.

"Don't even think about shifting unless you want your evil gray throat ripped out."

Damdid stared up at him with dazed eyes.

"You think Bora is a nightmare? Give him a message from me. Tell him there's a Caspian tiger after him and there's no place he can hide where I won't find him."

Since the alternative would have meant spending forty-eight hours on the road, they had decided to fly from Ulaanbaatar to Ölgii in the extreme west of the country. Houlun drove them to the airport.

"I wish I could come with you." Jiran's father shook his head regretfully. "But I have to work and my employers have no idea that I am a werewolf."

Khan laughed. "I can imagine the news that you need time for werewolf duties might come as a bombshell. Anyway, we need you here to watch what's going on at the Chanco Party headquarters. Let Jiran know if you notice anything suspicious."

Jiran snorted. "How will that happen? He refuses to use a cell phone. And even if he did, we are unlikely to get a signal in the mountains."

"When you do get a signal, you can call me on my landline." Houlun's voice held a mild rebuke. "I'll watch the headquarters for any new developments."

Sarange kissed his cheek, making him blush. "Thank you."

The three-hour flight on a small plane tested Khan's patience more than the longer flight from Los Angeles to Beijing. Being confined in one place didn't suit him. He needed to be able to get up and walk around. The larger aircraft had given him that freedom. This felt—his mind shied away from the comparison, but he forced it onward—this felt like captivity.

Sarange placed her hand over his and he saw understanding in her eyes. "It breaks my heart that there are more tigers in captivity than in the wild."

He shrugged. "Hopefully their experience of imprisonment will not be the same as mine. And many places are doing valuable conservation work. The blue wolves are not the only ones in danger of becoming extinct."

No matter how many chances she gave him, he couldn't talk to her about it. About the living hell of it. About the pain and degradation of being the mightiest beast of them all, yet brought so low. Of how the hardest part had been believing he would never see her again.

"I don't understand why they didn't kill you." Tears shimmered briefly in her eyes as she said the words. "When they first captured you, it would have been so much easier to murder you then than to keep you alive for all those years."

"I've thought about it. A lot. And the only reason I can come up with for them to keep me alive is that they couldn't find a way to kill me. Silver can't do it."

Sarange frowned. "How is that possible? I'll admit my knowledge is limited, but I thought all shifters could be killed with silver swords or bullets."

There was a time, not so long ago, when he wished his captors had killed him. Now, looking into the clear blue depths of her eyes, he was glad they hadn't. He still couldn't think of that time with anything other than pain, but he had come through it. He was here again with Sarange, doing what he was meant to do. Caring for her, protecting her, fighting at her side. Was it wrong to wish for some time to just enjoy being with her?

As if she read his mind, Sarange stretched. "When all this is over, we should take a vacation."

"Did you have somewhere in mind?"

"Somewhere warm, just you and me—" a smile curved her lips "—where clothes are optional."

A growl left his lips as he pressed them to her ear. A little shiver ran through her as he spoke. "When we're alone, you can always dispense with the clothes."

When the plane landed at Ölgii, they disembarked at the tiny airport in the mountains and he stretched his long limbs in relief. Breathing in the pristine air, he looked around him at the stunning landscape, framed by high peaks. They were in a beautiful, remote part of the world to which very few foreigners ever ventured. They were met by a guide from the ger camp where they would be staying. His name was Surkh, and as he loaded their belongings into his jeep, he explained that Radin's film crew had been in touch. They would be arriving in a day or two.

"What is a ger camp?" Khan asked as the jeep commenced a bone-rattling journey along an uneven track.

It was Jiran who answered. "A ger is a traditional tent used as a dwelling by nomads in the steppes of Central Asia. It's portable, round and covered with animal skins or felt."

"So I'll be sleeping in a tent in the mountains?" Khan studied the snow-covered peaks with dismay.

Sarange laughed. "Many ger camps are quite luxurious."

"Let's hope ours is one of the many." The chill wind was already whipping through his clothing.

The jeep journey took almost as long as the flight, and by the time they arrived at the camp, Khan was tired and hungry. The scenery they had traveled through was incredible. They had passed through several river valleys and seen hollows with semidesert landscapes, Alpine peaks, narrow river canyons and broad valleys. They had caught glimpses of deep limestone gorges, open steppes, as well as lakes, wild rivers and waterfalls. The mountains above them rose as high as forty-five hundred meters and were covered with permanent snow, glaciers and vast tracts of forest.

It was already dark when they descended from the jeep and Surkh's wife, Merkid, gestured for them to accompany her into the largest of the gers. There, an authentic meal of boiled sheep's head had been set out on a table. Once they had eaten, they were shown to their luxurious ger tents. Khan's spirits rose when he learned that the camp was equipped with flushing lavatories and showers with hot and cold water. The camp also had cell phone accessibility, but Surkh explained that the signal could be problematic.

"I don't care." Khan pulled Sarange down onto the bed next to him. "I could live here forever."

"No adoring crowds?" Her voice was teasing.

"You can be my audience." He started to unbutton her blouse.

"You would miss the limelight."

He shook his head. "Not when I have you."

There wasn't a door to the ger, but a bell at the entrance was the signal that someone wanted to enter.

Khan muttered a curse when it rang. "I was going to say 'and no interruptions…'"

Sarange smiled as she rebuttoned her blouse. When she went to the entrance, Surkh was waiting just outside. He pointed to the nearby mountain ridge. "Blue wolves."

Putting on warm clothing, Khan and Sarange stepped outside. Maybe it was the utter isolation of the location, the vast darkness of the sky above them and the sheer number of stars scattered across it. Or perhaps it was the story he knew had unfolded here. The curious, yet enduring, love story between two creatures who were such complete opposites. *Our story.* Whatever the reason, Khan felt a shiver run down his spine. At the same time, from the ridge above the ger camp, a howl echoed into the night. Long, low and mournful, the single voice was soon joined by others.

"It is strange." Surkh turned his head in the direction of the sound. "The blue wolves do not usually venture this close to the camp."

Sarange translated his words for Khan.

"How does he know they are blue wolves?" Khan asked.

"Their cry is not the same as that of the gray wolves." Sarange answered his question herself. Her expression was confused as though she was unsure how she knew that information.

Surkh spoke again.

"He said it is almost as if they are offering a greeting." Khan saw a single, shining tear slide down Sarange's cheek as she stepped forward into the clearing beyond the camp and faced the ridge. "And that's exactly why they're here. We have waited a long time for this reunion."

Khan stood back, trusting her instincts, even though

a tremor of fear ran through him when he realized what she was doing. After a few minutes, he noticed a change in the howling. It was hard to pinpoint the difference. *Wolf-song.* That was the only way he could describe it. They were celebrating. Singing without words. Offering their own unique music.

Then, out of the darkness, they came. Silvery shapes, gliding out of the shadows. They moved toward Sarange like blue-eyed ghosts.

Khan held his breath. Could he close the distance between them in time if the wolves became aggressive? There was no sign of hostility as they approached in a triangular formation, one large male in the lead, others following, fanning out into a larger group at the rear. Wolf hierarchy. Pack dynamics always came first.

The lead wolf reached Sarange and they gazed at each other for a moment or two. Then the wolf nudged her hand with his nose. It was the trigger to release Sarange from an apparent trance. She dropped to her knees and wrapped her arms around the animal's neck.

Across the distance that separated them, Khan heard her sobs as the other wolves surrounded her and she hugged each of them in turn.

Chapter 15

Sarange had always felt an affinity with animals that was beyond anything she had with other people. Believing it came from her upbringing and Golden Wing's own connection with the natural world, she had embraced it. As her fame and fortune grew, she had used her influence to speak out as a force for good. Becoming an ambassador for the creatures she loved had been a beacon in her life. Until she met Khan, it had been her passion.

Because she was high-profile, she had been fortunate enough to have many moving and exciting encounters with animals. Radin wasn't the first person to see the potential of putting her in front of the camera. She was charismatic, beautiful and passionate about wildlife. Her biggest problem was the number of projects she had to turn down.

Orangutans in Indonesia, elephants in Nepal, gorillas in Uganda…they had been just a few of the memorable moments, but nothing had prepared her for how she would feel when she encountered the blue wolves.

She had been raised to believe that humans and animals shared a common spiritual plain. Golden Wing had explained that humans identified strongly with certain animals—their guardians—and that the attraction was mutual. During life's important moments, it was possible that those animals would present themselves as guides or comforters.

But Sarange's meeting with the blue wolves was so much more than anything that had happened to her before, or anything that Golden Wing had spoken of. The closest thing she could compare it to was coming home.

When she heard that first wolf howl, it had resonated deep within her, calling to her personally. She knew how that made her sound like the ultimate narcissist. A celebrity who turned up in the wilds of nowhere and believed the wolves spoke just to her? But it was true. This pack of blue wolves had come to greet *her*. That was the only reason they were here.

And when they touched her, nudged and nuzzled her, let her hug them…it was the most incredibly moving moment. Both parts of her psyche—human and wolf— felt the surge of emotion equally. It was so much more than the feelings she had experienced in the past from the trust of a wild animal. This was about *her* animals, her pack. They were hers and she belonged to them. Past and present collided in that instant. Rolling around on the hard ground together, they reinforced those bonds and it was wonderful.

Tears of pure joy ran down her cheeks. These majestic and beautiful animals were part of her. Her feelings about their plight became clearer now. She loved all animals, but this was more. Her family was endangered. For them she would take the fight higher and further. She would stop at nothing to ensure their survival.

With a final few nose bumps, the wolves faded back into the darkness. Sarange remained kneeling, sitting back on her heels. The intensity of the moment took time to fade. She knew now that no matter where she was in the world, that connection would feel as strong as if she were right here with the wolves, burying her hands in their thick fur and rolling on the ground with them. She had discovered a part of her life that had its meaning imprinted into her soul.

Wolf. It's who I am. She would wear that badge with pride from now on.

She was aware of a movement at her side and turned her head to see Khan kneeling beside her. His eyes were filled with wonder. "That was incredible."

She nodded, not sure she could trust her voice.

"It's cold out here."

Sarange had barely noticed the icy temperatures, but his words drew her attention to the iron-hard ground beneath her knees and the chill wind cutting through her clothing. "Shall we go inside?"

He rose and slid a hand under her elbow, helping her up. For a moment or two, she leaned against him, looking up at the star-splattered sky. "So many life-changing moments within a month. It all started when I walked out on that stage and saw you."

His smile took some of the chill out of the air. "What can I say? I do my best to be out of the ordinary."

Khan's arm was warm and strong around her as they walked back to the ger. Once or twice, Sarange glanced back at the ridge. She couldn't see anything in the darkness, but she knew they were there. Her family was watching over her.

The following day they set out early, hiking deep into the interior of the mountainous region with Surkh as their guide. He explained that the area was considered sacred to the local population.

"There are rock carvings, standing stones, burial mounds and Kazakh cemeteries right across this area. And, of course, there are the remains of the fortress that was said to have belonged to the mighty Chinua."

Sarange halted abruptly, her heart suddenly developing an extra beat. "Can you take us there? To the place where Chinua lived?"

Surkh pursed his lips. "It is many miles from here."

"That's where we want to go."

Something in her voice must have convinced him, because he nodded and changed direction, striding out toward a steep incline that took her breath away. They made their way across steep ravines and into deep valleys with towering ice peaks in the distance.

"Is this the territory of the blue wolves?" Sarange asked as she walked alongside Surkh.

"Yes. Many rare and threatened animals live in this region including the snow leopard, ibex, lynx, wolf and bear. The gray wolves are more common at lower altitudes, and the blue wolves live here among the peaks. They used to roam right across the Altai region, but their numbers have dwindled and they are now found in smaller packs."

"So the gray wolves and blue wolves don't compete for the same habitat?" Sarange asked.

"That used to be the case. But as the gray wolf habitat has been threatened by man, the two species have been forced to fight for territory. The blue wolves, having a smaller population, are usually the ones to suffer in a confrontation."

It seemed that nature reflected the shifter world. The gray wolves dominated in both realms, while their blue counterparts were suppressed. Yet there had been a time when both packs were equal, even when the blue werewolves had dominated. And the change had come when Chinua had been defeated. When Khan had been taken from her. Now they were planning…what? To do the same thing again? She cast a glance in Khan's direction. No, that was not going to happen. She would fight that with every fiber of her being. Besides, the first werewolf attack had been an attempt to abduct her. Bora had other plans for her. The thought worried her and aroused her fighting instincts at the same time.

Surkh had brought food and they halted, sitting on a rocky incline to eat sausages, yak cheese and noodles. They washed this feast down with hot sweet tea. Jiran explained that he had been to this region before on climbing expeditions.

"I have climbed Mount Khuiten, one of the highest peaks of the Altai Mountains. It borders Russia, China and Kazakhstan."

Surkh regarded him with new respect. "That is a difficult climb. You look like a gray werewolf, but you must have other skills." It was the first time he had given any sign that he knew they were anything other than human.

Jiran blushed. "My mother was a blue werewolf. I am proud of both sides of my heritage."

When they set off again, the terrain became more difficult and a mist descended, making it hard to see more than a few feet in front of them. At the thought of having to turn around and make the return journey, Sarange was beginning to regret her request to come and see the fortress. She had no memory of this place, and all that was left of the fortress was likely to be ruins. What was the point of traveling all this way to look at something that would be meaningless? Just as dejection was taking over, Surkh halted.

"There."

She followed the direction of Surkh's pointing finger. And gazed into her own past.

Standing high above them, the fortress rose out of a spur of craggy brown rock, appearing to float on a bed of cloud. The vast, multitiered citadel clung to the mountain ridge like a sleeping snake. Its walls gleamed white, and its roof tiles had survived the test of the centuries, retaining their bright red color.

"Oh." Instinctively, Sarange reached for Khan's hand, and he was at her side immediately. His powerful torso pressed against her shoulder and she could sense his own emotion as he gazed at the beautiful image before them. "Can we go up there?"

Surkh looked up at the sky. "If we do, we will not get back to the ger camp before nightfall."

"We'll risk it." Khan was already heading toward the fortress, taking Sarange with him. "Jiran, are you okay with this?"

The young werewolf had been gazing openmouthed at the spectacle before him, but he nodded in response. "My mother told me stories about this place. I never believed it was real."

It took them another half hour of climbing before they reached the entrance to the fortress. There was an eerie feel to the place as they walked through huge double gates that hung open as though they were waiting for them.

Perhaps they are.

The thought was like a voice spoken out loud in Sarange's ear.

"How has it been so well preserved?" she asked Surkh.

"It is not perfect," he warned. "The exterior is impressive, but once we get inside, you will see that time has caused damage."

As they entered the building, she saw immediately what he meant. It was a shell. The exterior walls had survived the test of time, but the interior had crumbled. It didn't matter. Her memory supplied the missing images. She knew that the circular area in which they stood had once been the great hall.

"We gathered here each evening." Her voice was dreamy as she said the words, her mind filled with pictures. She could see her followers. The brave blue werewolf warriors, their female mates and the cubs playing in the center of the hall. She could hear the laughter and the chatter, smell the food and the scented rushes on the floor.

"The hunters would bring the kill to the kitchen." Khan pointed to his right. "Over there. There was always plenty to eat."

Sarange smiled. "Even for you, my tiger."

Jiran and Surkh stood back and watched them as they walked through the ruins, reminiscing about the rooms and galleries that had once occupied the space. It felt like she'd been here yesterday. At the same time, it felt like they were intruding on someone else's reality. As they stepped into the section that had been their bedchamber, Sarange felt light-headed with a combination of joy and grief.

"We thought we had forever." The words were squeezed out through throat muscles that were too tight.

"We did, until they took it from us." Khan's features were as harsh as the jagged mountain peaks.

A shout from Jiran brought them back to the present. "Men. Dozens of them." The young werewolf pointed over the battlement into the valley. "Coming this way."

"What shall we do?" Sarange looked around. "We're trapped here. There is no way of getting out and nowhere to hide."

"We'll stay and face them." Khan took her hand. "This is our territory."

The four of them walked out to the great gates. Khan and Sarange stood slightly ahead of Jiran and Surkh as they anticipated the appearance of the men. They didn't have long to wait. Within a few minutes, the men Jiran had seen from the battlements were approaching the gates. All of them wore the traditional dress of the nomadic Tuvan people of the region. As a group, they halted a few feet before the gates.

One of the men stepped forward. "We wish to speak to your leader."

Khan made a movement to restrain Sarange, but she stepped forward. "I am the leader you seek."

The man studied her for a moment before dropping on one knee and bowing his head. "When we knew that Chinua was risen, we came to offer our allegiance."

When Sarange moved forward to greet him, she saw his eyes were as blue as her own. All the men surrounding him had the same blue fire in their eyes. Her heart expanded with pride. Her werewolf army had found her.

* * *

Galba, the man who had led the werewolf army to them, told them that a shamanka had visited each of the blue werewolf tribes in the area to inform them that Chinua had returned and that she needed their help to defeat the gray werewolves.

"What was this shamanka's name?" Sarange asked.

Galba looked puzzled. "I don't remember if she told me. Does it matter?"

"I suppose not."

Khan could tell from Sarange's expression that it did matter, but he didn't get an opportunity to ask her why.

They made their way back to the ger camp together with the werewolves. Luckily, since the blue werewolves were nomadic, they had brought their horses and equipment with them, including tents. Surkh was relieved that he wouldn't have to find accommodation for all these people as well as the camera crew who would be arriving the next day. When he tentatively raised the subject of food, Galba assured him they would fend for themselves. The nomads would set up their own camp close to a mountain stream and hunt for their own food. It was what they always did.

"Radin's team may get more than they expected if the gray werewolves arrive and there is a werewolf fight in the middle of their filming schedule," Khan said.

"I'm sure you could use your tiger powers of persuasion to get them to part with any footage we didn't want made public."

He was pleased to see Sarange's spirits had been restored. When they had walked around the fortress, he had felt her sadness and understood its cause. Although it was many centuries ago, it had been their home. They had lived, loved and laughed there. Yes, they had fought constant battles to keep their place in the world, but it had been a happy one. Seeing it now, an empty shell, was a reminder that what they once had was in the past.

Reincarnation. The word had a hollow ring to it. Could past lives ever truly be recaptured? Almost a thousand years had passed since they last stood at those battlements. The view was unchanged and the feelings remained as strong as ever, but so many lifetimes had gone by. A great warrior, born of the dynasty they had created, had shaped this country. They were the same people, yet so very different, marked by the passage of time and the experiences they had endured. Khan's spirit had been broken by his captivity, Sarange's by their separation. They were together now, but the wounds inflicted on both of them ran soul deep. Once this nightmare was over, could they recover? Heal the injuries so that only scars and memories remained?

Even if that was the case, for Khan there was still another question. One that refused to go away. *Who am I?* When he was asked that question in his rock star life, his first response was always a swaggering *"I am Khan."* But who was Khan? What was his reality? He had uncovered part of his story. Now he wanted it all.

He watched Sarange as she walked with Galba, discussing the forthcoming fight with the gray werewolves. *I want it all.* She was what he wanted. The certainty gripped his heart like a vise, triggering an emotion so strong it made him gasp. It was like sunlight breaking through cloud. He wanted his mate, his love, his life. At his side, in his bed, forever. He wanted to see her smile first thing every morning and last thing every night. That militant light in her eyes when she disagreed with him? He wanted that to be a permanent fixture in his life. He wanted them to have the little things.

Although fighting monsters was one way to bond, he wanted walks on the beach, nights at the movies, pizza and beer. Ordinary...but not ordinary because she would be there.

He knew Sarange felt the same way. He saw it in her eyes when she looked at him, felt it in her body's response when he touched her. It was always there, electrifying the air between them. *How can I offer her all of me when I don't know who I am?* She wouldn't care. He knew that. *But I care. I won't give her a lie.* And that was what it would be. Until he had his full story, he was pretending to be whole. The thought stripped away his newfound happiness and confidence. Almost sent his mind hurtling back into that hellhole where he had been imprisoned.

Almost. Just at the right moment, Sarange turned her head and looked his way. The blue fire he loved so much shone from her eyes, restoring his balance. *I won't lose this. Won't lose her.* A thousand years of hell was worth it for that one smile.

So I don't know who I am. He added finding his identity to the list of impossible tasks facing them.

Radin's camera crew arrived at noon the next day. The team of three was led by an experienced wildlife photographer called Jenny Monroe. She explained that many of the shots they took would not require Sarange or Khan to be present.

"The final documentary needs your voices, obviously, but that will be done back in the studio. The wildlife shots here will be captured by the team, and could take weeks—" she grinned at Khan's look of horror "—which we appreciate that you can't commit to."

Khan gave an exaggerated sigh. "My manager would

kiss your hands and feet in appreciation if he heard that. He's already tearing his hair out that I've interrupted the making of a new album to be here."

"I promise not to keep you on location any longer than necessary," Jenny said. "Radin has been honest about what he wants. The two of you together on screen as much as possible in the blue wolf habitat. That's what will bring in the money."

Sarange grimaced and Jenny shrugged an apology. "Look at it as a way of raising awareness of the plight of these animals. If we can get some shots of you with the blue wolves in the background, great. If not, we'll see what we can do in the editing."

If the camera crew noticed the presence of dozens of nomads just beyond the confines of the ger camp, they didn't mention it. Possibly they believed this was a normal situation, or that the region was more densely populated than it had first appeared. The only comment Jenny made was that it looked like they would have to travel to find the blue wolves, since they were unlikely to come this close to so many people.

"They will come," Sarange said.

Jenny gave her a pitying look. "Don't count on it. I've been doing this job a long time, and wolves are one of the hardest animals to film. There are legends that paint them as aggressors, but the reality is that they're naturally cautious around humans. There is fear on both sides. We have to start by building up respect and trust. That's one of the reasons this shoot may take some time."

"You will have no problem getting your pictures." Sarange maintained her serene expression. "And you will not have to edit me into them."

Khan could tell Jenny thought she was dealing with

an eccentric, or possibly egotistical, celebrity. He decided not to enlighten her. It would be more entertaining to watch her reaction when the truth unfolded.

It happened just as he expected. The sky was the color of indigo velvet and the first stars had made their appearance when the alpha wolf gave a single, mournful howl from the ridge.

"What the hell is that?" Jenny dashed out of her ger, her face ashen.

"It's a greeting." Sarange pulled on her sweater as she walked past the edge of the camp and into the open. "One that is older than time."

Khan beckoned for Jenny and her team to follow him. They stood back, observing, as Sarange waited. Before long, the huge alpha male came into view, his coat gleaming in the moonlight. High on the ridge, his pack continued to howl, filling the night with their wolf song.

The silver-gray male reared up on his hind legs to at least seven feet. Towering above Sarange, he paused before placing his huge paws on her shoulders.

"We should do something." Jenny's voice shook with nerves. "He'll tear her apart. Doesn't anyone have a gun? A tranquilizer dart won't work fast enough."

"Watch." Khan kept his own eyes on Sarange, still fascinated by her relationship with the wild wolves.

The huge wolf brought his face down to Sarange's, rubbing his muzzle along her jawline. Jenny stifled a cry as he opened his mouth, revealing canines like daggers. Sarange tilted her head back and the wolf gently licked her cheek.

"Did he just…?" Jenny turned to look at Khan, her jaw dropping in shock.

"He kissed her," Khan confirmed. "And here come the others. They wish to pay their respects as well."

As Sarange wrapped her arms around the alpha wolf's neck, the rest of the pack came into view. The hierarchy was evident as the wolves approached Sarange in order of rank. Starting with the alpha female, they greeted her with nose bumps and wolf kisses until each of the adults had paid homage to her. Then the cubs were finally allowed to rush forward as a group and frolic around her feet. Laughing, she returned the embraces of the adults, played with the youngsters and spoke to them in a half language only she and they appeared to understand.

"Can you start recording this?" Jenny spoke quietly to one of the mesmerized camera team. She turned to Khan. "Tell me this isn't staged. Those are wild wolves, right? They're not from a sanctuary, or someone's private zoo?"

"This is one of the endangered wild blue wolf packs that roam this area. They have had no interaction with humans that we know of. Surkh tells me they had never ventured close to the ger camp until two nights ago when Sarange arrived. If anyone else tries to go near them, they take to the hills."

"What is she? Some kind of wolf whisperer?" Jenny looked across at where Sarange had almost disappeared under a mass of worshipful wolf bodies.

Khan laughed. "Still worried you may not get enough footage of Sarange with the wolves?"

"What about you?" Jenny asked. "Can we get you in there as well?"

Khan grimaced. How was he going to explain this to her? He could hardly tell the truth. That where he was standing now was just about as close as he could get without sending the wolves skittering away in fear. If he tried to get any nearer, even Sarange's presence wouldn't be enough to soothe their nerves. *Put a tiger among the wolves? I don't think so.*

"That's where you will have to get creative with your editing."

Chapter 16

Sarange called Khan, Jiran and Galba together at dawn a few days later. "The blue wolves are restless. I think it means the gray werewolves are close."

"My concern is the camera crew," Khan said. "Surkh and Merkid practice shamanism. I'm not saying they will take a werewolf battle in their stride, but they understand the mysteries of the universe. Three foreigners caught up in the middle of an ancient blood feud? I'm not sure I want that on my conscience."

"We need to distract them." Sarange felt a surge of confidence. The part of herself that was Chinua thrived on this sort of situation. The legendary general leading her troops. She bit back a smile. There was no trace of the pampered A-lister. "Galba, I need your men to reconnoiter the area. Find out where the gray werewolves are. When we have that information, we'll send the camera crew on a false trail. Tell them a blue wolf pack has been sighted somewhere in the opposite direction and make sure they're gone overnight." She turned to Jiran. "You can be their guide."

He had been listening with an expression of eager anticipation. Now his mouth turned down at the corners. "I want to take part in the fight. I owe Bora."

Sarange placed a hand on his arm. "I need you to do this, Jiran. Although the camera team members are vulnerable, they're also dangerous. If they get caught up in the fight, they could be killed or injured, but if they witness a werewolf fight, or even worse, get a recording, they'll endanger every shifter living in the human world."

Jiran hunched his shoulders. "If it means that much to you…"

"It does."

His expression lightened, reminding her of a schoolboy given a reprieve after being caught in a misdemeanor. "Maybe I should go with Galba's men when they survey the area?"

"That sounds like an excellent plan."

There was a slight swagger to Jiran's walk as he followed Galba to the nomad camp. Sarange was aware of Khan's eyes on her face, of the amused expression in their golden depths. "You never had any intention of letting that boy fight, did you?"

"I hoped to avoid it," she confessed. "But, like you, I was never quite sure where his loyalties lay."

"Now?" A smile quirked his lips as he continued to gaze at her.

"Oh, now I have no doubt he's on our side. Which is why I'm not prepared to expose him to any danger."

He placed his hands on her hips, drawing her to him. "You are a formidable woman, do you know that?"

"I think you may be confusing me with someone you once knew. Name of Chinua."

He rested his forehead against hers. "I remember her. A wolf on the battlefield and a tiger in the bedroom."

She choked back a laugh. "You are shameless."

"Is that a challenge? Because when it comes to shameless, I can take this to a whole other level."

"I believe you." She sighed. "And your shamelessness is deeply tempting, but we have work to do."

"Work?" He frowned. "No one told me about that."

"Jenny wants footage of us both together. A bit like a wedding photo shoot without the party." She paused, biting her lip. "I didn't mean…"

"Sarange, I think a thousand-year-old engagement gives you the right to talk about marriage without worrying that I'll take to the hills." He looked amused.

"But you're Khan." As soon as she said the words, she regretted them. She wasn't even sure what she meant. Yes, he was Khan. *Her* Khan. Her beloved tiger. He wasn't the person the fans saw. The arrogant, whirlwind rock star was an act. She knew that better than anyone.

He was the same man she had loved all those years ago, but he was different because of what had been done to him. She could see how deep the hurt and insecurity went. And it cut her like a knife. *They did that to him because of me.* Took his majestic tiger spirit and tore it to shreds. She didn't know if it was the same men who were coming for them now, or their ancestors. She didn't care. If Bora had been Chinua's enemy, they had an ancient score to settle. If he was new to this fight? Well, he was going to regret the day he got involved.

"Yes, I'm Khan." The pain in his eyes almost cut her in two. "I only wish I knew what that meant."

She took his face between her hands, tracing his beloved features with her fingertips. "It means you're mine." She felt him relax beneath her touch. Grasping her wrist, he turned her hand so he could press a kiss into the center of her palm. "You know what else it means?"

His smile melted her. Just turned her into a helpless puddle of longing. "Tell me."

"It means, no matter how hard you try, you're not going to get out of doing some work this morning."

"We are outnumbered." Galba's expression was troubled. "My scouts tell me the gray werewolves are coming in great numbers from the southeast."

"You know what we need to do." Khan spoke in an undertone to Sarange. She would reach this conclusion herself, but time was running out and he wanted to help her along.

"I do?" Her expression was puzzled as she turned her head to look at him.

"Think about what lies east of here."

He could see her considering and discarding different options. Then the frown lifted from her brow and she nodded. "Of course." She straightened her shoulders. "Galba, get your men ready. We're going to the fortress."

The werewolf regarded her with even greater respect. "Chinua's fortress? From there, we cannot fail." He bowed low before leaving them.

"What about me?" Jiran asked. "Is the plan still for me to distract the photographers?"

"Yes," Sarange said. "If you don't, they're going to think it's mighty strange when Khan and I disappear with the entire nomad tribe."

"Have you been in touch with Houlun?" Khan asked. "I can't help wondering what's going on at Chanco head-quarters while the gray werewolves are on the march."

"I spoke to my father earlier today. He said every-thing seems quiet in Ulaanbaatar, except for the prepa-rations for the big celebration."

"Let's see if we can't spoil the gala by defeating their army when they reach the fortress," Khan said.

"There's no time to lose." Jiran became businesslike. "I'll take the camera crew in the opposite direction of the fortress." He went away and a few minutes later they heard him calling to Jenny that he knew where the larg-est pack of blue wolves could be seen.

"There is hope for that boy yet," Khan said.

"Yes, Grandpa." Sarange's smile was mischievous.

He groaned. "You're right. I sound like someone's grandfather. Or a stern father, at the very least." She hesitated and he frowned. "What is it?"

"I wondered..."

He ducked his head to look more closely at her face and was surprised to see tears in her eyes.

"Did we have children? If we did, why don't I re-member that?"

"I don't recall either. I wonder if the fact that nei-ther of us remembers means that we didn't." He drew a breath, preparing to talk about the thing that hurt him most. Every time he thought about leaving her, his heart splintered and his mind scattered into a thousand fragments making rational thoughts impossible. Deter-minedly, he held them together. "And maybe, if we'd had a family, you—Chinua—would have kept going, for them, instead of searching for me?"

The tears spilled over, streaking her cheeks, but Sa-range appeared not to notice them. "If we didn't have children, how did we build a dynasty? Chinggis Khan was supposed to have been descended from the blue werewolf pack we established."

He held her close, cradling her against his chest. "That's just it. He was descended from the blue wolves. There is no mention of a tiger in his family tree."

She stood very still for a few moments. When she raised her head, the tears were gone but her face was pale. "Are you trying to tell me we couldn't have a child because we are different species? We can be mates, but we can't have children? Just like in the natural world, dogs and cats don't have hybrid offspring?"

This was not the conversation he wanted them to have just before they went into battle. But they had always been honest with each other and he wasn't going to change that now. He took her chin between his thumb and forefinger, tilting her face up to his. "I honestly don't know the answer to that. But we are shifters. We have human genes. And I guess there's only one way we're going to find out the answer to this question."

"You mean…?" She gulped back another sob. "We try?"

"Yes, I mean we try. But first we have to go and kill some bad guys." *And I have to figure out where the hell I came from.*

As Sarange went to gather a few items of warm clothing together, Khan speculated on that conversation. Of course he wanted children with her. He wanted everything with her. But he was fearful that he might have felt the same way a thousand years ago, with no outcome. Could Sarange be right? Her cats and dogs comparison was a clumsy one, but it was true. This wasn't a question for even the most skilled human doctor. It would rock the scientific world to its core and blow the anonymity of every shifter in the world wide open. It wasn't even a problem he was going to take to Ged, the shifter oracle. Right now it was one he was going to put to the back of his mind while he focused on the immediate problem of keeping Sarange safe.

Galba and his men were ready and waiting. Sarange explained that her childhood had been spent with a different nomadic group. Her tribe had been reindeer herders in the northernmost part of the country. Here in the Altai region, the Tuvan nomads used horses to navigate the difficult terrain. Now Galba was insisting that she should ride his horse.

"You are the leader. It is not fitting that I should ride while you walk."

To please him, Sarange acquiesced to his request. It meant the long hike to the fortress was a boring one for Khan. The horses, obviously used to their werewolf masters, were skittish around him. Khan had come across this issue once before. Ged was always careful about photo shoots. Generally, shifters tried to avoid causing distress to animals. Horses were particularly sensitive to the genes of a shifter.

On one occasion, an overenthusiastic photographer had decided to introduce an equine theme into a magazine cover without warning Ged in advance. The result could have been carnage. The poor horses with their highly developed awareness, not only of the presence of big cats, a werewolf, a bear and a dragon, but also of the mysticism of the shifter world, had reared and plunged in terror. The situation had only been resolved when Beast left the scene immediately.

These horses, more accustomed to the presence of shifters, were not exhibiting the same signs of distress. Nevertheless, it had been evident the first time he met

Galba that they were not comfortable if Khan got too close. For that reason, he was staying in sight of, but slightly apart from, the group.

His boredom was relieved slightly by the sight of a golden eagle soaring overhead. With its giant wings outstretched, it hovered briefly over the group before circling away toward the higher peaks. Within minutes, the bird had returned to hang in the air over their group once again. It repeated this pattern over and over until Khan might almost have believed they were being followed by a bird of prey.

Despite the warm clothing provided by Surkh, several hours of hiking through strong winds blowing fast and cold through the valleys and down the ravines, disturbing the freshly fallen snow and taking the icy edge off the glaciers, had Khan shivering when they arrived at the fortress.

"Oh, my tiger." Sarange held out her arms as she dismounted. "Come here and let me warm you up."

"At least I didn't get overpowered by the eagle." He stepped into her embrace, enjoying the sensation of her rubbing her hands up and down his arms.

"What eagle?"

"The one that followed us most of the way." At least his teeth seemed to have stopped chattering. "You can't have missed it. It was so big it blocked out most of the sky."

Sarange looked bemused. "I didn't see an eagle. Galba, did you notice an eagle following us?"

Galba shrugged. "No." *A man of few words.* He went away to help secure the horses.

"Ah, hell. You're telling me I'm seeing imaginary birds? What next? Fake gorillas? Fictional buffalo?"

No, joking about it didn't make it go away. "That damn eagle was real."

Sarange looked up at him in surprise. "Khan, it really doesn't matter."

Was it worth pursuing? Trying to convince her? For some reason, he thought it was. Before he could make any further attempt, a shout went up from the battlements. "They are here! The gray werewolves are just across the valley."

Although the gray werewolves outnumbered them, they had two disadvantages. As far as Sarange could see, they had no clear leader. And they didn't have a tiger on their side. Those were two of the things she was counting on as she surveyed the scene below her.

Emerging from the surrounding hills, they moved closer, their thick fur providing them with protection from the cruel wind that blew off the snowy peaks. It was the same wind that cut into Sarange's skin, blanching her cheeks and bluing her chattering lips. *And this was once my home.* She had obviously once been acclimatized.

At first the gray werewolves were little more than moving shadows, their warning howls carried away on the bitter wind. As they neared, their gray fur became obvious. With the killer instinct of a wolf pack but the intelligence of humans, they communicated in barks and growls, spreading wide and encircling the fortress, cutting off any means of escape.

Where are you, Bora? Because he sure as hell wasn't with them. She could tell because there was no one to whom they turned for leadership. Having formed their circle, they waited. The next move was in the hands of the blue werewolves. *I am leading this.* She gave a bring-it-on shrug. *Not for the first time.*

"Two to one in their favor?" Khan studied the opposition, trying to analyze the odds.

"I rate our chances a little higher than that. And we have you." She spared a moment to glance in his direction. "A tiger among wolves. Always an advantage."

"Except for the time they captured me." His expression clouded. "I wish I could remember how the hell they did that."

"That was then." Knowing her touch soothed him, she took a moment to grip his hand. "This is now. I wish I knew what Bora's game was. Why isn't he here?"

"Could he be down there?" Khan nodded at the waiting werewolves. "Just because there is no obvious leader doesn't mean he's not there. He's already proved he's tricky."

"I remember enough about my past to know that once those werewolves shift, they become a pack of wolves. They follow their alpha." She pointed into the valley. "Look at them. They don't have an alpha. They have been sent here. They formed a circle around the fortress because someone told them to. When we attack them, they'll fight back because they're wolves and that's what they're conditioned to do. But no one is guiding them. They have no one looking out for their welfare."

"You sound almost sorry for them." Khan scanned her face.

"In a way I do. A week ago, I had no idea I was a werewolf. Then I found out that, not only am I a werewolf, I was once a legendary leader who lived almost a thousand years ago. It's taken some getting used to in a short time." She smiled. "But some things were easy, probably because Chinua has always been there inside me. And I know she took care of her troops. There is no way she would have sent them into a battle without being with them. She would call that the sign of a coward." Her lip curled. "And I would agree with her."

"Maybe Bora thinks he's already won this one. He does have a lot more fighters than we do."

"If that's the case, he's making a big mistake."

"So you won't go easy on them because you feel sorry for them?" Khan asked.

Sarange shook her head. "It's sad, but they have to die."

They stepped down from the battlements and she called Galba to her. "Assemble the men. I want to talk to them before we go into this fight."

The blue werewolves gathered in the ruins of the great hall, and Sarange stood on a fallen stone in the area she knew had once been Chinua's place at the head of the table. The thought sent a prickle up her spine. It was a combination of feelings. There was pride, responsibility and honor. Together with a healthy dose of fear. But the fear was necessary. It gave her the edge she needed to remain focused on the task ahead. And she would never show her apprehension to the men who gazed at her with such adoration and respect.

"When we fight, the temptation is to become wolves. To immerse ourselves completely in the fighting mode of the pack. That is what our opponents will do." The warrior spirit of Chinua was strong in her as she spoke. "The way to win this battle is to use your werewolf strength and cunning, but retain your human reason. We know how to do this. It will be brutal. We are not planning to take prisoners. As we attack, keep ahead of the enemy by staying part human."

"What do you mean?" Galba asked.

"If you retain your human senses, you can recall those things that will help you defeat a wolf. The worst thing in the world for a wolf is to be pinned down. Normally, in a fight, both wolves are trying to avoid that. Let your opponent bring you down. It gives you the advantage of surprise and exposes his throat and belly to you. Do what you do best. Claw, bite and tear. But also kick, jump and—" she looked around, unsure how her next suggestion would be received "—consider running away."

As she had anticipated, the proposal that a group of brave warriors should contemplate retreat as a strategy wasn't well received. There were frowns and mutterings.

"Until Chinggis Khan, Chinua was the greatest leader this region had known," Khan said. "Her brilliance in battle was renowned…and she never lost a fight."

"We are outnumbered." Sarange gestured toward the valley. "Our advantage lies in doing the unexpected. I'm not suggesting you run and keep on running." There was a ripple of relieved laughter. "Run and turn when your foe least expects it. Or work together. If you see another blue werewolf being chased by the enemy, seize the initiative and attack the pursuer."

She felt the mood change. Her approval ratings were going up. Khan gave her an encouraging grin.

"One final thing…if they retreat, we will not pursue them." She nodded to Galba. "Let's get out there and start winning."

Before she could step down from her makeshift stage, the entire pack of blue werewolves dropped onto one knee, bowed their heads and placed their hands over their hearts.

Just as they used to before they followed Chinua into battle.

Chapter 17

"You should stay out of the fighting." Galba's face was serious as he accompanied Sarange to the gates. "Every one of the gray werewolves will have orders to kill you first."

"I know." She smiled as she started to shrug off her warm clothing. "It makes it even more exciting."

This time when she prepared to shift, it was like a surge of electricity along every nerve ending. She guessed it was the anticipation of what was to come. She spared a brief thought for her organized celebrity lifestyle. Flowers delivered every Tuesday, workouts with her personal trainer each morning, emails answered by her personal assistant within twenty-four hours, her slightly obsessive habit of organizing her closets according to color *and* fabric. *And all that time I never knew I was a bloodthirsty wolf general.*

As the men around her started shifting, Khan spoke quietly in her ear. "You know I've got your back."

"Always."

"Then let's go."

The blue werewolves exploded out of the gates with Khan slightly ahead of them. As Sarange had expected, the gray werewolves waited for their approach instead of advancing to meet them. Within minutes, they were in the valley. The blue werewolves spread out, charging into the circle of attackers.

The time for thinking of anything except this fight was over. As she had told the men when they were up in the fortress, if they were to win, they needed to take the gray werewolves by surprise. As she darted like a silver streak through the gray bodies that snapped and snarled around her, Sarange felt a rush of adrenaline powering her along. It was like stepping back in time. Or stepping into Chinua's body.

She took advantage of the fact that she was lighter and faster than the male werewolves. Leaping up and onto the backs of the warring males, she used her razor-sharp canines to rip at the ears and muzzles of the gray werewolves, harrying the enemy and moving on before they could respond.

Around her, she was aware of the blue werewolves carrying out her instructions and causing chaos. Throughout it all, there was the giant, comforting figure of the Caspian tiger, plowing through the fight, shredding wolf muscle and bone with his fangs and claws as if he were slicing through butter. Khan tossed the mangled bodies of his victims aside with a triumphant roar. It was brutal, but effective.

Sarange kept going, driving deeper into the enemy pack. Galba was right, of course. She was the one the gray werewolves were all seeking. As she darted among them, huge jaws snapped dangerously close to her hind legs and she used her superior speed and agility to dodge them.

Before long, the stench of blood was thick and cloying in her nostrils and she had to fight to ignore it. In normal circumstances, blood was a pleasant smell for a werewolf, but when it was the blood of another wolf it was cause for distress. All around her snarls, howls and cries of pain rang out. It was sensory overload, none of it good, all of it distracting.

When two gray werewolves came at her, one on each side, Sarange tried to dart away. Too late, she realized her mistake. A third opponent was blocking her escape. They moved closer, pushing in on her from three sides. Taking her own advice, she dropped to the ground.

The werewolf nearest to her grunted in confusion, his teeth snapping dangerously close to her throat as he stood over her. She pressed herself tighter to the cold earth, waiting for him to attack. When she felt him move, she twisted beneath him, sinking her teeth into the soft fur of his belly and holding on.

The other two gray werewolves tried to come to his aid, but Sarange's position made it almost impossible for them to get to her. As long as she remained crouched beneath her larger adversary, there was nothing they could do. Keeping her teeth locked in place as he writhed and howled, she felt his blood splatter her fur. The harder he tried to shake her off, the worse the wounds she was inflicting became. Eventually, he stopped fighting, flopping onto his side, breathing heavily. Sarange didn't have time to go in for the kill. She had to get away from his companions.

With blood dripping from her muzzle, she darted

back into the thick of the battle. Working her way toward the point where she could see Khan hurling werewolf bodies high into the air, she continued to lash out left and right, ripping apart flesh. Moving on without pause.

Teeth closed on her shoulder and she howled in pain and rage. Swinging her upper body around, she was in time to see one of Chinua's tactics in action. One of the blue werewolves threw himself onto her attacker, sinking his teeth into the gray werewolf's neck. Blood, bright red and warm, sprayed in a fine mist, coating Sarange's face and temporarily blinding her. When she blinked it away and cleared her vision, the wolf that had bitten her was lying on its side, gurgling as blood gushed from its wounds.

Sarange continued to dart through the battle, never losing sight of Khan. This strategy began to make sense to her. Although she was in charge, she wasn't as physically powerful as the males. With her tactics, she remained highly visible to her own troops, annoyed the hell out of her enemies and retained an overview of the battle. The only problem was the drain on her energy. She was running on adrenaline, her chest heaving, every muscle aching, heart pounding like the hooves of a wild stallion.

Just as she thought her lungs might explode with her next breath, she realized it was all over. The ground beneath her was littered with dead and dying werewolf bodies, almost all of them gray. The remaining enemy fighters, after giving voice to a united, anguished howl, turned and ran. True to Sarange's orders, her fighters let them go. The valley fell silent as the blue werewolves watched their enemy retreat.

This remembered feeling was in her bloodstream.

The movies had it all wrong. There was no elation in victory. No joy in killing. Later, there would be a sense of satisfaction in a job well done, a feeling of relief that, once again, she had kept her pack safe. Right now all she felt was overwhelming sadness. So many lives lost. And for what? Because one man's desire to destroy her was so strong he was willing to send his followers here in great numbers with orders to kill her?

Why, Bora? What did I do to make you hate me so much?

Above all else, there was exhaustion. A tiredness that seeped into her bones. She wanted to lay her head on the hard, cold ground, gaze up at the clear skies and just drift away.

Being in charge brought great responsibility. She shifted back, signaling for the blue werewolves to follow her lead. Blood and gore covered her body as she faced them. *How would I ever explain this to my stylist?* She was able to quash her initial human instinct to cover herself as she stood before dozens of naked men. They were shifters. In that instant, they weren't viewing her as a female. She was their leader. Before she could find the words to thank them, they were bowing before her once more.

The river water had been bone-jarringly icy, but at least it had washed away the blood from their bodies. Sarange had a bite on her shoulder, but the wound wasn't deep. Khan had scratches and bruises. Getting dry enough to put their clothing back on had been the hardest part. Now, at last, the shivering and teeth chattering had stopped.

Sarange and Galba had walked the valley floor, organizing the best way to dispose of the bodies. Khan marveled at the way she slipped into her leadership role. When she talked to the blue werewolves as a group, he had seen tears glimmering in the eyes of many of the big, tough men. Afterward, she found time to speak to each of them individually.

Before Galba and his men prepared to decapitate and bury the bodies, Sarange spoke a few words. Her voice was a soft, soothing sound that carried high on the icy breeze. When she walked away toward the fortress, a new peace seemed to settle over the bloodstained valley.

"What did you say?" Khan asked.

"It was a chant my grandmother used when one of the animals died. It helped them on their way."

A shadow fell over them and Khan looked up. "Still think my golden eagle was imaginary?"

He grasped Sarange's shoulders, pointing at the sky above them. The giant bird circled the fortress several times before swooping down and landing on the outer wall of the battlements. It almost appeared to be waiting for them. As they approached the giant bird, Khan watched in surprise as an incredible transformation took place. The eagle gradually drew its body up, becoming taller and thinner in the process. Its head grew rounder and its wings disappeared, arms appearing in their place. Within minutes, the bird had gone and a woman stood there instead.

Although she was old and lined, there was a vigor about her that energized the surrounding atmosphere. She wore a dull brown robe with a white sash and a gold silk scarf around her neck. On her feet were reindeer-skin boots and her coat was made of animal hide. She could have been eighty years old. She could have been older than time. Stepping down from the wall, she held out her hands in a sweeping gesture.

Khan's attention was diverted from the woman when Sarange gave a cry and fell to her knees. A suspicion entered his mind. Could it be?

Sarange covered her face with her hands. "This can't be happening."

Khan knelt beside her, wrapping his arms around her in an attempt to comfort her.

"This is the shamanka who told us the gray were-wolves were coming," Galba said. "She is the one who told us Chinua was risen and that we must prepare for battle."

"Golden Wing?" Some deep instinct, the same sense that had drawn him to the bird as it followed them from the ger camp to the fortress, was telling him he was right. That inner pull was so powerful he had blurted out the words before he had time to consider the consequences. If he was wrong, it would cause Sarange pain. She talked about Golden Wing all the time, but she was unlikely to be impressed by him mistaking this mystical stranger for her beloved grandmother.

"A wolf storm brought me back to you, my child." The woman's voice was low and melodic, almost like singing. Ignoring everyone else, she spoke directly to Sarange. "The skies are yours this day."

Sarange uncovered her face. "Is it really you?"

"It really is." The smile on the shamanka's face dispersed the clouds.

Sarange shook her head. "I don't know how, or why, this is happening, but I'm glad it is."

"You can hug me," Golden Wing said. "I am a spirit, but I am not made of vapor."

With a sound between a sob and a laugh, Sarange ran to her and was enveloped in an embrace. She caught hold of her grandmother's hand and drew her forward. "There is someone I want you to meet."

"Khan." Golden Wing took his hand. "You have a tiger soul, but your heart seeks peace. Will you find it?" Coal-black eyes studied his face. "I think the answer lies within yourself."

It was an unusual introduction, but it was the first time Khan had met a shamanka. He didn't know how he was supposed to respond. Casting a pleading glance in Sarange's direction, he encountered only an encouraging smile. "Um, thank you."

In the valley below them, Galba had returned to his men. They were beginning the ritual of disposing of the dead gray werewolves using short, leather-handled silver swords to decapitate the bodies and digging the hard ground to make graves.

"Walk with me, my children. My feet can only touch the land on this day and only while the sun is high."

Sarange cast a fearful glance at the sky. "Can't you stay?"

Golden Wing shook her head as she led them to the highest point on the battlements. The three of them stood together looking out across the sweeping valley to the highest of the snowy peaks beyond. "The spirits may cross into this realm, but we cannot linger."

"Why did you come today?" Khan asked.

"It was not in my power to intervene, but I called upon the spirits of blue wolves past to watch over you."

"It seems they did." Sarange looked back down the curving lines of the fortress at Galba and his men.

"Perhaps, but the strength came from within you. You have grown stronger than Chinua herself." Golden Wing's serene expression clouded briefly. "But the gray werewolf leader was not vanquished in the fight."

"It was obvious they had no leader. I don't know why he chose not to come here today. Can you explain it?" Sarange asked.

"I can ask the spirits."

Sitting cross-legged on the dusty floor, Golden Wing closed her eyes. Swaying slightly from side to side, she began to chant under her breath. Sarange tugged on Khan's hand and they sat opposite her, watching her in complete silence.

After several minutes of her incantation, Golden Wing opened her eyes. Although she looked directly at them, Khan had the strangest feeling that she wasn't seeing them. "The gray werewolf leader wants you to die, but he does not want you to see his face when it happens."

"Is he Bora?" Khan asked.

"That is one of his names."

"Do you know the others he uses?" Sarange leaned forward eagerly.

"I know he is one man who is three."

What the hell kind of answer was that? Khan got the feeling the spirits might be offended if he blurted out that response.

"He has been fighting you for a long time."

"Why did he hate me—hate Chinua—so much?"

"The answer to hate often begins with love." Golden Wing's smile was sad. "The gray werewolf leader wanted Chinua. When she chose the tiger instead, his love became hatred. It turned pack against pack and ignited a feud that has lasted a thousand years."

Sarange turned her head to smile at Khan. "How did I find myself a tiger in a world of wolves?"

"The gray werewolf leader was putting pressure on you to tell him you would be his. You decided to spend some time alone here in the Altai Mountains. It was here you met a man who was good. A man who said 'I am yours' instead of 'You are mine.'"

Khan placed his hand over Sarange's. "I may not remember the details, but I know you made me the happiest man on earth."

"You also made a powerful enemy. From that day on, the gray werewolf leader swore to destroy you." Golden Wing closed her eyes briefly. "He was unrelenting in his desire for vengeance. You found great joy in each other, but he did not allow you to find peace."

"That was why we built this place." Sarange gestured at the mighty fortress around them. "Because we always had to fight, and we had to have somewhere to keep our people safe." Her expression was sad. "Even today, the blue werewolves are persecuted and the wild blue wolves face extinction, because Khan and I fell in love."

"Do you know where Bora is now?" Khan asked.

Golden Wing's black brows drew together and she clasped her hands in front of her as though in prayer. "The spirits cannot tell me his location, but his followers are getting ready to celebrate a great triumph." She shook her head. "It is strange because victory did not come their way today."

"The gala dinner in Ulaanbaatar," Sarange said.

Khan nodded. "Maybe that was the plan all along. Bora didn't want to get blood on his hands. Instead, he gets to put on his tux and deliver the keynote speech."

Golden Wing cast a look at the sky. "The sun is sinking…"

"Don't go yet. Please." Sarange's voice throbbed with emotion as she placed a hand on her grandmother's arm. "There are other things I need to ask you."

"Then you must ask me quickly, my child." There was a note of amusement in Golden Wing's voice.

"You found me miles from anywhere, wrapped in reindeer hide. But you knew I would be there, didn't you?" Sarange asked.

Golden Wing nodded. "The spirits told me where to find you. I know what you are going to ask me next, and I have no answers for you. I don't know who your birth parents were. I only know that you are Chinua born again."

Sarange was silent for a moment or two, considering her answer. "Is it possible that my parents were not human? Could they have been blue wolves?"

Khan remembered her interaction with the blue wolf pack. Recalled the bond between them. The love between them. Could a shifter child be born of wild animals? It made its own kind of sense.

"Anything is possible in this great universe of ours," Golden Wing said.

Sarange bowed her head. With his ability to read her emotions, Khan felt a feeling of peace emanating from her. It was a story come full circle.

When she raised her head, Sarange's expression was serene. "I have one final question for you."

Golden Wing looked from her upturned face to Khan's. "This is not your question to ask, my child. This must come from the heart of the tiger."

Khan regarded them in confusion. "Would someone mind telling me what's going on?"

Golden Wing took his hand in hers. Although her fingers were cool, a curious feeling of heat spread outward from the point where her flesh connected with his, tingling along his nerve endings. It felt as though she was connecting with a deeper part of him than the surface of his skin.

"The question Sarange wants me to answer is one only you can ask me." Golden Wing's dark gaze probed his face.

Khan stared at her, confused and unsettled. How could he ask the right question, when he had no idea what she was talking about? He was a shifter, but the mystical world to which Golden Wing belonged was beyond his experience.

A voice in his head—a voice that sounded a lot like Golden Wing's—prompted him to open his heart. To see what she wanted him to. But he was afraid of what she was offering. There was a strange sort of comfort in not knowing, there was familiarity in the belief that he would never remember it all and there was fear in hearing a shamanka's voice inside his head telling him to let go, to soar with her, high above the earth and into the clear sky.

Without knowing anything about him, Golden Wing was giving him hope and compassion, wrapping him in them as if they were warm blankets. Her dark eyes promised him magic and miracles…if he was brave enough to take them. If he could ask her the only question that mattered. Drawing in a shaky breath, he finally found his voice.

"Who is Khan?"

Chapter 18

Who is Khan?

Even though they weren't touching, Sarange felt the tremor that ran through Khan as he asked the question. She saw the pain in his eyes and knew how scared he was of hearing the answer. It was the question that haunted him. The world thought it knew Khan. They saw the image he wanted to project. The flaunting, arrogant egotist. He created a new headline every day, each one more outrageous than the last. That was his hiding place. Because the truth was, he didn't know himself. And he was terrified of what he might discover.

She also knew this was a barrier he had to cross if they were to ever find lasting happiness together. It was a difficult admission. *Because we are happy.* Theirs wasn't even a once-in-a-lifetime story. It was once-in-forever. But no matter how hard he tried to hide it from her, Sarange felt Khan's pain as if it was her own. And the source of his hurt was beyond her control. She could move armies and defeat a centuries-old enemy, but she couldn't help him with this.

Maybe I can't help him, but I know a woman who can.

Her emotions were still in turmoil over Golden Wing's surprise appearance and disclosures. Her grandmother's death almost fifteen years ago had left her bereft. Bek and Gerel had done their best to fill the void in her life, but nothing could really compensate for the loss of the woman who had raised her. Golden Wing had been a unique figure. Sarange's guiding light, her constant companion, and her only family for so long. Not being able to say goodbye had also hit Sarange hard. It had been a double blow. Like a death within a death. First there was the pain of knowing Golden Wing had gone; then there was the heartache of false hope. Being so far from home, she hadn't seen a body, hadn't been part of the funeral rites. Her heart had played a game of disbelief. What if it wasn't true? Someone had gotten it all horribly wrong? When reality sank in, grief hit a second time. She had mourned all over again.

Will this be a third time? She watched as Golden Wing placed her hands on either side of Khan's face and pressed her forehead against his. Would the joy of seeing her again be the roller-coaster high that was followed by a low of sorrow when she left?

And what about Khan? What if his worst fears were realized and Golden Wing told him something now that meant they could never be together? If he walked away from her, the heartache that had sent Chinua wandering this great land until her spirit faded away would pale in comparison. *I would not survive.* There was no drama in the thought. Only certainty.

"The spirits speak to me of the Xinjiang region." Golden Wing kept her hands on Khan's face. Her voice was low, almost a whisper.

Khan jerked as though she had delivered an electric shock. "That is where I was held in captivity."

"It is also where you were born." Golden Wing remained silent for a moment or two. "When you shift, you are a Caspian tiger."

"That's what Sarange said."

Sarange knew her grandmother had to enter a mystical realm as part of her shamanistic rituals. Golden Wing's eyes fluttered closed now and her body trembled as she received messages from her spirit guides. "But you were not born a shifter. Your parents were human."

"I don't understand." Khan frowned. "Do you mean I was bitten by a weretiger?"

Sarange cursed her limited knowledge of shifter lore. All she had was what Khan had once told her, but she needed more detail. She weighed her options. While she didn't want to interrupt Golden Wing's vision, these revelations affected her. She needed to know it all, no matter how bad it got. "What does that mean?"

"A shifter is either born or made," Khan said. "Although it is rare, a shifter can be transformed through a bite. It happens in one of two ways. Often the bitten shifter has agreed to the process because he, or she, wishes to make the transformation and live alongside a shifter mate. The other way is during an attack. If bitten humans don't die, they take on the form of the shifter that attacked them."

"So there is a grain of truth in those old movies about feral werewolves waiting on misty moors to jump out on unsuspecting humans?"

A brief smile lightened the strain on his features. "More than a grain."

Sarange swallowed hard. "Was Khan bitten in an attack…or by a mate?"

She had believed she wanted to know it all, but did she really want to hear the answer to this question? It was all very well to tell herself that Khan had been hers for a thousand years as if that conferred some sort of entitlement on her. Although she didn't know much about shifter tradition, she knew there were creeds and rules that ran deeper than the ties of emotion. Immortality brought benefits and responsibilities. If there was a mate who had a prior claim on him, Sarange didn't like her own chances of holding him. Her inner wolf was already rising in rebellion. Tenacity and loyalty. Wolf traits. *This isn't about my wolf. This is about me. About not letting him go because I love him. With everything I have in me. And I cannot—will not—give up on that.*

"Your story is a strange and tragic one." Golden Wing continued to speak directly to Khan. "You were only eight years old when you were taken from your parents. They called you the Tiger Boys. Children who were converted from human to weretigers by a bite from a rogue shifter."

"Why?" Khan's voice was little more than a croak.

The anguish on his face flayed Sarange's nerves until they were raw. She wanted to wrap her arms around him until the pain went away, but she was afraid of breaking the connection between him and the shamanka. Instead, all she could do was take the hit of physical pain to her chest and stomach and know it was only a fraction of what he was feeling.

"Sometimes evil needs no reason. This shifter kept you as his playthings until, one day, there was a rebel-

lion led by the largest and bravest of the Tiger Boys."
Golden Wing tilted her head to one side as though listening to an invisible voice. "That was you, Khan."

"I remember. All of it." Khan's eyes widened in
shock. "Twice in my life I have been a prisoner. Once
when I was first transformed and then again when I
was captured by the gray werewolves."

Sarange pressed a hand to her lips to stifle the sobs
that were threatening to escape.

"You killed the shifter who stole the Tiger Boys
from their homes. You freed them from their captivity," Golden Wing said.

"And I will kill the leader of the gray werewolves."
The strength was returning to Khan's voice, the determination to his features. With his memory, he was gaining resolve. "Both my captors will die."

"Now that you know it all, you have a new decision
to make." Golden Wing took her hands from his head.
Her voice returned to normal and Sarange guessed that
she had parted from her mystical guides.

"I do?" Khan quirked a brow at her. "This sounds
interesting."

"It is. Your childhood was stolen from you. This is
your chance to turn back time." Golden Wing's eyes
rested briefly on Sarange, a flicker of sympathy in their
depths. "The spirits will let you remain as you are, or
they will reverse the wrong that was done and allow
you to return to your human form."

Khan had his memory back. Finally, he could begin
to understand the events that had shaped him. So much
of his life had been about sadness and despair. He remembered the brief time he had spent with his parents.
His happy family home. Then, when the tiger-shifter

took him and transformed him, it felt like all the hope and happiness had been sucked out of the world. His future had been stolen, and in its place there was a desolate expanse of endless gray. The loss had been all-encompassing.

Even when he had taken the initiative and escaped from his tormentor, his life had been empty. He had felt like an observer watching his own story unfold. No longer human, he was a reluctant shifter, learning the lifestyle. Tiger. Shifter. Human. He had become fluent in all three. But human was the one with which he struggled. Emotions were never his strong point.

Until he met Chinua. She had made him whole. All three parts of his persona had finally been aligned. He had made sense at last.

Then the gray werewolves had taken him. Khan couldn't be killed. That was one of the unique features of the Tiger Boys. Unlike other shifters, they could be weakened by silver, but not killed by it. During a battle, his enemies had surrounded him and tied him up with bindings made of silver, before placing a hood woven with silver thread over his head. Even then he had fought like the tiger he was, injuring several of them. But the silver had done its job. The gray werewolves had taken him back to the Xinjiang region. Back to a new prison. One that was to be his home for almost a thousand years.

Although the silver had contained him, so had his own broken heart. His captors had tried everything they could to kill him. In the end, they had resorted to weakening him with the silver and by depriving him of food, water, exercise and sunlight. But it was the loss of his love that had broken him. It felt like they'd taken his heart and dropped it into a bucket of boiling oil. Without her, every part of him had turned to lead and he had been unable to think, to move, to do anything except ache. It didn't matter if that had lasted a minute or a thousand years. It felt the same.

Now Golden Wing was offering him a choice. And he didn't need to think about it. Because the answer was sitting right next to him with a hint of tears and a whole lot of fear shimmering in the blue depths of her eyes.

He reached out his hand and placed it on Sarange's knee. "My *koke gal* is a shifter. My life is nothing without her. I choose to stay as I am."

Sarange leaned closer and rested her head on his shoulder. He felt the quiver of relief that ran through her. As he held her closer, it was as if the pieces inside him that had been broken were gradually coming back together.

Golden Wing got to her feet. "I may be biased, but I think you made a good choice. Although it wasn't the path you chose, you are a strong weretiger who has brought much good to your species. And through your union with Sarange, you have helped save the blue werewolves…many times."

"Why did the Fates bring us back together at this time?" Khan asked.

"I only know there was a reason." Golden Wing looked at the sky. "The shadows tell me I must go."

Khan stood, holding out a hand to Sarange to help her up. "Thank you for giving me my identity."

"It was inside you all the time. I simply helped you find it," Golden Wing said.

He moved away, leaving the two women alone. Golden Wing held out her arms and Sarange stepped into her grandmother's embrace. He couldn't hear what they were saying, but he knew they were both crying.

They stayed that way for long minutes before separating.

"I am always here, even though you may not see me."

With those words, Golden Wing's transformation went into reverse, and within seconds, the great eagle was in her place. Spreading its wings, the bird gave a single, harsh cry before wheeling away into the sky.

Khan came to stand at Sarange's side, placing his arm around her shoulder as they watched the eagle until it was a distant speck among the high peaks.

"Does it feel better or worse that you got to see her again?" Khan asked.

Sarange gave it some thought. "Better, I think. She died when I was in America and I never got to say goodbye." She lifted a hand and brushed away a tear. "So, although it hurts that she's gone again, at least I got to hug her and tell her I love her. Speaking of which, if your memory is back, how did you first tell me you loved me?"

"I think I said 'Chinua, I love you.'"

She gave a tearful chuckle. "Mr. Romance."

"My animal guardian is the tiger. They're good at the hunting and killing. They're not big on the romance. But let me try." He turned her to face him. "A thousand years ago, you stole my heart and I will never ask for it back. It's yours to keep. Forever won't be long enough for me to tell you how much I love you."

She gave a little gasp. "Oh, Khan—"

They were interrupted by Galba's approaching footsteps. "The gray werewolves are all buried."

"And I thought tigers were bad at romance." Khan murmured the words into her hair and got an elbow in his ribs in response.

"Thank you," Sarange said. "Your loyalty has been remarkable."

Galba bowed his head. "Is it your wish that my men should return to their tribes?"

"Not all of them." Khan answered before Sarange could speak and she raised her brows in surprise. "We need you and some of your best fighters to accompany us to Ulaanbaatar."

"Do we?" Sarange asked.

"Yes. We have a gala dinner to attend."

By the time they reached the ger camp, the moon was full, the stars were putting on a brilliant display and Sarange was almost asleep in the saddle. Her feet had gone numb in the stirrups, her fingers were tingling inside her gloves and her mind was blank. The well-trained horse was doing all the work. She was certain he could sense her tiredness and was picking his way carefully over the rough terrain to avoid jolting her.

When they finally reached their camp and she slid from the horse's back, Khan was there to catch her.

"Always," she murmured, resting her cheek against the hard muscles of his chest.

"Pardon?"

"Always there to catch me." She was so weary it was hard to put her thoughts into words.

Some of her tiredness melted away at the smell of food coming from the large tent. When they entered, Merkid had made enough stew to feed the entire nomad camp as well. The task of helping to distribute the food and then eating her own meal took some time. During the feast, Jenny emerged from her ger and came to sit with them.

"From her expression, I'm guessing Jiran did a good job of distracting the camera crew," Khan murmured.

"Where did you go?" Jenny helped herself to some bread.

"To the mountains in the east." Sarange bit back a smile as Jiran entered and gave her a cheery thumbs-up. "Did you have a good day's filming?"

"No." Jenny sent a look of dislike in Jiran's direction. "Your friend over there told us he knew where we could find one of the largest blue wolf packs in the area. We spent an entire day following him up and down ravines and valleys. Ask me if we saw a single wolf."

"Did you see a single wolf, Jenny?"

"We may have caught a glimpse of one in the distance. Once. But it was so far away it could just as easily have been an antelope." She took a long slug of Surkh's homemade beer. "If he wasn't with you—" she nodded at Jiran "—I'd be tempted to think he deliberately took us on a false trail just to cause mischief. He certainly seemed to be enjoying himself."

Sarange had grown to like Jenny in the short time she had known her. She wished she could explain that Jiran had saved her life and that of her team with his trickery. He had also protected the anonymity of the shifters in the region, of course, something that Sarange could never reveal.

"How much longer will we need to be here?" Khan's question to Jenny was a key one. If they were to get back to Ulaanbaatar in time for the Chanco Party gala dinner, they needed to leave soon. Sarange knew Khan's choice would be to depart the next day. Every minute they could spend preparing for the coming encounter was crucial.

"I think we're done." Jenny gave a relieved sigh. "A

big part of completing this so fast has been Sarange's
relationship with the wolves. Everything else is a background to that. We have the two of you together in this
glorious setting, some shots of the wolves in their natural habitat, and we caught some wonderful footage of
cubs playing near a waterfall. We have a lot of work to
do back in the studio, but I know we have the start of
something special."

"Does that mean you're ready to leave?" Sarange
said.

"First thing in the morning."

Khan beckoned Jiran over. "Can you get us on the
first available flight to Ulaanbaatar tomorrow?"

Jiran nodded eagerly. "Three seats?"

"It's not quite that simple." Khan got to his feet, drap-
ing an arm around the younger man's shoulders. "We
have a few other people coming with us."

She watched as Khan and Jiran walked away. As
Jiran's expression became increasingly thunderstruck,
she knew Khan was sharing with him the details of the
next part of the plan. Since this included taking Galba
and twelve of his men to Ulaanbaatar with them, Jiran
was clearly trying to come to grips with the logistics
of the journey ahead of them.

When Khan returned to her side, she held up her
hands so he could pull her to her feet. "Take me to
bed, tiger."

"I thought you'd never ask."

She chuckled as they made their way across to their
ger. "Khan, I hate to disappoint you, but I may not stay
awake long enough to get the entrails out of my hair."

"I love it when you talk dirty to me."

Sarange was still laughing as she switched on the
shower, getting the water as hot as she could stand it.

As she stepped under the heated jets, she decided her weariness was only partly a reaction to the physical exertion of the day. It was also, she reflected, her psyche's way of coping with the emotional roller coaster she had been on. Leading the blue werewolves into battle, coping with the aftermath, seeing Golden Wing again, discovering the secrets of her own and Khan's past lives... all those things had drained her. And they had happened within the space of a few hours. This intense tiredness was her body's way of giving her time to assimilate everything the day had thrown at her. Sleep was the balm she needed to heal the bruises on her soul.

When she emerged from the small bathroom, warm, clean and scented, her gaze sought Khan. A tender smile curved her lips when she saw him. Sprawled like a starfish across the bed, her hard-living, rock star tiger was sleeping like a baby. Sarange removed his boots, socks and as much of his clothing as she could without disturbing him. Switching off the light, she curled up close to him in the small space available to her, pulling the comforter over them both. Sleep began to overwhelm her almost immediately.

When Khan woke, the patch of brilliant sunlight streaking through the heavy drapes that weren't fully closed told him they'd slept late. Sarange was a sweet, warm weight tucked into his side. They still had a long way to go before this was all over, but it felt like the tide was beginning to turn in their favor.

He had Bora in his sights—even though he had never looked his enemy in the eye—and he wasn't letting this go until the gray werewolf leader had been destroyed. Something about that thought brought him fully awake and he stirred restlessly.

He had never looked his enemy in the eye. Was that true? Had Bora always kept his distance, or had he gotten up close at some point? Was it even possible he was someone Khan or Sarange had met? Even someone they knew?

His restlessness must have disturbed Sarange, because she murmured something unintelligible and opened her eyes. For a moment, she blinked away the remnants of sleep; then she smiled. "I like waking up with you."

She reached up a hand to touch his face, but Khan caught hold of her wrist, kissing her fingertips. "I fell asleep before showering last night. Although I washed in the river, I'm still battle bloody and sweaty."

"I don't mind you sweaty, but bloody…." Sarange's eyes sparkled as she propped herself up on one elbow. "How about I join you while you shower away the blood and the sweat?"

"You have some good ideas, but that has to be right up there among the best ever."

The shower cubicle was barely big enough for one, so some ingenuity was needed to fit them both under the jets of warm water. Once Khan was clean, he pushed Sarange up against the wall. Wrapping her legs around his waist, she wriggled into position until she could feel his cock pressing between her heated folds.

Khan's appreciative growl echoed off the tiles as he lowered his head and bit the tender junction where her neck met her shoulder. Without pausing, he drove into her velvet heat. Sarange's gasps mingled with his urgent groans. Sarange's scent, her taste, her pelvis rubbing and grinding against his own…she fitted him perfectly and drove him wild. Slowly, tormenting them both, he drew out, one hand moving down so his thumb could tease her clit. Then he slammed his cock back into her so hard he almost blacked out. Sarange threw her head back and cried out his name.

Her hips moved in time with his, rocking and pounding, slamming and jerking. She grabbed his ass, driving her nails painfully into his skin. Khan snarled, raking her shoulder and neck with his teeth, before moving along her jaw. When he reached her lips, he plunged his tongue into her mouth, kissing her with an intensity that increased the fire in his blood.

The pleasure building within him was driving him crazy. Sarange pressed her breasts against his chest, sinking her teeth into his pecs. Khan cried out, whether in pain or pleasure, he didn't know. Didn't have time to care. The pressure continued to build, his rock-hard erection driving in and out of her, his thumb grinding out its insistent demand.

She was whimpering now, biting him anywhere she could. He felt the tension spiraling in her as her climax neared. She jerked him closer to her, urging him on with her hands and legs. Khan slammed relentlessly into her, groaning each time their bodies connected. At last it hit, taking Sarange first, and the spasms racked her, stiffening every muscle all the way to her curling toes. She threw her head back and howled. Still Khan drove into her, and still she came, her muscles clenching hard around him. Khan's own harsh growl followed, his release molten heat pulsing deep within her as the world emptied of everything except mind-numbing pleasure.

Sarange went limp and Khan lifted her higher so he could ease out of her. Turning off the water, he wrapped her in a towel and carried her through to the bedroom. Placing her on the bed, he returned to the bathroom and tucked another towel around his waist before he lay down next to her. Drawing her into his arms, he held her close, stroking the long, wet length of her hair.

"What time do we have to leave?" When she finally spoke, her voice was slightly dazed.

"In about an hour."

"You take my breath away. Every time." She traced a finger along the ridge of his abdominal muscles. "You consume me, Khan. With desire, with love, with joy. I never thought it was possible to feel like this. To have felt it twice—" she shook her head "—I must be the luckiest woman alive."

He crushed her hard to his chest, his voice husky. "If we didn't have packing to do, I'd show you all over again how much I love you. Unfortunately, since I don't like our chances of Jiran not bursting in on us to see where we are, this conversation—and any follow-up action—will have to be put on hold until we get to Ulaanbaatar."

Chapter 19

Jiran had taken on the role of tour guide and Sarange had to admit he was unexpectedly—and quite frighteningly—good at it. Since they didn't want to draw attention to themselves, using a hotel such as the one they had stayed in on their last visit to the capital wasn't an option. Thirteen blue werewolf nomads might not have gone unnoticed. With that in mind, Jiran had organized accommodation in a hostel frequented by backpackers.

Before they left the ger camp, Sarange had said goodbye to Jenny. "Is it official that you and the bad boy of rock are an item?" Jenny had paused in the act of loading her cameras into the film crew's hired jeep to give her a searching look.

Sarange had felt a blush warming her cheeks. "I'd appreciate it if you'd keep it to yourself."

Jenny shrugged. "Your business." She frowned. "There is something here, isn't there?"

"I don't know what you mean." Sarange had regarded her warily.

"Oh, you do, but I don't suppose you'll tell me." She had glanced across at where Khan was talking to Jiran. "It's about you and him and the way you generate enough electricity between you to light up a small city…and yet it's even more than that. This is going to sound crazy, but there is magic in this place. I could even feel it coming off your crazy friend when he was leading me on a blatantly false trail yesterday. And don't tell me you have no idea what that was all about, because we both know you do."

Her mock outrage had amused Sarange. "Believe me, it's better if you don't know."

Jenny had given an exaggerated sigh. "Just take care. Khan is too gorgeous for his own good, but rock stars can be dangerous." She had regarded Sarange with bewilderment. "What have I said to make you laugh?"

"You wouldn't understand, but believe me, there are more dangerous things than rock stars in this world."

Now they were back in Ulaanbaatar, planning their next steps, and those words came back to her. Because Bora was the greatest threat to their safety and, on the following night, they would be invading his territory.

Houlun was their source of information on what was happening at the Chanco Party headquarters. While he hadn't been able to get into the building to observe the preparations—security had been stepped up since their last visit—he knew the layout and he had a source on the inside. He had even brought with him a plan of the building.

"This is no ordinary gala dinner. Something big is happening," Houlun said.

The hostel had once been university accommodation.

Because Jiran had rented so many rooms, the booking clerk had allocated them their own meeting room. Seventeen people were crowded into a space that contained three sofas and a coffee table. Still in full-on organizational mode, Jiran had ordered takeout and beer. From the stains on the furniture and the lingering smell, Sarange had a feeling this room had seen more than its share of those items.

"How do you know this is out of the ordinary?" Khan asked.

"Security is cast-iron, and not only to prevent unwelcome visitors. Everyone concerned has been vetted to within an inch of their lives. From the caterers to the musicians and serving staff. My source tells me the checks on their backgrounds were more intense than if they'd been working for foreign presidents or royalty."

Khan was silent for a few moments, a faraway look in his eyes. "What are you thinking?" Sarange asked at last.

His wicked smile dawned. "I'm thinking...musicians?"

She caught his meaning instantly, his daring astounding her so much that she gave a little gasp. "Seriously?"

He laughed. "You're the wolf general. When you attack, it's in the open. Let's do this the tiger way. We'll sneak up on them and take them by surprise."

"I have no idea what you're talking about," Jiran grumbled.

Khan turned to Houlun. "I need to know who the musicians are for tomorrow's gala."

Houlun frowned. "I can find that out for you. But why do you need to know?"

"They're going to be joined by a guest duo." He

grinned, and caught hold of Sarange's hand. "The Chanco Party is going to get an A-list performance tomorrow night."

"What about the rest of us?" Jiran asked. "How will we get in?"

"Good question. Houlun, find out which company is providing the serving staff."

"Very well, but—" Houlun blinked as he looked at Galba and his nomad companions "—do any of you have any experience serving at a black-tie function?"

Galba paused in the act of tearing a fried chicken portion apart with his teeth, bones and all. "How hard can it be? You put food on plates, don't you?"

Sarange turned away to hide a smile at Houlun's horrified expression. "We'll need to give them a lesson in the basics."

"That's settled," Khan said. "Jiran, your next job is to organize fifteen waiters' uniforms…"

Persuading the band who was booked to play at the dinner to allow a guest duo to join them on stage for part of the performance was surprisingly easy, for one simple reason… Sarange accompanied Khan when he visited their manager.

From the minute they walked into his office, Tod Qatun was unable to take his eyes off her. "This is incredible. Your likeness to her—to the real Sarange—is uncanny. You must make a fortune from your tribute act." Since it was Khan who had made the appointment, Tod spoke in flawless English.

Khan could sense Sarange struggling to contain her mirth. She managed to keep a straight face as she answered, "I do okay."

With obvious difficulty, Tod dragged his attention

to Khan, looking him up and down. "No offense, but, although you have a passing resemblance to Khan, this act of yours must rely totally on your partner."

Khan shrugged. "What can I say? She's the star. I tag along for the ride."

"Ah, um..." Tod glanced from one to the other, then relaxed slightly. "I see. You're joking."

"We're a team." Sarange cast a mischievous smile in Khan's direction. "One of us has the looks. One of us has the musical ability."

"And it may, or may not, be the same person who has both." Khan figured Tod was sufficiently confused by now. "We're in town for a few nights. We heard about your big gig at the political function, and wondered if we could get in on that. It's not often you come across such a perfect Sarange look-a-like with whom you can wow your clients."

He could almost see the moment at which Tod's brain kicked into money mode. It was evident in the alteration in his expression, the switch from awed to avaricious. Leaning back in his chair, he studied them in silence for a moment or two. "I get why having a Sarange-a-like— especially one who is almost identical to the original— would be a good idea. But I'll be blunt. I don't see why I also need a second-rate Khan impersonator."

Khan had heard stories about celebrities who jokingly entered look-a-like talent contests and didn't win. Being told he was a poor imitation of himself was a whole new experience. Even though the underlying reason for their presence here was deadly serious, he couldn't help appreciating the humor in the situation. Since he could tell Sarange was close to dissolving into helpless giggles, he decided it was time to get things back on track.

"Maybe the whole Kha-range thing hasn't hit here the way it has in the US, but we're cashing in on the publicity while it lasts," he said.

"Kha-range?" Tod looked bemused.

"Speculation is rife that Khan and Sarange are in a secret relationship," Sarange said.

"Oh, I saw something about that on social media. After that duet they did at the Animals Alive concert. I see what you mean. Very topical." Todd lapsed into silence again. "How much?"

Before Khan could speak, Sarange surprised him by naming a figure. They hadn't discussed this, but when he took a moment to consider it, he saw what she was doing made sense. If they offered to perform for free, or too cheaply, they would arouse Tod's suspicions. With no concept of Mongolian currency, Khan didn't know how reasonable Sarange's suggestion was. All he knew was a hundred thousand togrog amounted to about fifty dollars, so the huge amount she was asking probably wasn't as high as it sounded. From the gleam in Tod's eyes, he thought she had judged it just about right.

"The band isn't going to like the last-minute change. And they might feel you're upstaging them—" It was unmistakably a negotiating tone.

"Okay. Sorry we bothered you." Sarange made a movement as if to get to her feet.

"How about fifty thousand togrog less?" Tod spoke quickly before she could move.

"What time do we need to be there?" Sarange gave him her most dazzling smile. Khan wanted to throat-punch Tod as he almost slid under the desk with a look of pleasure on his face.

The rest of the day was spent in a whirlwind of preparation. Sarange went shopping for a dress. Khan, having no expectation of finding the sort of clothing he wore on stage in the stores of Ulaanbaatar, decided straight-out-of-the-backpack grunge would be his look for the night.

They found Jiran on the point of tearing out his hair. Carrying the wad of cash Khan had given him, he had bribed the manager of the serving company into replacing some of his existing staff with Jiran, Houlun, Galba and the other nomads. He had even ensured that everyone had a uniform.

"As soon as they start serving, the guests will know something is wrong." He pointed at the grass outside the hostel. The nomads had found a soccer ball and were engaged in a noisy game. "They aren't interested in learning how to do it properly."

Khan took charge. Before long, Galba and his men were receiving detailed instructions from Jiran, who had spent a summer working in an upmarket hotel, on how to wait tables at a formal function. Sarange returned while this was going on and stood beside Khan, watching the proceedings for a few minutes.

"This isn't going to work." Her words echoed Jiran's mood.

"The guests will have more important things to worry about than the presentation of their dinner." Khan's voice reflected his grim determination.

What they needed was to get inside that building when the leaders of the Chanco Party—including Bora—were there. Everything else was an elaborate pretense, and possibly also a way of distracting themselves from the reality of what they were about to do. But walking into a den of wolves? It shouldn't frighten any of them, not after what they'd already been through. *It's not the werewolves.* How could it be, when his companions were werewolves themselves? It wasn't the thought of another confrontation and the possibility of more bloodshed. Even the prospect of finally coming face-to-face with the elusive Bora wasn't responsible for the curious jittery feeling he was experiencing, one he knew was infecting his companions.

No, it was the prospect of coming face-to-face with concentrated evil. That was what the Chanco Party represented. It had been replicated all too often throughout history. With no respect for time or place, these groups sprang up. Hiding behind sugarcoated messages and charismatic leaders, they rose to power on a wave of false promises. But underneath it all, there was hatred and poison, old hostilities and new atrocities. Humans had long memories, but shifters? They could make a grudge last forever.

The Chanco Party had one policy. To wipe out the blue werewolves and their descendants. Once that was over, the Chanco people would move on to another shifter minority, then another. They were bullies in suits. They appeared more credible than other extreme groups simply because most of the world didn't believe in werewolves. They had been able to rise to power rapidly because they could deliver their popular, secondary pledges while all the time keeping that main goal in their sights. And from what Houlun said, because they were dirty, using bribery and rigging votes to get to power. Now they were close to their ultimate aim. Government. When they got there, no one would be able to stop them.

No more. It ends tonight.

"Did anyone tell them they lost the battle?" Sarange whispered to Khan as she sneaked a look from between the heavy velvet drapes that spanned the stage. "Because they don't look like a group of people who have been defeated."

The glittering crowd who were assembling represented Mongolia's elite, along with a number of foreign dignitaries. Wealth, fame, political excellence, business acumen...all were present in the huge, lavishly decorated ballroom.

She wouldn't have believed from its ugly exterior that the building could hide such a beautiful venue inside. Sarange had been catapulted into fame at an early age, so she had never earned her stripes the way many artists did. Launching her career on a nationwide TV show meant she hadn't toured small venues building up a name for herself.

Khan had clearly played some unsavory places before Beast made its name, as had Soyombo, the band whose gig they had so abruptly crashed. They were all agreed that this place was the height of luxury.

"I've sung in places where the smell of damp makes you feel sick." Chen, the lead singer, was a beautiful Chinese woman who offered to share her cramped dressing room with Sarange. "Or the plaster is falling off the walls and the dust chokes you."

"You're sure you don't mind us joining you?" Sarange asked.

"No. But I'm going to add to my résumé and say that I sang with Sarange." Chen grinned mischievously. "I just won't mention that you aren't the real one."

Sarange bit back a smile, wishing for a moment that she could tell her the truth. Maybe when this craziness died down, she could do something for her. Offer her an endorsement? Invite her to LA? She was getting ahead

of herself. They had a long night in front of them before
she could start thinking about "what next."

"We have to get the band, and the other people who
have been hired to work here for the night, out before
we put our plan into action. I don't want any innocent
people to get injured." She whispered the words to Khan
when no one else was around.

"I'm already on it. Jiran knows what to do."

"That's a sentence I never thought I'd hear you say."
Sarange smiled as she took another quick look through
the curtains and saw Jiran surreptitiously supervising
the nomads. "Jiran has come a long way."

It was true. Their plans for this night were com-
plicated, but Jiran had followed every one of Khan's
instructions meticulously. Getting every piece of equipment they needed, plotting out positions on the floor
plan, organizing the getaway vehicle…he had done it
all with precision. When they left this building tonight,
they wanted to be sure the Chanco Party was destroyed
with no danger it could rise again.

Once the guests were all seated, Soyombo took to
the stage. Chen sang a few popular songs, both international and Mongolian, while the first course was served.
Sarange, observing from the shadows at the edge of
the stage, noticed a few minor incidents, but nothing
that would draw too much attention to the ineptitude
of the waiters.

From her vantage point, she watched Damdid Gandi
circulating the room. Focusing on the men, he was pat-
ting shoulders, stooping close to his companion's ear
to be heard above the sound of the music. Laughing.
Joking. Assured. His whole attitude was that of a man
convinced he was a winner. It didn't make sense. They
had lost the battle…

That was when it hit her. This was the real prize. Seizing power was all that mattered.

"Bora didn't lead his troops into battle because they weren't important."

"Pardon?" Khan bent his head closer so he could hear her.

"They were a sacrifice to keep us away from what was important to him." She waved a hand to indicate the elegant gathering. "From this."

"I don't understand."

Sarange pressed her fingertips to her temple, trying to gather her thoughts. "You and I didn't understand why fate brought us back together at *this* time. All Golden Wing knew was that there was a reason for us to be reunited. The blue werewolves were being persecuted and the blue wolves were facing extinction, so we believed that was why. But it wasn't. At least, it wasn't all of it. Those were consequences of a bigger picture. Our true purpose was to fight these people. This evil. They are going to do anything they can to win this election. When they fight, they are dirty." She turned her head to look at him. "Look at their confidence. They know they have it within their grasp. They will do it if we don't stop them. Once they win, the blue werewolves will be the first of many groups they come for."

"You think that's why Bora was so determined to kill you? Because he knew why fate brought us together?"

She could see Khan trying to catch up with her thinking. "Maybe he didn't know for sure, but if he even suspected, it would be enough for him to take drastic action."

"How would he know about us?" Khan asked.

"Think about it. He's not just anybody. He has known our faces for a thousand years. We didn't get back together privately. We did it in the most public manner possible, in front of hundreds of thousands of people. We lit up TV screens, the internet and social media." She laughed. "He was onto us the minute we sang that first note together at the Animals Alive concert."

"He let all those gray werewolves die in battle as a diversion?" Khan's growl was only audible to her because she was standing so close. "His own followers?"

"We knew how ruthless he could be when he sent those students to my house simply to test Beast's strength. Or to show us how evil he is."

"But we still don't know who *he* is because he's in disguise." Khan's jaw was tight with frustration as he surveyed the room. "He could be any one of the men here."

As Chen finished her number and turned their way, Sarange took his hand. "I guess we're about to find out."

Chapter 20

No matter the size of the stage, Khan's impulse was to dominate it. It was what he did best. This time, with Sarange at his side, he reined in his controlling instincts and worked with her. Although they were there for a different purpose entirely, he knew the result was incredible. The song was one Beast's former bass guitarist, Nate Zilar, had written at a time when he thought he might lose the love of his life forever. Called "My Only," it was a declaration in which the sense of yearning and hope for the future were palpable.

Clad in a thigh-skimming, backless black dress, with her trademark braid slung over one shoulder, Sarange took his breath away, along with that of most of the audience. The crystal simplicity of her vocals perfectly matched his smoky, rasping growl. The haunting melody didn't allow for Khan's usual acrobatics, but they swayed together in perfect harmony, losing themselves momentarily in the public love letter.

Out of the corner of his eye, Khan observed Damdid. The Chanco Party secretary was a danger. He had met Khan and Sarange before, and knew they were in Mongolia. Sarange had threatened him. Damdid's jaw plummeted as he realized what was happening and he made a move toward the door, presumably to alert security. His exit was halted by a quiet but powerfully effective punch to the throat from Galba. The nomad leader had been warned by Khan at the start of the night to take Damdid out before he could cause problems. Damdid dropped like a stone, and because all eyes were on the stage, he was carried out by Galba and Houlun before anyone noticed.

Khan also noticed there appeared to be a few problems with the food service. One or two of the elegantly clad women were complaining that half their meal had found its way down the front, or even the back, of their designer dresses. Some of the men appeared unhappy at the attitude of the waiters. Luckily, Khan and Sarange's duet was coming to an end.

The closing bars were the cue. Jiran sprang into action, hustling surprised people out of the room. The nomads abruptly stopped serving and started removing their shoes and socks. Khan took Sarange's hand as the last notes died away and thunderous applause echoed around the vast room.

Where are you, Bora? The gray werewolf leader must have recognized them, must have known this was no tribute act. *Nothing.*

"Ladies and gentlemen, I just have one thing to say—" if Bora wasn't coming to them, they were taking the fight to him. And wiping out his evil Chanco

Party at the same time. "If you are not a shifter, get the hell out of here while you still have time."

As he finished speaking, he launched himself from the stage, shifting in midair. There were screams of horror as the guests stared into the open jaws of a giant Caspian tiger before scattering in every direction. Sarange was right behind him, the remains of her black dress clinging to her fur as she raced to keep up with him. There was a surreal moment as they faced designer-clad werewolves before the fighting began in earnest.

They had two main aims. Find Bora, and create a diversion while Jiran and Houlun got into the offices. Their job was to get as much evidence as they could. Paperwork, laptops, hard drives. Anything that would damage the Chanco Party forever. Their plan wasn't just about tonight, it was about ensuring that nothing could rise from the destruction they were about to inflict. As for the remaining partygoers? Khan had issued a warning. They were dealing with a weretiger and a pack of werewolves. They knew what to expect and it wasn't going to be negotiation. The gala dinner was about to get bloody.

Most of the guests headed for the exits, which was good and bad. It limited the opposition, but it also meant the police would be arriving soon. There were about twenty male gray werewolves left in the room and a few females. Although Khan figured Bora must be one of the males, he was disappointed when he couldn't feel his presence. He wanted the moment he faced his sworn enemy to be memorable. Right now, he didn't even know who he was seeking.

Galba and his men had shifted and were plowing

through the opposition. Khan experienced a bizarre confrontation when a female werewolf in a tiara hurled herself at him. Brushing her aside, he continued on toward the males.

Show yourself, you bastard. Stop hiding behind your disguise.

The ballroom had become a scene of carnage. Led by Sarange, Galba's blue werewolves fought with a strength and fury that couldn't be matched by the shocked gray werewolves. Crushing and slashing, they inflicted terrible wounds on each victim before tossing it aside and moving on to the next. The floor became slippery with blood and littered with bodies.

When he judged the enemy was finished, Khan shifted back and gave the signal for the others to do the same. He wasn't looking for annihilation. Jiran would step up and put the next part of the plan into action.

"Rear exit." Khan jerked a thumb over his shoulder, indicating the direction Houlun had shown them on his plan of the building. He called Jiran's cell phone. "The police are on their way. Make your call, do what you have to and get out."

Sarange cast a look over her shoulder as they left the ballroom. There was no sign of movement. "Bora?"

They piled into the truck that was waiting at the rear of the building. Jiran and Houlun had already stacked the haul of items they had removed from the offices inside. Khan and Sarange jumped into the cab. Jiran joined them a minute or two later. Climbing into the driver's seat, he gunned the engine.

"Everything go according to plan?" Khan asked as Jiran pulled out of the narrow road at the rear of the building.

"We disabled the security cameras at the start of the

night. I just called the police and the fire department and told them there had been a terrorist attack at the Chanco Party headquarters, which was now on fire." After driving for a few minutes, he halted the truck on an incline from which they had a clear view of the area they had just left.

"You're sure the fire you set will spread quickly enough?"

"Look." Jiran pointed at the building where bright orange flame was bursting from the windows and clouds of smoke poured into the night sky. "I used a fast-acting accelerant. Fire investigators will know it was arson, but I already told them that."

Khan viewed the spectacle for a moment or two. "It's a pity Torque isn't here. He loves watching things burn."

Jiran drove back toward the hostel. "We'll never know which of them was Bora." There was a note of dissatisfaction in Sarange's voice that Khan understood. The Chanco Party had been destroyed, its leaders killed, and he was confident that Jiran and Houlun would find evidence of corruption in the items they took from the offices. But it still felt like unfinished business. *We didn't get to look Bora in the eye. That's why it feels this way.*

"It's over. We go home tomorrow." Home. For the first time since his release from captivity, he felt like he knew where that was. It was any place where he had Sarange at his side.

"And I suppose you want me to arrange to get Galba and his men back to the Altai Mountains?" There was a note of resignation in Jiran's voice.

Khan patted his shoulder. "I knew we could rely on you."

* * *

Khan swam several fast lengths of the pool before climbing out and dropping onto a sunbed. There was a misconception among humans that tigers hated getting wet. While most big cats were land hunters and tended to avoid water, the tiger's environment was different. In the wild, its prey didn't form nice, neat herds, which meant a stalking tiger often had to swim long distances.

Not that Sarange's pristine pool resembled a tropical river, or that he was likely to have to hunt down tonight's dinner. The thought made him smile. But he was smiling a lot this afternoon.

The jeweler had dropped off the ring and it was perfect. Khan had designed it himself. The central stone was a sapphire—of course—surrounded by a circle of diamonds that reflected the deep blue color over and over.

"Blue fire." That was what he had told the jeweler, and the guy had delivered a piece Khan would feel proud to place on Sarange's finger.

He had picked up on a hint of impatience in her demeanor lately. Caught her watching him once or twice as though wondering when—*if*, even—he was going to ask. Once or twice he had wanted to confess, to tell her he wasn't being arrogant and doing that whole *"I am Khan"* thing. He was simply waiting for the perfect moment to ask her to be his wife.

Tonight would be that moment. The table was booked. The champagne was chilling. To hell with protecting their privacy. He was going down on one knee in the most public manner possible. He didn't care who saw it.

When Sarange came home, he would tell her they were going out to dinner at her favorite restaurant. He frowned. Where *was* Sarange? She had gone out to pick up a few things to get ready for their trip to New York the next day. Beast was getting back on track with the album, but luckily Sarange had no immediate commitments so she was able to travel with him. The other members of the band were already on their way to the airport. Khan had negotiated with Ged for an extra twenty-four hours.

He reached out a hand for the cell phone that lay on a table at his side and glanced at the time. Sarange had been gone for hours. Far longer than she'd said…

With perfect timing the phone buzzed at that exact moment and he smiled, assuming it would be her. With a frown, he saw it was Jiran's number. As he answered, his mind was registering that it was 5:00 a.m. in Ulaanbaatar.

"Hey."

"Khan? It is Houlun."

The words made his stomach drop as if he were on the worst kind of roller-coaster ride. "Jiran said you don't use cell phones."

"I don't, but this is important." The sinking feeling intensified. No one called at 5:00 a.m. if it was good news. "I have discovered from my sources that Bora wasn't at the gala dinner."

Khan jerked upright, shaking tendrils of damp hair out of his face. "What?"

"He wasn't here in Ulaanbaatar on the night the Chanco Party held its celebration."

Even across the miles that separated them, Khan could hear the other man's distress.

"He was never in Mongolia."

"Where the hell was he?"

"He was in America the whole time. In California."

Khan got to his feet, pacing along the edge of the pool. His thoughts were a whirlwind, but one phrase was pushing itself to the forefront of his mind. He kept hearing Golden Wing's voice. *Bora is one man who is three.*

"Houlun, what is the Mongol word for 'three'?"

He could hear the confusion in the other man's voice as he answered, *"Gurav."*

"Close, but not exact."

"Khan, what is going on?" Houlun was starting to sound concerned.

He's concerned? He should try being me.

"I'll tell you when it's over. Right now I need to call someone else." Khan ended the call abruptly and found the number he needed. Why did his memory still have so many holes? Especially when it came to the ancient language his people had spoken? And why the hell did this have to be one of the missing details?

"Bek? No, Sarange is not here. Look, I'll explain this later, but I don't have time to chat. Sarange said you have a framed document on your study wall with the ancient Mongolian words and symbols on it. I'm hoping that means you have some knowledge of that language. Can you tell me what the number three was?"

When the other man spoke, it only confirmed what Khan had already guessed. *"Gurban."*

He finished the call to Bek, promising he would bring Sarange on a visit soon. Hoping he could make it happen. She had been right. Bora had used the battle against the gray werewolves as a distraction from his bigger plan. More than that, he had *created* the diversion by sending them to Mongolia. Because Bora was Radin. *Gurban* Radin.

I stopped protecting her because I thought we were safe. And now he has her. He was sure of it.

Breaking into a run, Khan was calling Ged on his cell phone as he burst through the bedroom door and grabbed clothes from the closet, pulling them on with the phone tucked awkwardly between his ear and his shoulder.

"Radin has Sarange." The words came out in a garbled *whoosh.*

"Slow down." As always, Ged's voice had a calming effect. "Radin the filmmaker?"

"Yes. I don't have time to explain. All you need to know is that he's Bora. Tell me it's not too late for you to turn around."

"We were just about to board, but that doesn't matter. All that matters is Sarange. Tell me where to meet you."

Khan gave him the address of Radin's West Hollywood office, hoping he was right and that was where he would have taken Sarange. He figured Radin's plan would only work if he got Khan and Sarange together. Destroying one of them wouldn't be enough for the man who had hated them for a thousand years. And Radin would want Khan to see his revenge up close. The thought caused sour, choking panic to rise in his gullet. He quashed it back down. Grabbing up the keys to his rental car, he dashed out of the house.

Golden Wing had been right. Their enemy was one man who was three. First, he was the gray werewolf leader who had loved Chinua and sworn revenge when she didn't return his feelings. He was also Bora, the shadowy figure who had orchestrated the fight against them in this life. And now Khan had the third and final piece of the puzzle. He was Radin, the man who had always looked at Sarange with a mix of admiration and agitation.

Now Khan knew the reason for those glances. Admiration, because, like Khan, Radin had loved Sarange for a thousand years. Agitation, because he was trying to hide his feelings.

He won't harm her unless I am there to witness it. As he pulled out of Sarange's driveway, he kept telling himself that. *He wants to hurt us both.* Khan didn't know how to call on the spirits in the way of the shamans, but he tried his best.

Let me be right about this. Watch over my koke gal.

As she was dragged into Radin's office, Sarange didn't know which emotion was strongest. Yes, she was scared. Now that she knew who he really was, she was very, very afraid. But she was also angry. And most of that anger was directed at herself for allowing him to dupe her this way.

She had been going about her shopping with a slight smile on her face. Khan thought he was being enigmatic. Clearly, he imagined he had tricked her into believing he wasn't going to propose to her. The thought almost made her laugh out loud. A tiger with a secret was something to behold. All the sneaking glances at his cell phone? Jumping up and bolting out of the room for surreptitious conversations when he thought she might overhear? The way he kept watching her as though he thought she might be reading his mind? Then, this morning, he hadn't been able to get her out of the house fast enough. He had practically pushed her out the door. No, either he was having an affair—and, after a thousand years together, she knew him well enough to trust him unconditionally—or he was buying a ring.

Wrapped in her pleasant thoughts, she had left the drugstore where she had called to collect some pain medication for the headaches she recently started experiencing. A brief conversation with the pharmacist had convinced her that she should see her doctor. It was probably nothing. That was what the pharmacist had said. Had she been under any recent stress? That could be the cause. Sarange had bitten back a smile. Yes, there had been a few things going on lately. Stress might just be the reason.

She hadn't heard anyone come up behind her as she reached her car. Hadn't known anything until a hand was clamped over her mouth and her hands were being roughly jerked behind her. As soon as the handcuffs were snapped onto her wrists they burned like red-hot iron fresh out of the furnace. At the same time, the stench hit her nostrils. It was like nothing she had ever smelled before. It was like rotten meat and bad eggs mixed with verdigris. Her werewolf senses told her instantly what it must be...

...*silver.* It was already making her feel weak and light-headed. That was how her attacker had been able to get so close without her noticing.

"If you struggle, the sensations will get worse."

She knew that voice. As she was pulled away from her vehicle, she fought off the silver fog enveloping her brain in an effort to identify it. "Radin?"

"Don't bring her too close to me, Jason." Radin's voice was sharp.

Sarange tried to turn her head to see who he was talking to, but the mysterious Jason was already placing a dark hood over her head.

"The silver affects me as well."

Radin was affected by silver? Even in her con-

fused state Sarange could work out what that meant.
It meant Radin was a shifter. It meant he had tricked
her. It meant…oh, hell, did it mean he was *Bora*? One
thing was for sure. It meant she was in a whole world
of trouble.

The man who had grabbed her had forced her into
the trunk of a car and she had been driven across town
to the underground parking lot of Radin's office building. From there, they had brought her, still hooded, up
to Radin's office.

Now she was seated on a chair near the window. The
hood had been removed, but the silver handcuffs were
still in place. Radin was standing across the room from
her, clearly trying to keep his distance from the effects
of the silver. Another man, presumably Jason, stood
near the desk. He was a huge, bulky figure with muscles like carved concrete. He had a gun tucked into the
waistband of his jeans and Sarange was willing to bet
it contained silver bullets. It seemed Radin had thought
of everything.

She found if she focused, she could fight off the
mind-numbing effects for a few minutes at a time. If
she relaxed, the silver acted like a hypnotic drug, pulling her under and making her forget how to think.

"What now?" Her speech was slurred as though she'd
had too much to drink.

"Now we wait for the heroic tiger to come to the rescue." Radin's smile was serene.

"Doesn't know where I am." She tried to shake her
head, but her neck muscles weren't working.

"I reckon he'll work it out," Radin said. "I may not
rate tiger intelligence very high, but he has a sixth sense
where you are concerned."

Something wasn't right about this. Trying to draw

some air deeper into her lungs was a mistake. The silver scalded as though she'd breathed in acid. Hanging her head, she coughed and spluttered. When she finally regained enough breath to speak, it took her a few moments to remember what she wanted to say. "Bora was here. Attacked you."

Radin laughed. "I thought that was a particularly clever trick. Pretending to have been attacked and robbed...it was just too easy. I was worried that you might start making connections. Maybe even think that my insistence on you and Khan making the documentary together could be more than coincidence. I wanted to kill you, not arouse your suspicions."

"Can't kill Khan."

"Some things are worse than death. For Khan, the worst torture will be to watch you die." The smile deepened. "When he gets here, that is what I will make him endure. Then, when he has nothing left to live for, he can return to his captivity with the image of your death in his mind for all eternity."

"No." Sarange wouldn't plead for herself, but she would do it for Khan. "Don't make him go back there. Please."

The smile vanished. "You think begging for his miserable life is going to change my mind? You are a werewolf—" he spat the words at her "—but you chose a tiger over one of your own kind."

"We don't choose who we love." Her wrists were on fire, her head felt like it had been stuffed full of cotton candy, and all she wanted to do was sleep. But she had led an army against this man and defeated him. She wasn't going to give in easily. Determinedly, she forced herself to focus.

Radin had said he would kill her and make Khan

watch. *Get him mad. Make him want to kill me before Khan gets here.* It wasn't much of a plan, but it was the only hope she had of getting him to come close enough so that she could lash out with her feet, maybe even her teeth. Okay, it might provoke the circus strongman into shooting her, but that was going to happen anyway... If only these damn cuffs weren't making it impossible for her to summon the energy to shift.

"You are saying you didn't choose your tiger lover?" Radin sneered.

"That's right. We're mates. The Fates decreed that we should be together." Ignoring the awful silver stench, she drew a deep breath. "But if I lived a thousand life-times, I would choose him in every one. Never you."

He lunged toward her, his features suffused with rage. "You will regret those words."

"But not for long." Even though every muscle ached with the effort, she forced herself to shrug. "From what you've just said, I'll be dead soon."

The anger in his face hardened, but another emotion shone in his eyes. "I could make you change your mind."

Dear heaven, did he mean what she thought he did? Snatching victory from the jaws of defeat was what she did best. But this? She had never faced a personal challenge of this magnitude. A man whose arrogance was so great he believed he could make her love him...by forcing her? As the effects of the silver dragged on her psyche, she felt her fighting spirit—Chinua's spirit—surge. "I don't think so."

"Take the cuffs off her and then get out." Radin barked the words at Jason without taking his gaze from Sarange. Yes, she had been right about that gleam in his eyes. It was lust, and it sickened her.

"You said she was dangerous."

"Don't question me!" Radin's growl echoed around the room.

The muscleman hesitated for a second or two, then moved forward to remove Sarange's handcuffs. He did it carefully, watching her the whole time as if she were a coiled snake. She didn't have any energy to waste on him. If she did, she'd have explained that she didn't have the strength to lift her head, let alone attack anyone. Even though the silver was gone, the impact lingered.

When the door closed behind his accomplice, Radin moved closer. Slumped as she was in her seat, all Sarange could see of him was his expensive, handmade shoes. A discordant thought flickered through her mind. As diversionary tactics went, it would certainly be unusual if she threw up over those shoes. And that was exactly what she felt like doing right now...

Radin caught hold of her hair, jerking her head back. The blaze of triumph on his face increased her nausea. He reached out a hand as if to touch her face, but before it connected, the door flew open. Expecting to see Jason return, Sarange blinked at the unexpected vision that met her eyes. Her sight was slightly blurred from the effects and she decided she must be seeing things.

Because that couldn't be Diablo? And Dev? Could it? As Beast's drummer shifted into a black panther and the rhythm guitarist became a snow leopard, Sarange realized she wasn't imagining this. They were real. The rock-star-shifter rescue party had arrived.

Radin snarled, his hold on her hair tightening as he jerked her to her feet. Sarange's leg muscles refused to cooperate, and she stumbled to her knees. As the two big cats moved closer, she heard a sound from the window. Now things were getting even more surreal. The beating of dragon wings ten floors high was like a small hurricane hammering against the glass. With a single flip of his tail, Torque shattered the window and Khan, ever the showman, leaped from the dragon's back, landing in a crouch in the center of the room.

"You rode on a dragon for me?" Despite her weakness, Sarange couldn't keep the emotion—and a touch of laughter—out of her voice.

"Didn't I tell you I would do anything for you?" Khan swept her up, cradling her against his chest. Immediately, some of the mist swirling in her brain started to clear. She nestled her head gratefully into the crook of his shoulder.

"Jason…" Radin made an attempt to reach the door, but Diablo blocked his path.

"You used the silver trick on me all those centuries ago." Khan's voice was silky smooth and dangerous as he turned on Radin. "That was bad enough. But to try it on Sarange?" He shook his head. "Just one more thing you are going to pay for."

Radin's lips drew back in a snarl so awful it brought a fresh wave of nausea washing over Sarange. "Do your worst, Tiger Boy."

The words provoked a rumbling growl from somewhere deep in Khan's chest. "I intend to. But first…" He raised his voice slightly. "Ged!"

The big werebear came into the office. He was rubbing his knuckles and his expression was one of distaste. "You could have warned me that guy would be carrying silver. Knocking him out was no problem, but that stench lingers for days."

Khan moved toward him. "Get Sarange back to her house. It looks like she's been exposed to a strong dose of silver. Rest is the only cure for that." Tenderly, he transferred her to Ged's strong arms. "You don't need to see him die, *koke gal*. You only need to know it will happen."

As Ged carried her out of the office, she heard Khan growl to Diablo and Dev, "Stand back. This is one kill that belongs to me."

Chapter 21

Khan sat beside Sarange's bed, watching her face as she slept. Exactly the way he had done that first night together. He corrected himself. *The first night of this lifetime.*

He was worried about her. He knew the silver would weaken her, but its effect had been stronger than he'd expected. She had been asleep since Ged brought her back from Radin's office. Khan glanced at the clock. It was now over twenty-four hours.

Her skin was waxwork pale, her breathing shallow and her pulse slow. When he rested his hand on her forehead, she felt cold. The burns on her wrists stood out, angry and raw, scorching into her tender flesh. But it was the injuries to her psyche that scared him. He knew what silver had done to him, but he had an immunity that Sarange didn't possess.

The poison hadn't killed her. That meant she wouldn't

deteriorate further from this point. But what if this was it? If this was the damage that had been done? What if she didn't recover from this debilitating weakness? What if his beautiful *koke gal* remained frozen like a statue for all eternity?

He couldn't think like that. It had been a day since he found her. The sun had risen and set once since he finally faced and killed Bora. One thousand years avenged in a single swipe of his claws across Radin's throat. Khan had left his friends to clean up while he raced back to be with Sarange.

Because of everything that had happened in his life, all the barriers that had been thrown up between them, he supposed he was hardwired to believe the worst. By clinging to gloom, he was able to avoid hope. Because faith and belief…they were his enemies. As soon as he went down those twin roads, he was lost. Yet how could he allow his mind to dwell in bleakness when this was Sarange? When his whole life was wrapped up in the slender figure beneath that comforter?

If he gave up on her, he gave up on himself. Lifting her hand to his cheek, he watched her eyelids with their black fan of lashes, willing them to open. "For me, *koke gal*."

He glanced up at a sound from the balcony. Although Sarange felt cool, the day was warm and he had left one of the doors open. Not again. Physically, he felt as strong as ever, but if this was another attack, he didn't feel mentally prepared…

Getting to his feet, he went to the door and pulled back the lightweight drapes that covered it. When he stepped onto the balcony, it was empty. He took a moment to glance back at Sarange before going to the balcony rail and looking out over the yard. Everything was still and quiet.

Paranoia. He shook his head, going back inside. As he reached for the handle of the door to pull it closed behind him, an unmistakable noise reached his ears. Here? In Los Angeles? He would know the sound of those giant wings anywhere. He tilted his head skyward in time to see the golden eagle circle the house once before disappearing into the distance.

Hurrying to the bed, he scooped Sarange up into his arms. Her head flopped against his shoulder as he carried her onto the balcony.

"We are both here." His voice was a croak as he scoured the sky for another sighting of the mighty bird. "Golden Wing and I."

Even before the eagle reappeared, he felt Sarange stir. Her hands came up to clasp his neck. As the great bird hovered directly overhead for a few minutes, casting her shadow over them, Sarange opened her eyes.

"Thank you," she murmured, half raising a hand toward the bird.

The eagle appeared to dip its head in acknowledgment before wheeling high over the rooftops with a single, echoing cry.

When they could no longer see it, Khan carried Sarange back inside and placed her on the bed. Carefully, he lifted the glass of water that had been on the bedside table to her lips and she sipped gratefully.

"How long have I been asleep?" She lay back on the pillows.

"A full day. You went out shopping yesterday morning and it's now four o'clock in the afternoon."

She shook her head, clearly struggling to believe

what he was telling her. "The silver…it made me feel like I'd been drugged. I could barely think or move. Every second I had those handcuffs on made it worse."

"What I don't understand is why Radin removed them. He had you in his power, which meant he had control over me. Why would he throw away his advantage?"

Sarange shivered. "He thought—" She paused, clearly struggling with the memory. "He thought he could force me to love him."

"You mean…?" Khan struggled to fight off the waves of fury.

She nodded, her fingers plucking at the coverlet. "I think he was going to rape me. Golden Wing said hate springs from love, and she was right. Radin said he could make me love him, but the only thing I saw in his eyes was hate."

"If I'd known what he was planning—" Khan could barely think, let alone speak. "I wasn't there to protect you from him. I made an assumption that you were safe, and I was wrong."

Sarange reached out and placed her hand over his. "You are always there to protect me and you were again. You arrived in time to save me. Radin is dead and the nightmare is over."

"After all this time, it's hard to believe it's true."

She tilted her head. "The house seems very quiet. Are we alone?"

"Yes, apart from your efficient, unobtrusive staff. Beast has gone back to New York. Ged wanted to stay and help me take care of you, but I persuaded him your recovery wouldn't be helped if you had a shifter rock band living in your house."

Although she still looked weary, some of the magic

was back in her smile. "You were right. I am fond of your friends, and grateful to them for rescuing me, but I'm not sure I can cope with too much Beast right now. And even when I haven't been wearing silver handcuffs, I like it best when it's just you and me."

Khan's heart expanded so rapidly his chest hurt. Everything he once thought he could never have was right here in this room. He realized now how frightened he had been. Ged had released him from his prison, but Sarange was the one who had finally freed him from fear. Until her, he had been afraid of living a normal life in case someone discovered he didn't know how to do human emotion, terrified of commitment in case he got hurt, or hurt another person in return. Worst of all, he had been unwilling to give even the tiniest part of his heart because he was scared of losing it forever.

But now he finally knew where all that fear had come from. And he knew how to deal with it. As long as he had Sarange at his side, he could have all the things his heart craved. The life they had once shared could be theirs again, without the need for constant battles…and with one or two obvious, modern-day bonuses such as running water and air travel.

What am I waiting for? The romantic proposal had been a nice idea…yesterday. Before he almost lost her to the crazed enemy who had made their lives hell for so long. After yet another stark reminder of how much Sarange meant to him, perhaps it was time to just get on and do it… "I'll be right back."

He was aware of Sarange watching him in some surprise as he dashed out of the room. He had hidden the ring in a drawer in the kitchen and he retrieved it now, taking the stairs two at a time in his impatience to be back with her. When he burst through the bedroom door and hurled himself onto his knees beside the bed, he was out of breath and could feel his face burning.

Sarange had moved into a sitting position against a bank of pillows. She regarded him in some surprise. "Are you rehearsing a new move for your next tour?"

The question, and the whole situation, struck him as so deliciously funny that he started to laugh. Still kneeling, he leaned his elbows on the bed and kissed her. "This is not a rehearsal. This is the most real thing I've ever done in my life." Flipping open the ring box, he presented it to her. "My Sarange, my *koke gal*, I'm already the happiest man alive because of you. Will you make my life even more perfect and become my wife?"

"Khan…" Her voice trailed off as tears filled her eyes. "Damn. I decided I wasn't going to cry."

He slid the ring onto her finger. "You knew?"

"I had an idea." She smiled through the tears. "You're a tiger. Subtlety is not your strong point." Lifting her hand, she turned it from side to side to admire the ring. "It's the most beautiful thing I've ever seen."

"Is that an acceptance?" Khan tried to growl, but his emotions were still on high alert and his voice was too husky.

Sarange held out her arms. When he rose and went to sit next to her on the bed, she slid her arms around his waist and rested her cheek against his chest. "You are all I have ever wanted. We complete each other. This—" she held up her hand, and the ring sparkled its blue fire just as he had hoped it would "—just makes it even more special." She tilted her head back, the fire in her eyes even brighter than that of the stones on her finger. "I love you, my tiger."

Khan managed the growl he had tried earlier. "And I adore you, my *koke gal*."

One Year Later

Diablo regarded the baby in Khan's arms with interest. "So, what is she? A wiger? Or a tolf?"

"She is Karina, and she's unique," Sarange said. "And we won't know what her inner animal is until she shifts. She could be a tiger, or a wolf, or she may be a hybrid. It doesn't matter." She smiled up at Khan. "After everything that has happened to us, she is our reward."

"And there were no ill effects from the silver to which Radin exposed you?" Gerel asked, when Diablo had gone. The change in Gerel over the last year had been remarkable. Now that she had embraced her shamanistic abilities instead of subduing them, her health had improved steadily so that she glowed with vitality.

"Fortunately not. Of course, I didn't know I was pregnant then because it was at such an early stage. Strangely, I was already experiencing some symptoms. My human hormones hadn't reacted, but my inner wolf had registered the change and I was getting headaches. Once I knew for sure, I was worried that the silver could have harmed the baby, but the shifter doctor Ged recommended did some checks and everything was fine." She stroked her daughter's head and Karina gurgled with pleasure. The baby was a perfect combination of them both, with Khan's red-gold hair and Sarange's light blue eyes. "More than fine. She's perfect."

Everyone who mattered to them was gathered here for the baby's dedication. It wasn't in any sense a traditional ceremony. Led by Gerel, it was a simple, shamanistic statement of thanks to the spirits for the gift of their child. And there were special thanks for one particular spirit. *I am always here, even though you may not see me.* Golden Wing's words. Sarange felt her grandmother's presence more strongly today than ever.

As well as Gerel and Bek, Ged and the other members of Beast were gathered on the lawn of the Los Angeles house. Sarange was delighted that Jiran, Houlun and Galba had agreed to make the long journey. Getting her personal assistant to ensure that their journey and accommodations were first class and luxurious had given her immense pleasure. She could never thank the three men enough for what they had done for her and Khan. An all-expenses-paid vacation was minor in return.

Jenny was also present. Leaving her movie cameras behind, she had taken one picture of Khan, Sarange and Karina. They had agreed to release it to the press in return for donations to the Animals Alive Foundation.

"I'm just sorry I never got footage of the story everyone has been talking about for months." Jenny's eyes quizzed them over the top of her champagne glass.

"What story was that?" Khan asked.

"The one about a dragon flying up to Radin's office block with you on its back. That was the same day Radin disappeared. He hasn't been seen since."

Khan shrugged. "Must have been some sort of stunt."

"Right." Jenny gave them one of her piercing stares. "Strange things always seem to happen around the two of you, don't they?" She went away and started to talk to Jiran.

"She is frighteningly observant," Sarange said.

"Is it just me, or is she not as hostile to Jiran as she'd like us to believe?" Khan asked as he watched them.

Sarange regarded him in surprise. "Since when did you turn matchmaker? Anyway, Jenny is not a shifter."

"That's true, but she may well be talking to a future president of Mongolia."

The demise of the Chanco Party had caused a major stir in Mongolian politics. No suspects had ever been identified over the attack. Several weeks later, evidence of widespread corruption, vote rigging and voter intimidation within the party had been made public by an anonymous source. Since then, Jiran's interest in politics had become serious.

Sadly, the ger camp was fully booked for the next few months and Surkh and Merkid had not been able to get away. Sarange, who kept in touch with them by email—erratically because of the signal problems in the Altai region—promised them pictures and a visit when Karina was old enough. She and Khan would take their daughter to see the fortress where it all began.

"We will have quite a story to tell her," Khan said.

"Did you read my mind?" They stood slightly apart from their guests, content to spend a few moments alone. Just the three of them.

Their wedding had taken place soon after Radin's death with no fuss or frills. Just the two of them with Bek and Gerel as witnesses. The simple ceremony had been a final confirmation of the commitment that had begun a thousand years ago. Sarange hadn't been sure how much it would matter to them. They already had so much history, so much depth of emotion. Their legend was told and retold as one of the greatest love stories the world had ever known. Could a few words and a piece of paper make a difference?

In many ways, it didn't. In one way it did. It brought the peace they had been seeking. Maybe it was wrong to place too much emphasis on the wedding. Perhaps the peace came with Radin's death, but Sarange liked to think it had started the day they exchanged their vows. She wanted to forget the blood, the fury and the vengeance and focus on the fresh start. It worked for her.

Since then, there had been logistical details to take care of. They had made this house their home, but they both needed to travel for work. After a few months of barely seeing each other, they sat down one day and reorganized their lives. The strategy had coincided with Sarange's pregnancy. They had come up with a strict policy that they wouldn't be apart for more than two nights at a time. And now that Karina was here, Sarange wasn't prepared to accept any work that took her away from her daughter.

"She's beautiful, isn't she?" They never got tired of rejoicing in the perfect little person they had made.

"Like her mother." Khan leaned down to kiss her. A thousand years and that kiss still had the power to weaken her knees. "And Karina is the first of many."

"Whoa, easy, tiger." Sarange placed a hand on his chest. "When were you planning on discussing this with me?"

"You don't want more children?" He raised his brows in surprise. "I thought you'd want your own pack."

"Yes, I want more. It's the 'many' part that's bothering me." She smiled. "Can we negotiate? Maybe bring it down to 'several'?"

The smile in his eyes contained just a hint of something that made her glad they were standing away from their guests. It was a little too Khan, just the wrong—or maybe the right—side of carnal, for sharing. "As long as we can get started on making the next one while negotiating each time, that's fine by me."

Sarange wondered how it was possible for her heart to hold so much love without overflowing. This was her forever. Her husband with their child in his arms. Their journey to this point had been long and tortuous, and every step had been a fight. Now that they were here, it felt like the iron hand that had gripped her spine and propelled her onward had eased. She could finally relax.

"Always."

* * * * *